LAURAINE SNELLING

HAWAIIAN SUNRISE

BETHANY HOUSE PUBLISHERS
MINNEAPOLIS, MINNESOTA 55438

Published by Bethany House Publishers
A Ministry of Bethany Fellowship International
11400 Hampshire Avenue South
Minneapolis, Minnesota 55438
www.bethanyhouse.com

Printed in the United States of America by
Bethany Press International, Minneapolis, Minnesota 55438

Library of Congress Cataloging-in-Publication Data

CIP data applied for

ISBN 1–55661–991–X

CIP

To WKB and JEJ
for sharing with me what you've learned of abuse.
May your lives continue to bless others,
knowing that our heavenly Father
never wastes anything.

Books by Lauraine Snelling

Hawaiian Sunrise

RED RIVER OF THE NORTH

An Untamed Land
A New Day Rising
A Land to Call Home
The Reapers' Song
Tender Mercies

HIGH HURDLES

Olympic Dreams   *Storm Clouds*
DJ's Challenge   *Close Quarters*
Setting the Pace   *Moving Up*
Out of the Blue   *Letting Go*

GOLDEN FILLY SERIES

The Race   *Shadow Over San Mateo*
Eagle's Wings   *Out of the Mist*
Go for the Glory   *Second Wind*
Kentucky Dreamer   *Close Call*
Call for Courage   *The Winner's Circle*

LAURAINE SNELLING is an award-winning author of over thirty books, fiction and nonfiction, for adults and young adults. Besides writing both books and articles, she teaches at writers' conferences across the country. She and husband, Wayne, have two grown sons, four grand-dogs, and make their home in California.

L eaving is always hard.

Maddy Morton glanced around the decrepit, empty apartment one more time. She stared at a familiar crack in the wall and listened for the continuous drip in the kitchen sink. The management, if you could call their landlord that, hadn't fixed anything in the two years they'd been there. No, leaving this shabby place wasn't hard, but friends . . . friends were a different matter.

But you never left your memories. Memories, both good and bad, came along whether you wanted them to or not.

"Come on, Nicholas, it's time."

"I don't want to go and you can't make me."

She stared at her ten-year-old son. Right now Nicholas reminded her so much of his father, she could scream in frustration. Instead, she clamped her jaw shut and anchored her hands on her hips. She leaned forward, looking him square in the eye. And waited.

Her teeth ached from the clenched jaw.

Nicholas stared right back, his jaw a miniature of her own. Gray eyes that matched hers flashed to storm-cloud hue, and a lock of dark hair flopped forward over his left eye.

She started to brush it back and stopped. In the last few weeks, he'd avoided her touch. Gone, too, was the merry laugh that made her life worthwhile. In its place slunk this sullen caricature of her son.

Fear sucked the moisture from her throat. Would he turn out like his father in spite of her efforts? Gabino, better known as Gabe, Hernandez now occupied a cell in the state penitentiary for spousal abuse and illegal possession and sale of drugs. She and Nicholas were safe for ten years, according to the judge. At that time Gabe would be up for parole, if he could behave himself in the interim.

Since the notion of Gabe controlling his temper had yet to be even a possibility, Maddy was counting on her ex-husband's inability to change. She only let his threat to "get them when he got out" intrude on her mind in moments of utter despair. This wasn't one of them—yet.

She waited.

First Nicholas's shoulders drooped. The motion was so faint she'd have missed it were she not looking for that reaction.

"Why can't we stay in Honolulu? All my friends are here." His voice transformed from defiance to a plaintive whine.

She knew she'd won. Accepting his defeat gracefully, she went down on one knee so they could be eye-to-eye. "Nicholas, you know why. I can't pay the rent and—"

"We could move in with Juan. His mom said it was okay." He switched to reasoning mode.

Oh, to gather him in the shelter of both arms and heart! But the skinny arms he locked across his chest still kept her at bay.

"Rita didn't mean permanently, just for a night or two." Maddy waited again. It seemed like she'd spent half her life waiting. Waiting had never been her strong suit. Getting in and getting it done was more her style, no matter what "it" was.

"I hate you." His eyes narrowed to slits. "You're the meanest . . ."

He then used a local word that she had forbidden. His lashes flickered and he sniffed, fighting to maintain his tough-boy facade.

Maddy debated between throwing him over her shoulder or paddling his behind. She knew how badly he needed a hug just now but feared he would resent it all the more. Inside she wasn't sure who needed the hug more—she or Nicholas.

If only she could hold on to her own temper long enough. "Sorry about that, son, but right now I'm not liking your behavior too well either. So you just go get your backpack and help me carry these last things down to the truck—Rita's waiting. We'll be on our way before they come and kick us out." She stood and looked down at him, shaking her head.

"It's going to be all right, Nicholas, I promise." Her voice had dropped to a whisper.

He shot her a look that told her quite clearly what he thought of her promises and stamped off to the bedroom.

She breathed a sigh of relief. Another skirmish done. The language he'd used was just one more reason to be leaving Honolulu; the gang he'd taken to running with, another. Life on the Big Island, living on her father's ranch, would be much slower and would give her renegade son enough to do to keep out of trouble. The cows would be calving now, and there was always at least one calf that needed bottle feeding, a good job for Nicholas.

If Pop would let them stay.

She brushed a lock of dishwater blond hair back from the corner of her eye and put that thought as far out of her mind as she had others. At least there they would be safe. She'd taken back her maiden name after the divorce was final, and neither Gabe nor his "friends" would look for them there . . . she hoped. He knew how she despised anyone running home with her tail between her legs. He also believed she was *his* property, to knock around when he wanted, divorce or no. Thinking of others was as foreign to Gabe's nature as the sun rising in the west.

What Gabe didn't understand was that she'd do anything to save her son, even broaching her father—something she'd sworn never to do.

Nicholas stomped by her, his pack slung over one shoulder, eyes averted. The long, furry ear of Mr. Mops hung out from the pack. The rabbit had been his constant bed companion since the Easter he turned three. Like the Velveteen Rabbit, Mr. Mops wore the patina of love.

With only a cursory glance around the place that had been their home for two years, Maddy closed the door and followed her son down the two flights of stairs. She felt like stamping her feet as he did, but that took far more energy than she had at the moment.

If only she hadn't dumped that man's drink in his lap, she'd still have a job. But he'd been trying to pick her up all night, and when he pinched her rear as she carried a tray of orders out, the camel's back had broken. Even though her boss had shaken his head sadly, she'd known a parting of ways was coming.

She slung her pack into the back of the pickup and climbed in the passenger side.

"You sure about this?" Rita asked for the umpteenth time.

"Sure as I'll ever be." Maddy reached to tousle Nicholas's hair as he hunkered in the narrow space between them, but he ducked away. "We'll miss our flight if we don't get a move on."

"There's always another." Rita shifted into first gear and the pickup whined its way down the steep grade.

Maddy didn't have much to say as they drove out to the Honolulu airport. While she watched the passing palm trees and gigantic hibiscus blossoms, she felt nothing. Honolulu had never been home.

"Where will you go if he won't let you stay?"

Rita voiced the thought that had kept Maddy awake more nights than she cared to count.

"He'll let us." Maddy knew that in spite of himself, her father wanted to see his only grandson. She was counting on that being enough incentive. How could she ask Nicholas to put on a happy face if only to gain them a home where they weren't wanted? Anyone, including her father, would be able to tell that her son didn't want to be there. It was a shame she hadn't told Nicholas more about the ranch and his family, but whoever dreamed *she*'d be skulking back home?

She shook her head at the memory of her arrogant answer to her father's threat of cutting her out of his will if she ran off with Gabe Hernandez. As if she were leaving that much behind. Besides, the baby she was carrying made staying impossible.

She shook her head. Why did her father always have to be right? He'd said Gabe would end up in jail one day.

It was only unfortunate it hadn't been a whole lot sooner. She was now finally gaining back the strength in the arm he'd broken the last time he got mad at her, just before his trial. One lesson she'd learned with impeccable success through all this mess was there'd be no man in her life from now on. Men were far more trouble than they were worth. And to top it off, they always left.

"Here we are, then." Rita swung the truck into an empty space in front of the airline's open-air ticket counter. "You call if you need me?"

Maddy nodded. "Come on, Nicky, let's get our gear."

"Don't call me that." He shoved out the door and slung his pack on his shoulder again.

"Thanks, Rita, we'd never have made it without you." Maddy lifted their four boxes from the pickup bed and set them on the sidewalk. "Get me a cart, Nick, please."

He snagged one of the luggage carriers some departing guest had left loose and trundled it over.

After stacking the boxes on the cart, Maddy gave Rita a hug and, with promises to write or call, pushed all their worldly belongings up to the check-in counter. The horn honked and she waved. Looking down, Maddy saw her son's lip quiver. Rita had been like another mother as the two women swapped baby-sitting, meals, and anything else one had that the other needed, including a shoulder to cry on if necessary. Rita's son, Juan, had been Nicholas's best friend.

Once the scramble to board the plane was over, Maddy lapsed into memories again. She hadn't been home since her mother's funeral. If her mother had still been alive, there would be no doubt as to their welcome home. If fact, she'd probably have come for them if the news of Gabe's trial had made the Hilo paper. What would it be like without her waiting at the door? What if Pop really didn't let them stay?

Maddy stared at Mauna Kea, the highest peak on the island of Hawaii, as the plane circled to land at the Kona airport. The ranch lay on the eastern slopes, the leeward side of the island. A cloud hid the mountaintop and cottoned its flanks. Most likely it was raining in Waimea, the town nearest the ranch.

Maddy knew she didn't need to count the bills in her wallet again—hiring a driver to take them to the ranch would empty it completely. Why, oh *why* hadn't she kept in contact with any of the people she'd grown up with?

Get over it, she told herself. *The milk is all spilt and crying over it won't do any good.* She took a deep breath. *God, let him take us in.*

Her sigh was loud enough to make Nicholas turn from staring out the window and look at her with both questions and fear in his eyes. She'd given up on praying a long time ago and never planned on going back.

That one had sneaked up on her.

Once on the ground a short time later, with their packs and boxes around them, she shook her head at the man offering to drive her to the ranch.

"But I don't have that much." She raised her hands in defeat. So close and yet so far. Should she call her father to come get them?

That would happen the day a snowball rolled down the new lava flow. As the man walked back to his van, she glanced up to see a tall, familiar-looking Hawaiian looking her way. His broad smile invited one in return, but right now she was fresh out of smiles. In fact, she had been for quite some time, but he wouldn't know that.

She turned away when he began threading his way between the luggage and passengers toward them. Surely she'd known him from high school, though he was older. What was his name?

He didn't take the hint. "I heard you ask about Waimea. I'm going to Hilo and can drop you off in Waimea on my way."

Maddy stared at his scuffed cowboy boots, then followed creased khaki pants up to a turquoise shirt with peach hibiscus that covered a wide chest. Her perusal stopped at his smile. Wide and warm, just like the look in his eyes.

"I don't have much money." The words sounded flat, even to her ears. Who was he? *Come on, brain, what's left of you?*

"No matter. My name's Kam Waiano." He waited, the smile never leaving his face. It broadened when he looked down at Nicholas.

"I know! You played football." *But you wouldn't know me.*

"That was a long time ago."

Maddy understood Hawaiian courtesy. She'd been raised by it. He wouldn't take anything for the extra effort. She gestured to herself. "I'm Maddy, and this is Nicholas."

"Nick." Her son hadn't left his shoulder chip on the plane.

"Aloha, Nick and Maddy. Welcome back to the Big Island." He took a box under either arm, making Maddy feel petite. At five feet eight, she never felt petite. She picked up one of the remaining boxes, refusing to grunt in the process. All of them were heavy. Books and personal things weighed up quickly, but she found she couldn't leave all of her life behind. Just the hurtful parts.

After depositing the first boxes in the bed of the white pickup, he took hers and lifted up the rest. "I have to swing by Holuakoa."

When neither answered, Kam showed them in to the pickup cab and slammed the door behind them. "How long since you been here?" He turned the ignition as he asked.

The warmth in his voice and its musical tone made Maddy want to answer. He was only being his friendly Hawaiian self, she reasoned. Aloha was a way of life among the Hawaiians, not just a polite greeting. After all, she wasn't a *haole*, a visitor from the mainland. She'd grown up on the island. And left.

"Ummm. Long time." She looked out the window, doing all in her power to discourage small talk. Nicholas had retreated into the shell he'd become so expert at closing around himself. She could tell the man was trying to place her.

Kam hummed a tune as he drove, glancing at her frequently but honoring her silence. Even though she stared out the window, she felt each of his glances as if he brushed every nerve end she owned with the tip of an ostrich feather.

"I'll just be a minute," he said, getting out of the truck in front of a weathered building that looked like a giant had put a foot on one side and lightly pushed. He was whistling when he returned.

Maddy brought herself back from the land of *what if* and nodded at his greeting.

"You want a cup of coffee?" Kam pointed to a ramshackle restaurant off to the right.

"No, thanks." *One more cup of coffee and I might shatter*, she thought, trying to still her already shaking fingers. *Hurry up and go. Take your time and wait.* The two contradicting schools of thought warred in her head.

By the time they'd stopped at one of the shrimp farms and started up Highway 19, the sun had disappeared beyond the horizon banked by dark masses of clouds.

They drove right into the rain cloud, huge drops pummeling the windshield and creating rivers of red beside the highway. Nicholas slumped against her side, his backpack on his lap, his mouth slightly open in sleep. By the time they drove through Waimea, dusk was drowning in night.

The huge eucalyptus tree that marked the ranch turnoff was nearly undecipherable in the torrent. The headlights glistened briefly on the silvery bark.

"Up there." Maddy indicated the road they had to follow. When the truck stopped in front of a picket fence that had certainly seen better days, Maddy dug in her purse.

"Don't even think about it." The firm tone in his voice left no room for argument. "Hey, you aren't Mark Morton's baby sister, are you?"

She ignorned the question. After all, it was none of his business.

"Thank you for the ride." Maddy stepped out into the downpour, studying what she could see of her father's place by the headlights. The gate hung off one hinge and the rose arbor, her mother's pride and joy, tilted to one side, propped up by two sticks rammed in the red clay soil. A light shone faintly at the window.

"C-come on, Nicholas, we're home." She shook him awake with one hand and pushed a soaked strand of hair back from her eyes. She pointed her son toward the front door and, ignoring the sheeting rain, hoisted one of her boxes out of the truck bed. Kam came around and helped her carry them to the lanai that circled the front of the low building. Like other houses on the islands, posts held the floor up off the ground to allow both air circulation and the water to run by.

At their arrival a dog had crawled from under the porch and stood barking.

"Amos?" Maddy asked softly.

The barks turned to a whine of welcome, the stiff stance to a dance of delight. The mottled gray, tan, black, and white cattle dog yipped and wriggled, spattering Maddy's sodden clothes with red mud. She set the boxes down and, using both hands, rubbed the dog's ears and whatever part of him she could grab on to.

"Nicholas, this is Amos—and he obviously remembers me." She glanced up to see her son standing just under the porch roof, arms again across his chest.

"He 'bout bit me."

"Oh, he was just doing his job, weren't you, fella?" More wriggles and yips, plus a flashing tongue that tried to clear the rain from her cheeks.

Kam cleared his throat. "You sure you'll be all right?"

"Yes, thank you." Maddy stood from her tussle with the dog. When Kam turned to leave, she almost reached out a hand to draw him back. *What's with you, girl?* she silently questioned. *First man who's nice to you, and you want to keep him near? Where's your backbone?* She resolutely turned toward the house again and began petting the dog, who put muddy paws up on her leg to reach her hand better. She waited until she heard the truck slosh out the lane.

Maddy flung her dripping braid over her shoulder and straightened to her fullest height, hoping the action would put some steel in her reluctant backbone. "Well, here goes nothing." She mounted the stairs and, with one hand on Nicholas's shoulder, walked to the door.

"Who in tarnation. . . ?"

She heard him muttering even before she could knock. The door opened before her hand struck it. "Hi, Pop, we've come home."

Only her foot in the door kept it from closing in their faces.

W ait . . . please!"
As the door silently swung open again, she breathed a sigh of relief. Nicholas shivered beneath her clenched fingers.

When her father turned and shuffled back to the living room, she guided her son with one hand and followed the man who'd aged so much she hardly recognized him. Had he been sick? He wasn't that old, but the stooped shoulders and shock of white hair made her wonder. He looked to have lost fifty pounds or so, and though tall, he'd never a big man. Even the house smelled old and musty.

She shuddered when she entered the living room. He'd carved a nest for himself around the blue overstuffed recliner her mother had given him for his birthday the year before Maddy left home. A single floor lamp pooled light over the dishes left from far more than one meal, the newspapers of what looked like the entire last year, and an ashtray holding his well-worn cherrywood pipe. The boots beside the chair looked just like the ones he'd been wearing the day of the funeral.

Funny how she could remember such strangely intimate details.

He shook out his paper and settled wire-frame glasses back up on his once-broken nose. The grandfather clock on the walnut shelf ticked on ceaselessly, just as it had since the first day she could remember.

Nicholas looked up at her, wet hair plastered against his forehead.

She shrugged and, keeping her hands on her son's shivering shoulders, continued to inspect the room. Didn't look like it had been cleaned since her mother died. Dried roses in a dusty vase on the wicker corner table might well have come from the funeral.

Rain drummed on the tin roof, gushing through the downspouts and flowing down the drive. Her heartbeat sounded as loud in her ears as the clock on the wall. Would it chime the quarter hour and bong out the hours as well?

Maddy's unease increased. *Okay, we're in. Now what do I do?* She felt Nicholas move a step closer to her side, as if seeking the warmth from her body. That settled it. "Pop, I need to get Nicholas out of his wet clothes."

Her father looked up at her over the rim of his paper. "You know where the bathroom is. And the bedrooms." He rattled the paper again as if to say, "Don't bother me, I'm busy with *important* things."

Clenching her teeth, Maddy turned Nicholas with her hands and stepped back into the hall. She pointed to the bathroom door. "Take a shower to warm up, and I'll see about a place to sleep."

"M-my c-clothes?" Nicholas shuddered this time.

"I'll get them," she said as she gave him a gentle push in the direction of the bathroom. "Go now. You'll find the towels under the sink." At least, that's where they used to be. From the state of the house, she doubted her father had moved anything. Surely he did the laundry.

With Nicholas safely in the bathroom, she headed for the lanai and their boxes. Picking up the one with their clothing, she strode past the living room and mounted the stairs. If Pop didn't want to talk any more than that, neither did she.

The upstairs bedrooms remained the same as the day she left. Hers on the left and Mark's on the right. When they finally knew her brother had been killed on his second air strike in Vietnam, her mother had tried to clean out Mark's room to turn it into a guest room but her father had thrown such a fit, she'd backed down. It didn't look like it had been dusted since her mother died, like the downstairs.

Maddy pulled back the bedspread to find the bed unmade. She took sheets from the linen closet in the hall and made up the bed, resisting the urge to look in the dresser drawers. If the clothes were still there, they would be so full of mold the wood would most likely fall apart when she opened them. Best leave that for another day, if they stayed. If he let them.

"Mom?"

"Up here." She could hear Nicholas climb the steep stairs but heard nothing from the living room other than the hum of the televison.

Nicholas was too tired to even glance around the room. Instead, he fell into bed, then quickly got up to fetch Mr. Mops and crawled back under the covers.

"Good night." Maddy ached to kiss his cheek and smooth back his wet hair, but his mumble warned her away.

Crossing the hall, she gazed at her room. She could have left the day before, it was so familiar. She pulled off the plaid bedspread she'd received for her sixteenth birthday, sneezing from the mustiness. To-morrow she would wash everything and drag the mattresses outside in the sun. She resolutely forced herself to act and think as if this would be their home . . . until the next moment fear took over again.

She checked on Nicholas one more time before falling into her own bed. He slept like the worn-out child he was. At least he wasn't on the streets of Honolulu with the gang of boys who'd become his friends.

— — —

Next morning, with dawn lightening the black to blue-gray, from the state of her bed and the cotton in her head, Maddy knew she hadn't slept any better than she thought she had. She felt like she'd run fifty miles—always with Gabe chasing after her, screaming what he'd do when he caught her. The nightmares had been a nightly occurrence for longer than she took the time to count. Now she could hear birds beginning their morning song outside in the blue gum trees that shaded the house. She listened for the cardinals and the cooing of the doves. In Honolulu there hadn't been much time for birds. Here on the ranch . . . well, just like many other mornings in her life, she heard the doves calling her first.

She slipped into her jeans and shirt, then padded barefoot down the stairs and out onto the lanai. The wicker rocker there welcomed her as if it'd been waiting for her a long time.

The rain had quit sometime during the night. The last time she remembered listening, it had still been coming down like it didn't plan on ever stopping. But that was the way of rain in Hawaii. It could pour all night and be chased away by the rising of the sun. She'd heard haoles referring to that as one of the best things about Hawaii. That and the fact that no matter how hard it rained, as soon as the sun came out again you would be dry in just a matter of minutes.

Amos's toenails nicked on the wood as he padded up the front steps and came to sit beside her. He laid his muzzle across her knees and looked up at her with eyes that plainly said, "Where have you been for so long?"

Maddy stoked the silvery hair on the top of his head. "You've gotten to be an old gray dog in the years I've been gone. You might have been silver to begin with, but you're gray now." She stroked his muzzle and fluffed his ears.

He put one paw up on her knee and leaned against her. The gentle cooing of the doves, the twittering sparrows up in the trees, and the harsh call of the myna birds sounded like morning music in Hawaii. An unseen cardinal added his aria.

As the breeze rustled through the eucalyptus leaves, raindrops pattered down on the tin roof above her head. That, too, sounded like morning music. Maddy stretched her arms high above her head, pulling out all the kinks from the day before. Her bare toes scraped against the worn wood of the porch. She glanced around. Cushions that her mother had made were now so faded that the pattern was indistinct and ripped in places. The wicker badly needed repairing, just like the gate that hung haphazardly along the fence.

Her father had always been one to make sure he fixed things before they broke. If you fix it before it breaks, things will last longer. How many times had he drummed that into her head? Now the place looked like nobody lived there.

And now the question of the hour: Would he let them stay?

She stared out across the treetops toward the ocean, the sprinkling of rain already gone. Dawn painted the sky with gentle fingers of purple and pink. She knew it would soon brighten into the peaches and brilliant oranges of sunrise. For this moment, her whole world felt gentle.

It felt like home.

Maddy shook her head. She didn't really want this to feel like home—not when she returned like a whipped dog, though she had to admit it wasn't at the first sign of trouble. She rubbed the arm that still pained her since the last break. That had been the final fight, if you could call a man beating a woman into the floor a fight. She'd sworn if he ever touched her again, she'd kill him. But the government had intervened and thrown Gabe in prison, thank God—although she didn't want to go running to Him either.

She forced those thoughts from her mind and watched the sunrise. As the sun came up, the birdsong swelled into a triumphant chorus, as if the birds themselves brought forth the light. A cow bellowed for her calf. The baby bawled an answer.

Could she live here again? If he made them leave, then what? Either option left her with more choices, and making intelligent choices didn't seem to be her lot right now.

She stretched again. Amos whined and put both paws up on her knees this time. So what would she do first? She couldn't just sit here wasting the morning away, as her father would say. But then, where was he? Usually by now he'd be outside. She hadn't checked his bedroom, she'd just noticed that he wasn't still in the chair.

She breathed in deeply. Rain had released the medicinal aroma from the eucalyptus. The Plumeria were blooming right off the porch and she could smell that too. Rich, sweet. Again, an essence of home.

Shaking her head, Maddy pushed herself to her feet, gave Amos one last pat, and headed back to her room to get her shoes on and then go looking for her father. Nicholas would probably sleep away the morning. Since school had been out, he liked to stay up half the night, then sleep all morning. Just like his father. She'd give her son this one morning to sleep in, since yesterday had been shot off the stress scale.

She gave Amos's ears one last ruffle and opened the screen door back into the house. Nothing moved—not even the dust motes yet, although there certainly were plenty of those. She shook her head as she went down the hallway. Upstairs, Maddy grabbed a hairbrush, quickly brushed her hair, and with nimble fingers, braided the long blond strands into the single braid that hung down her back in its usual style. After brushing her teeth, she checked on Nicholas, who was sound asleep, spread across the bed like somebody had severed the puppet strings. Mr. Mops lay under his arm. She looked in the kitchen. Nothing there. Not even the coffeepot on yet. Her father's bedroom was empty, as was the living room. She'd been in the only bathroom, so she knew he couldn't be there.

Wandering back outside, she slapped her thigh for Amos to come with her. "How come you're not with him, fella? I thought you were his tail? Where did he go?"

Amos cocked one ear in the way that only he could. His one blue eye looked at her with wide-eyed innocence while the brown one appeared to smile.

She wandered down to the barn area, but she didn't find her father there either. The cows with their calves were scattered across the hillside, grazing the dew-laden grass. She checked the yard behind the house, where his fruit trees didn't show the meticulous care they'd had in the past. But at least he had pruned them in the last year or two. Several papaya hung on the stalk ready to pick, and a new stalk coming up showed that it had either seeded itself or her father had replanted like he should.

Maddy continued to gaze at the expanse of land before her, wondering where her father was. Then an idea came to her. The cemetery, of course.

She took the path up the hill, wandering toward the grove of mimosa. Halfway up she stopped. Sure enough, there he sat beside her mother's grave. She should have thought to look there first. Should she go up and talk to him? Or wait? Maddy turned and looked back out over the sea. The sun now floated above the edge of the ocean that seemed to go on forever. She'd heard the haoles say that they couldn't believe the color of the water. But to her island-born senses, the intense blue that changed to turquoise as the water shallowed was the way water should be.

With all her courage she turned and walked back up the path, stopping at the edge of the fenced-in plot. Here the fence stood erect, posts replaced, the gate firmly attached. No weeds cluttered the cemetery like they did along the edge of the backyard of the house. Her father had set a tombstone in since she left. Of course, she hadn't been back since the day they buried her mother next to Pop's mother and father.

"Pop." She whispered his name, afraid to disturb the stillness. When he didn't move she called a little bit louder. "Pop?"

Slowly he turned his head, as if the joints had frozen into immobility. The carved stone of his face told her more than the slump of his shoulders. While he'd never been one to show his feelings, the man before her looked wrung dry, as if someone had taken a dishrag and squeezed out all the water, tossing it down to be washed later. Or simply discarded. Shadows from the trees streaked across his face, deepening the contrast, lightening the gray to chalk white. Was he sick? Why had he not told her?

But of course he hadn't told her anything. The last he'd said to her was, *"If you leave now, don't come back."* And she hadn't, until now.

"Pop, I need to talk."

"Yeah." One word. Pulling those giant trees out by their roots by hand might be easier than getting him to discuss their situation.

"Can I come in?"

"Suit yourself."

She swung open the gate, which had been oiled recently enough that it didn't creak. Shutting it carefully behind her, she followed the steep path up to where a carved granite stone indicated the resting place of Amelia Jane Morton.

Tears made the carved words fade—tears she'd sworn never to cry again. She sank down on the clipped grass beside her father. Resting her elbows on her raised knees, she waited. With so much practice lately, waiting was one thing she was getting good at. "Would you rather talk later?"

"No need to talk at all, far as I can see."

Groveling had never been a trait Maddy developed or relished. In fact, the only reason she got down on her knees was either to play with Nicholas or scrub the floor. But now she knew she needed to be on her knees and it hurt.

"Can we stay here?" There. The words were out.

"What'd he do? Kick you out?"

"No. He's in prison."

"Now, that ain't no surprise." His tone cut like she knew it would. It was his way of saying "I told you so." And he'd been right.

"I know sorry isn't enough, but I am, and I have to say I wish I'd listened to you."

"Bit late for that now, ain't it?"

Two little gray-brown doves fluttered down from the trees overhead and landed on the grass not far from her. Cooing and bobbing their heads, they searched for seeds. She wished she'd brought something to feed them. Doves had been her mother's favorite birds. She'd often said nothing was more peaceful than the sound of the doves cooing. Maddy took a deep breath, breathing in the stillness and the peace as much as the clean air. The pink-tinged Plumeria bush spilled its fragrance as an offering from its place beside the granite.

"Well?"

"Well, what?"

"Can we stay?"

He knew what she wanted. Begging was hard; groveling was worse. But grovel she would if that's what it took to give Nicholas a home . . . not that he wanted this one. He'd made that abundantly clear last night and the days before. But then, he was tired and she was tired. When you're soul tired, there's no place for making sense.

"So can we stay?"

"You don't see me running you off, do you?"

"No. But . . ." She breathed a sigh of relief. They could stay. So now what? She pulled up bits of grass and tossed them one at a time, trying to think. First thing she ought to do was clean that house. "Mind if I clean the house up?"

"Suit yourself."

She took that as a yes, got to her feet, and strode back down the path. Well, at least they had a roof over their heads. She thought of the nine dollars and fifty-eight cents left in her wallet. And food to eat. Pop wouldn't let them starve. Now, if she could just get a job. But how do you get a job when you don't have wheels to get you back and forth? This wasn't like Honolulu, where there was a bus stop at every other corner. And if she did find a job, would Pop take care of Nicholas while she worked?

On her way back down the hill, her mind flashed back to the night before. She'd forgotten how everyone knew each other on Hawaii, just a small town, in reality.

Kam Waiano, football legend, had come back to the hometown too. Shame he realized who she was. Would he keep his mouth shut, or by nightfall would the whole island know she was home?

The next morning County Extension Agent Kam Waiano sorted through his files to find out what he could about Jesse Morton. As he read, he wished he could change the story he saw there. Morton had lost his shirt and nearly his land when the coffee market collapsed a few years earlier. While Kam had been away at school, he'd often heard of the devastation to the small farmers. And most of the farmers on the Big Island were indeed small-time, hardscrabble workers. That was why he preached the message of diversification. That way if something happened to one form of income, the other could fill in or at least keep them going.

A knock on the half-open door brought his attention back to the present. Kam looked up to see his supervisor, Carl Davidson, pausing in the doorway. "Come on in, man. I thought you were coming over the middle of next week."

"Seems I was forced to make it sooner than that." The man stroked his fingers through his thinning gray hair.

"You have to be forced to come visit this side of paradise?" Kam removed some papers from the padded chair to the side of his desk. "Here, have a seat. You look like you lost your last friend."

"Might be a lot worse than that." Davidson sighed. "You heard any scuttlebutt about some sick cows down the other side of Kona?"

Kam shook his head. "How sick?"

"Sick enough that we're being asked to test every herd on the island." He dropped his voice, as if whispering might make the horror go away. "It could be anthrax. A couple head died."

"You've got to be kidding. Between inoculations and quarantine, there's no chance anthrax could get loose here on Hawaii." Kam studied the man before him. Carl Davidson looked like he hadn't slept in three days and had been wearing the same clothes the whole time. "Besides, it hasn't been on either the news or the coconut telegraph."

Carl just stared at him.

"You're serious, aren't you?"

Davidson nodded. "Let's pray it's not dead serious." Carl studied the younger man. "It could have come from the soil, you know. Sometimes construction stirs up old spores that have been hiding in the ground."

"That's right." Kam rubbed the center of his chin. "So what's the plan?"

"We make one right now."

Kam picked up a pencil and drew circles and squares on his blotter while he thought of the ramifications of the report. He looked up a few minutes later to see Carl slumped in the seat, his chin on his chest.

He lifted the phone and, speaking softly to let the other man rest, asked his secretary to come in. He touched a finger to his lips and nodded to the sleeping man, then handed her a list.

"Call all these farms and tell them to have a sampling of their herds, both dairy and beef, ready for blood tests. I'll go with Sam and start up north; Mike can ride with Lew and start down on the southeast corner. Ask them to keep it to themselves. We don't want to start a panic." He tapped the paper with his pen. "And most of all, let's see if we can keep it out of the news."

Carl jerked awake. "Sorry."

Kam handed him the list. "Sue will make copies for all of us. Probably the biggest problem we face are the one- or two-cow families. Guess we'll put out a bulletin when we know more. Get everyone's cooperation."

"This looks good to me." Carl looked up at the muumuu-clad woman waiting. "Get as many as you need to help you call. We have to get this done quickly and without a lot of noise."

"Just answer any questions but don't volunteer information," Kam added. He then gathered up some papers from his desk and made sure his cell phone had a charge. "We tested for brucellosis like this, so maybe they'll think it's the same thing."

"What if it is anthrax?" Sue asked.

"Just get as many people praying as you know. I sure don't want to be the one to go out and tell any of those farmers they have to shoot and burn their cows." He checked the time and date on his watch. "We'll just have to see how far it has spread. If all goes right, I'll leave the Parker Ranch for last just in case we've already isolated it."

"Sounds like a good plan to me," Carl said. "Let's get started. I've never had to deal with anything like this in all my years. Why didn't I retire last year like Belle wanted me to?"

The men stood at the same time. "Not to change the subject or anything, but what do you know about Jesse Morton?"

Carl stopped. "Why?"

"Well, I dropped a young woman and her son off there last night. I think it's his daughter."

"Hmm. The Morton family's been farming on this island for several generations. Good solid folk." Carl squinted his eyes, thinking back. "I get the feeling I heard something about a daughter. Coconut telegraph, you know. Nothing substantial." He stopped. "I remember they had a son, lost in the Vietnam War." Shook his head. " 'Bout all I can tell you."

He took a step and stopped again. "I know what else. He took it bad when the bottom fell out of the coffee market back a few years ago. Someone interviewed him for a TV special. He was hot."

"Can't say as I blame him." Kam snagged his straw cowboy hat off the coat tree by the door. "Let's get on this."

— — —

By Monday morning Kam arrived at the Morton Ranch. When they drove in, he could hear cattle bawling. Sounded like they had some up in the chute. Getting out, he was met by the cow dog, who wagged his bit of a tail as usual. Good old Amos, he'd heard the old man call him on a previous visit.

Kam motioned to the veterinarian who rode with him. Together the two of them would draw blood from the cattle in the chute. Kam walked up the steps and knocked at the screen door. Music loud enough to rattle the windows and with a beat he could feel through his feet let him know his knock couldn't be heard. Now, if *that* wasn't something strange. Looked like the woman and her son had stayed after all. He knocked again. Still no answer. He walked to the edge of the porch, hands in his back pockets, and surveyed what he could see of the ranch. He knew most of the cattle would be up on the hills on the northeast flank of the mountain.

Shaking his head, he stepped down the stairs, waved for the vet to follow, and together they walked out past the barn and up to the cattle chutes. Dust billowed from the corral where the cattle were penned on the other side of the chute. He could see the old man opening one gate as the young woman he'd met those nights before drove the cows one at a time into the long chute.

"Looks like they've got five or six penned. Is that going to be enough?" Kam asked.

Sam Jones looked back at him. "Should do it. We don't have to test them all. If they've got anything, you know that we're in for it."

Kam looked around and didn't see any sign of the boy. That explained the so-called music shaking the windows back at the house. He'd bet an order of pupus that only happened when Grandpa was out of the way.

"Howdy, Jesse," Sam said when they reached the corral.

Jesse nodded and crossed his arms on the corral, watching the cows. The block of ice on his shoulder didn't appear to be melting, regardless of the hot sun.

Sam set his pail and syringes by the side of the metal squeeze chute and waited while the woman in the corral drove in one of the cows. He pulled the lever, locking the animal in place.

"Sorry to have to do this," Sam said over his shoulder to Jesse.

"Yeah, well, just get on with it."

While Sam drew the syringe full of blood, Kam looked around. He nodded to Maddy, who stayed a fair distance away, as if she didn't want to talk to or see anybody. But why should he care? She hadn't been friendly or hardly even civil—and he's the one who gave her the ride. But Kam found that more than once those eyes of hers had intruded on his thoughts. Gray eyes. Gray that changed with her moods. He wondered if when she really smiled her eyes wouldn't be blue. Like the ocean which changed from gray to blue depending on the sunshine. He thought again. It was more than that. He'd seen a hurt deep in her eyes that was too big to conceal, no matter how hard she tried.

Kam knew he was a sucker for wounded critters, be they two-legged or four.

Jesse said nary a word as they finished with the next three cows.

"How's your calf crop this year?" Kam asked.

The old man glared at him. "If'n what you're intimating is true, don't matter what kind of calf crop I got, does it?"

Kam knew that giving out false hope wouldn't help. "We'll have all the results back in three days. If they're clear, you'll still need to inoculate."

Neither the man nor the woman said thank you, but then, Kam

didn't expect them to. He and Sam waved and left without trying to make any more small talk.

"Where's that boy of yours?" Jesse turned from his study of the bawling cattle.

"Huh?" Maddy stopped herself. The sound of her father's voice caught her by surprise. He'd hardly spoken three sentences to her since their arrival three days earlier.

"Your boy. Where is he?"

"You mean Nicholas?" Her brain felt like it was slogging through mud. She blinked and shook her head. "Down at the house, I suppose."

"Tell him to get out here and help me run these cows back up to the high pasture."

"Pop, he knows nothing about running cows. I'll help you." She whistled for Amos and headed for the gate that kept the cows and calves in the corral.

"Looks to me like he don't know much about anything."

She heard his mutter, as she was sure he had intended. At this point Nicholas had refused to leave his room. Maddy figured she'd give him one more day to come out of his cave, and then she planned a full frontal assault. How to handle such a maneuver, she wasn't sure. For this kind of behavior to have carried on so long was totally foreign to her. But then, sulking had been one of Gabe's favorite tactics.

Why did her son have to take up his father's worst traits?

The eucalyptus leaves rattled in the breeze above her as she swung the gate open and whistled for Amos to round up the animals. With a bark that showed he understood, the dog darted to the other side of the fenced area and, between sharp barks and darting attacks, got the cows moving again. Red dust stirred by sharp hooves rose to mingle with the pungent fragrance wafting from the tree. After the cows passed, Maddy ambled over to the other side of the tree and picked up a cluster of seed pods. She sniffed them again as she followed Amos and the cows. The fresh pods with their silvery green bodies looked like someone had stitched them a skin of leather and applied furry caps. Her mother used to use all manner of local dried seed pods, leaves, and flowers on the wreaths she made by hand and sold at local shops.

Harvesting for the things to dry had been one of Maddy's chores, one that she'd never groused about since anything having to do with the outdoors was pure pleasure. Halfway up the hill, seedlings had sprouted all about an aged coffee tree's drip line and further afield. Coffee cherries hung heavy on the unpruned branches.

Maddy picked a couple of the clusters and held them to her nose like she had the eucalyptus. Fragrances of home. Promising herself to return and harvest the crop as it ripened, she followed Amos up the hill.

Her father couldn't lose the cows, too, not after the loss he'd taken on the coffee fields a few years ago. It just wasn't fair. He'd worked so hard.

"But who said life was fair?" She tossed the eucalyptus pods across the fence and hurried to open the gate. Since they lived on the rainy side of the island, the grass grew lush with a green that brought a smarting to her eyes. Now that she was home, how had she ever thought she could live happily in a city?

After the cows and calves bawled their way through the gate, she swung it shut and dropped the wire latch again. Leaning over, she ruffled Amos's ears and scrubbed her fingers down his shoulders and the length of his back. He beamed his grin up at her, a lightning tongue catching the tip of her nose. When she stood again, he leaped in front of her, yipping his delight at her attention.

She turned, studying the cows ranging on the field above them. Most of them were crossbreeds with a preponderance of white-faced calves, showing her father had employed the services of a Herford bull. The calf crop looked really good, the green grass making their white faces and pink noses stand out like neon lights. She laughed as one calf chased another and a third stood nursing, his tail twitching like a metronome.

Turning back, she lifted her face to the sun, resting her elbows on the rail of the fence. Was that peace she felt seeping through her skin and bones and winding its way into her soul? She stood like an ancient sun-worshiping statue, as if afraid the slightest movement might send the strange feeling into hiding. It persisted, tugging the corners of her mouth upward and the moisture in her eyes out and down over her cheeks. *Peace.* Her heart seemed to deepen its beat and slow its pace, pulling her back to the rhythms of the earth.

The tears continued, and as each one fell, quiet calm took its place. Washed of fear and insidious anger, she welcomed the serenity that invaded her being. *God, where did I go wrong?* It seemed she had shouted the words, sending them up to flutter the leaves and bend the mighty trees with their gale-force wind.

She dug at the bark on the top bar of the gate until her fingers ached. A sliver pricked her skin. Trying to remove it with her teeth, she looked up toward a mountaintop hidden in cotton-ball clouds. *"I will lift up my eyes to the hills; From whence comes my help?"*

Maddy waited in silence. So many years ago she and her mother had memorized that psalm. Her mother had quoted it often, reminding her daughter that the help didn't come from the hills, but from the Creator of the hills.

But as usual, there was no answer. There hadn't been any answers for longer than she cared to remember. Which was why she no longer consulted the God of her mother . . . or hadn't until a few moments ago.

"Remember, I said I wasn't talking to you anymore?" She looked heavenward, then scuffed her toe in the dirt. "You never answer anyway. Gabe said you don't exist and I . . . I guess I believe him." *Why I'd believe him is anyone's guess.*

"So I got a deal for you. You leave me alone and I won't bug you either. Fair enough? After all, you didn't hold up your part of the bargain—in taking care of me, I mean." Amos put his foot up on her knee so she absently scratched his ears.

Like all those promises Mom taught me. There'd be someone to love me. . . .

"Just a mess, that's what it's been." She shook her head. "Mess" didn't begin to cover her life to this point.

A cow bellered up behind her. She couldn't hear the cattle cropping the knee-deep grass. Amos whined. Life went on.

High enough now to see the Pacific tossing sparkles back at the sun, she breathed deeply to clear her mind of the crazy conversation.

What could she do to earn a living for her and Nicholas? Her father couldn't afford to support them, and that had never been her agenda anyway. Like the surly man now tinkering with the ancient tractor down by the barn, Maddy was determined to earn her own way, asking no quarter from anyone.

"If that were the case, why did you just show up on his doorstep?" The words unexpectedly escaped her lips.

Doves cooed from under the coffee bushes and a myna bird strutted among the grass clumps. None of them answered her, however. At her feet, Amos looked up and whined. She stared down at the dog.

"I showed up on his doorstep because I had no where else to turn." She thrust her hand in her pocket and pulled out two pennies. "That's about all I have, and two pennies won't even get you a piece of candy anymore." She stared at the two copper coins in her hand. Granted, she had nine bills in her wallet, but right now she couldn't even buy a fast food lunch for all of them, let alone pay rent and all the other bills that constituted life in the present.

"You think he'll let us stay here?"

Amos put his front feet up against her thighs and whined again, pink tongue lolling out the side of his mouth.

"*You* would, wouldn't you, fella?" She laid her cheek against the silky fur on his head. "Think you can get that son of mine out here to run the hills with you and forget that bunch of rotten kids he hung out with in Honolulu?"

A nose dampened by Amos's tongue was her only answer.

"Well, I know one thing, boy. There'll be no more tears shed from these eyes, you can bet your life on that."

Amos whined again and tucked his muzzle under her hand so she'd pet him.

She ambled back down the hill, her hands shoved in her rear pockets. Kicking a red clay dirt clump ahead of her, she caught herself whistling under her breath. That old trait, like many others, had long been missing from her life.

Her mother would call it the miracle of the mysterious, her joyous response to everything that happened. Maddy seriously doubted she would ever learn to praise God in all things, like her mother. Not that she really had any desire to do so. But it was hard not to thank Him for that interlude up on the hill.

The words coming from the barn let her know in no uncertain terms that her father was talking the tractor into submission. At the moment it sounded as though the tractor were winning.

She used to be the one to hand him the tools. In doing so, she'd become a better than average mechanic herself, not that she'd used her skills in the city. Gabe had never let her touch his Beamer, informing her that public transportation was good enough for her. The costly vehicle had been confiscated along with his high-powered cruiser when the feds indicted him for drug smuggling. Now Maddy entered the dimness of the sun-faded, hip-roofed structure that held more memories for her, most of them good. "You want some help, Pop?"

"Consarn it!" He dropped a wrench and glared at her over his shoulder. "Quit sneaking up like that. Can't you let a person know you're coming?"

"Sorry." She bent down and retrieved the wrench from the inside of the front wheel of the arthritic John Deere. Handing the tool to him, she peered under the raised hood. "What seems to be the problem?"

"If I knew, I'da fixed it." He reached back inside the diesel motor and muttered a few words that brought a half smile to Maddy's face. Her father said more to the tractor than he had to her since she'd arrived. However, she wouldn't have tolerated the kind of litany he was using.

"How long since she ran?" Maddy glanced at the parts lined up on a tarp he'd laid out carefully beside his feet. Looked like the battery was new.

No answer.

A rooster crowed from the neighbor's. While nearer to noon than dawn, he was probably trying to impress his lady love. The sound reminded Maddy that she should go start lunch.

"You hungry?" She couldn't tell if the muttered response was affirmative or another invective against the machine.

She shrugged. "Lunch will be ready in about fifteen minutes, then. Unless you want me to stay and give you a hand . . ." When he didn't answer, she slapped her thigh for Amos to join her and headed back toward the house. "Ornery old buzzard," she muttered to the dog at her knee.

Amos didn't disagree.

She stopped with one foot on the bottom step. Waves of dissonance and discord flowed from the open door and window. "They call that music?" She could hardly hear her own grumblings as she mounted the steps. Nicholas knew hard rock was out of bounds. She figured he didn't really like the music, except for the heavy bass beat and the fact that he knew it annoyed her.

With one hand on the screen door, she glared at the wire patch by the handle that had rusted through. Another sign of her father's neglect . . . or of her father's decline. She banished that thought aborning and yanked open the door. "Nicholas Adam Her—Morton, turn that thing off!" She paused.

No response.

D r. Jones, is it really anthrax that is loose on the island?"
Kam stood back as a television reporter stuck a microphone in Sam's face.

"Ah . . . yes, we are dealing with anthrax, but in a very isolated case." Sam wiped his brow with his handkerchief. "There is no need to be concerned for human health."

"Then why have those cows been shot and burned?"

"That is the only way to deal with affected animals."

"Where did the anthrax come from?" "Why are you continuing to test herds?" "Dr. Jones . . ."

To control the flood of questions, Kam stepped forward and raised a hand. "Come on, folks, you know we will give you the information as soon as we have it. We have to test to see if the disease has spread."

"How is it spread?" Now the camcorder was in his face. He realized he didn't like it any better than Sam did.

"By contact."

"But Noshura said his cows had not been off the farm, no new ones brought in. And now he has no cows."

"Mr. Noshura dug a hole in his pasture to build a new barn. There must have been a cow or deer or a cloven-hoofed animal that died of anthrax there in the far distant past and was buried. The anthrax virus is spore laden and can remain viable in the ground for . . . well, we don't know how long. That it got disturbed is a sad fact of life."

"What about his neighbors?"

"We're not sure yet. The tests have to come back. For right now, all cloven hoofed livestock is quarantined to their home place."

When two more reporters got so close they pushed against him, he raised his hands again. "That's all we know at this time, and we promise to keep you appraised of any further developements."

And now you sound like a government bureaucrat, he chided himself as he and Sam closed the building door behind them.

"You did good out there. Someone shoves a mike in front of my face and I want to run, not talk." Dr. Jones wiped his forehead again. "And we still got the farms on this side to go."

Kam wanted nothing more than a very tall glass of iced tea. He shook his head. "Crazy world out there, Sam. Let's get on with it."

They stopped at a local drive-in to get drinks and headed back up Highway 19. A sign tacked to a fence post said Seaside Ranch. They could see the cows that grazed the lush hillside as they turned into the bumpy driveway.

Kam shifted into low gear and drove slowly enough to keep their teeth from rattling. Just as he turned off the ignition under an avocado tree, a shot rang out.

They both ducked, then peeked over the dash to see where it was coming from.

"Just get on out of here and you won't get hurt!" The shout rang through the stillness. Even the birds had ceased their normal conversation.

"We're just here to test your cows."

"I know why you're here. My cows ain't been nowhere, and you ain't bringing any disease onto my place." Another shot emphasized the shooter's point.

Kam tried to swallow, but without another drink from his glass, that was impossible. "I say let's do as the man says and leave—now." He looked at Sam, who rolled his eyes and shrugged.

"Didn't know we were in a war zone." Kam leaned out his window. "Okay, hold your fire, we're leaving. But I will have to report this to the State Board of Health." He lowered his voice. "And the sheriff and disease control and—"

Another shot. This time Kam heard it plunk into the body of his truck. He turned the ignition again and backed around enough to head out the way them came in. *Dear God, please don't let that have hit any essential part.* But he wasn't about to stop and check it out at that point.

When they got back to the highway, he turned to Sam. "You know that crazy?"

Sam shook his head. "But a lot of these farmers treat their cattle the old way—don't call a vet, don't inoculate; they figure if a cow dies, that must be the will of the gods."

Kam knew some of the old-timers felt that way, but the ranch they'd just left seemed more . . . more up-to-date, current. . . . He wasn't sure what word he wanted to use. He only knew he wasn't having a hard time calling the idiot with the rifle every name he could think of and then some. Up to this point, he hadn't considered being a county extension agent a hazardous occupation.

— — —

They learned they'd been driven out by an irate farmer on the evening news that night.

"How in. . .?" Kam stared at the television set. Someone must have been following them.

His phone rang. And rang. By the fourth call, he let the answering machine pick up so he could screen his calls. By now he had much more sympathy for famous people who put up with the press all the time. No wonder they hired bodyguards.

— — —

By the end of the week, Kam felt like he'd been run over by a semi that backed over him again before he could catch his breath. He stopped the car at the turnoff for the Parker Ranch headquarters. They'd saved the worst for last, as if the gun-toting rancher the other day hadn't been bad enough. They'd have to take the sheriff back with them for that one.

"You rather go for lunch first?" Sam asked, one eyebrow raised.

"I'd rather go mainland first, or China maybe." Kam crossed burly arms over the steering wheel. "Remember the old Greek saying 'They shoot the messenger'?"

Sam nodded. "Yeah, I feel that way too. Can't say as I blame them." He sighed and leaned his head on his hand, propped up by his arm on the windowsill. "But at least we're fairly sure it hasn't spread."

"Further than the three places, that is. The look on that girl's face when we had to shoot her 4-H steer about did me in." He could feel a lump form in his throat at the thought.

"I read a novel about some terrorists loosing an even more virulent strain of anthrax on an island just to test it out and see how fast it spread."

"That's fiction all right." Kam took in a deep breath and slowly let it out. "Well, let's go." He shifted back to drive and eased on the accelerator. The thought of a terrorist threatening his island with something as deadly as anthrax made his stomach churn and pop like the lava pots at the other end of the island.

Heading up the long drive, Kam looked over at Sam. "I'm just sick and tired of this."

"Well, that's sure no surprise." The vet shook his head. "Let's get it over with."

John Hampton, the head manager, met them when they parked in front of the long, low barn. "I got the cows up like you said. But you know it couldn't have gotten clear up here."

"Unless it got into the feral pigs and they transmitted it. You know we have no idea how far they range."

Hampton groaned. "I hadn't thought of that. Inoculating the thousands of head we have will be one expensive job, both in time and serum."

Hampton then swung open the steel-bar gate that led to the corral and the squeeze chutes. With a minimum of effort, thanks to the three employees of the Parker Ranch, they had the blood drawn and were on their way again in less than half an hour. There hadn't been any banter or return invitations this time.

"Feel like lunch?" Sam asked.

Kam shook his head. "I'd rather drop this batch off and check back in at the office. Somehow my appetite took a hike."

"I know what you mean." Sam took a bandana out of his rear pocket and, lifting his hat, wiped his forehead. "Just thinking about the possibilities of this disease gives me a headache."

"Is that one of the symptoms?"

Sam shook his head. "Not that I know of."

"So what's next?"

"We wait."

— — —

Back in his office, Kam flipped through his messages, returned a couple of phone calls, and emailed several replies before turning off his computer. After all the havoc and heartbreak of the last few days, what he really needed was beach time, preferably snorkeling and maybe even spearfishing. Fresh fish for dinner sounded mighty fine, but the silence of the sea and the feel of warm water buoying him were the real draw. Watching the gold-and-black butterfly fish, the tangs, and the wildly marked triggers grazing on the coral like cows in a pasture always returned him to a peaceful state of mind.

But as his mind equated the fish with cows, he thought again of the animals that might soon have to be destroyed. The unfairness of it all brought an edge to his jaw and an ache to his soul. *God, why are you doing this to these people? It's just not fair and you know it.*

Reminders of the stoic looks on some faces and the unmasked resentment on others sent him right to his knees. "What do you want me to do? How can I help?" Despite the despair he felt, he knew *why* wasn't the question to be asked. He also knew that his heavenly Father would bring good out of this too. He'd promised, and Kam Waiano believed firmly in the promises of the Almighty.

He waited awhile longer, hoping an answer would come quickly, then shut his door and headed for home. Maybe he'd go pick some papaya instead. He'd noticed several hanging heavy on the stalk in his backyard this morning. Or perhaps he'd work in his garden. God's presence always seemed near to him there.

— — —

The garden didn't help much, and when Kam read the newspaper, he found his irritation had peaked. Why couldn't they let it go? He flipped the pages savagely, noting that at least the story was off the front page and only taking up three columns at the end of the news section.

When the phone rang, he picked it up on the first ring. "Hello," he stated with a caustic tone to his voice.

"Whoa, sor-r-y." His sister Marlea's laugh grated on his nerves. "They're getting to you, huh?"

"No idea why. I've been called names, threatened with fists and a club, shot at, and hounded by the . . ." He refrained from calling the media what he really thought. He knew his voice wore machete edges, but at the moment he didn't much care.

"Easy, big brother. I hate to bother you, but the boys have been wanting to go fishing."

Kam's reply was harsh. "You could take them." *What in the world is the matter with me?*

"I could and I just guess I will—after I explain to them how rude their favorite uncle was."

The dial tone buzzed in his ear.

Kam sighed. Guilt didn't taste any better than fear. And he hated asking for forgiveness.

Nicholas's jaw stuck out farther than his nose.

Maddy steeled herself against the pain masquerading as anger she saw in her son's eyes. "You know we don't play that kind of music in our house."

"This isn't *our* house." His eyes narrowed.

"That makes the rule stand even more so. Your grandfather would hate that stuff more than I do." She forced herself to assume a nonchalant pose against the doorjamb. "Come on and help me make lunch."

"I'm not hungry."

"I didn't ask if you were hungry, and I didn't *ask* you to come help me make lunch. That was more on the order side." She waited. Nicholas had never openly defied her before. While he often grumbled, he always did what she said—up until now. She could feel anger bubbling in her midsection. She kept a clamp on it with superhuman effort, for if she let the monster loose, she might never get it caged again. *Nicholas, please! Now!* she silently implored.

Nicholas stared at the wall.

Maddy studied a battered cuticle while she kept one eye peeking from under her lashes to watch her son. Suddenly the boy on the bed heaved a sigh and flung himself to his feet. The stomp of his feet and the squint of his eyes left her in no doubt of his feelings, but still he came.

Maddy reached out to tousle his hair like she used to, but at the slightest movement of her hand, he glared at her and shifted away.

Oh, Nicholas, if only you could understand I—we—made the move more for your sake than mine. I couldn't let you go down the path you were taking. The lack of money was only the catalyst, not the cause.

In the kitchen, she removed the eggs she'd boiled the night before from the refrigerator and handed him the bowl. "You can peel these on the counter, but put a paper towel down first." While he stomped over to the sink, she searched the shelves for mayonnaise and mustard. She knew they were there, since she'd cleaned the mold and stale food out of the refrigerator during the night hours when she couldn't sleep. Someone would have to go to the store soon. The pantry reminded her of the cupboards of the old woman who lived in the shoe. She'd wondered what her father had been existing on until she dumped stuff in the trash and saw the soup and stew cans.

Amos whined at the screened back door.

She knew Nicholas had always wanted a dog. Perhaps Amos was the entry through the wall Nicholas had erected around himself.

"He can come in the house, you know."

Nicholas rolled his eyes, as if she'd asked him to climb Mauna Kea in his bare feet. He shook his head all the way to the door and pushed it open.

Amos darted through, a lightning tongue grazing the tips of the boy's hand on the way past.

If she hadn't been watching out of the corner of her eye, she'd have missed the grin that sneaked past her son's defenses. Quickly, before she could say anything, he reattached his scowly face and returned to the sink.

"There. I did that."

"Thanks. Would you mash them, please." Another major rolling of the eyes, along with a meeting of dark eyebrows and a tightening of the jaw again.

"Amos, you want to go get Pop?"

Amos wriggled at her feet, tongue lolling out the side of his mouth.

She broke off a bit of bread, tossed it to the dog, and waved him to the door.

"He doesn't know what you mean." *Dumb dog* was the portion of his sentence left unsaid.

"Oh really?" Maddy couldn't help but smile at the first words he'd volunteered since they left Honolulu. She walked to the door and opened the screen. "Fetch Pop."

Amos yipped and dashed out the door.

"Come here." She stood watching the dog hightail it to the barn, where her father still worked on the tractor. Nicholas joined her.

In a moment they heard the sharp bark. Amos darted out the barn door, waited, yipped, and spun back into the dimness.

Maddy glanced down at her son. A hug would be so easy.

Out in the sun again, Amos skidded in the red dust, yipped, and turned. He sat down and yipped again.

"I'm coming, I'm coming. Don't go getting your tail in a knot."

Only because they waited so silently could they hear the old man's voice.

Nicholas looked up at his mother. "Amos really got him." Wonder filled his voice. "He knew what you said."

Maddy didn't tell him that fetching Pop had been one of the first lessons her mother had taught the young cow dog. Sending Amos saved her lots of time and energy searching the farm for her husband. Amos knew "Fetch Maddy" also and a myriad of commands for rounding up the cattle, including hand signals.

"You take over feeding him, and he'll be your friend for life." She turned back to the table. "I'll finish the sandwiches while you pour the milk."

"Can't. I used up the last for breakfast." The stomps back to the sink were definitely muted in their intensity.

"Oh, then I guess we drink water. Looks like I'll be going to the store sooner than I thought." *Without any money. Now I have to ask for that too*. The thought of begging again twisted her stomach back into its square knot. At least there'd been a few hours of relief.

They sat down to eat as soon as Jesse washed up.

"No coffee?" Her father broke the silence, punctuated only by their chewing.

"Nope, nor milk either."

"I suppose you want to take my truck to town, then?"

"Better than walking." Maddy centered her sandwich in the middle of her plate.

Nicholas raised an eyebrow and continued to chew.

The desire to hear her mother tease her father about the surly tone of voice clamped around Maddy's throat, choking off her windpipe. She swallowed hard and raised her gaze to the mimosa tree outside the kitchen window, blinking all the while. *Oh, Mom, we need you so bad around here.*

"You got money?"

She coughed to clear her throat. "Umm . . . no." A deep sigh. "But I'll see about a job while I'm out."

"They're hiring at the Ranch House."

The Ranch House Restaurant claimed to have the best sixteen-ounce steaks in the islands and lived up to the boast. Situated right along Highway 19 in Waimea, with a parking lot big enough to accommodate eighteen-wheelers, the place never lacked for customers, both locals and tourists. Back when she was a kid, the help usually stayed, so openings were few. Most likely the position would be filled quickly. She hoped it would be with her.

"That be enough?" The abrupt voice brought her back to the table and the sight of twenty-dollar bills fanned across the tabletop.

"I . . . I reckon." She smiled up at him. But the solid line of his snowy eyebrows sent her smile back where it came from. "Anything special you want me to get?"

"Better get some soda." He nodded toward Nicholas and, without another word, headed for the door. With one hand on the screen door handle, he paused, dug in his front pocket with the other, and tossed the truck keys to Maddy. "I 'spect you'll need these."

I didn't have to grovel again. Relief made her feel lightheaded. She turned to Nicholas with a smile. "You want to go along?" *Come on, son, cut me some slack here.*

"To the grocery store?" He arched an eyebrow packed so full of disdain, it lost its curve.

"Fine, then you can stay here and clean up the kitchen." Disappointment put a snap in her voice. "The bathroom needs scrubbing too. You'll find the supplies under the sink." She looked him in the eye, daring him to change his mind. Wishing he would.

His eyelids draped lower, hiding the disgust she knew he felt. Thanks to his father, Nicholas had well-defined fences on what was "women's work" and what a male should do. Of course, had he continued to grow like his father, in another year or so he'd be selling drugs on street corners—if he waited that long.

How could I have been so stupid? The words had become a litany in the last years. But she had to remind herself over and over: If she hadn't married Gabe, she wouldn't have Nicholas. And in spite of his recent surly attitude, her son was worth any amount of suffering. If only she could break the chain of destruction that snaked from generation to generation.

Her father had recognized Gabe for what he really was. All she'd seen was a devastatingly handsome young man who always had enough money to play and could sweet-talk the wings off an angel—let alone an innocent teen who felt a need to defy her father. A father who thought his life ended with the death of his son in Vietnam. After that he never had or took the time to help shape his daughter.

Maddy let her shoulders drop. *Please, God . . .* She stopped the thought before it went any further. With all the mud she'd flung in His face, God surely didn't want her whining to Him now. Strange how she'd caught herself thinking of Him more in the days since she got home than in all the years since she'd left.

Maddy leaned back in her chair and crossed her arms over her chest, knowing she had to address the issue at hand. Should she let it ride? Decisions, decisions. She spoke the words softly but the meaning rang clear.

"The kitchen, then the bathroom. And if you think that's grossly unfair, I'll add in the walls in the hall."

"I was just getting to it."

"Good . . . then we understand each other. I'd thought maybe we could go for a drive, but since you didn't want to go along . . ." She knew this was like adding salt to an open wound. But she sensed that if she didn't break this streak in her son now, it might never happen. Pushing back her own chair, she stacked silverware and her glass on her plate and carried them to the sink. "See you later."

She could hear him muttering as she swung her bag over her shoulder and exited.

Driving down the lane a few moments later, she glanced in her rearview mirror to see her son standing on the porch. The slouch in his shoulders told her she'd won. She breathed a sigh of relief. What if he'd refused? What would she have done?

Since the turn for the Ranch House came before that of the grocery store, she wheeled into the asphalt parking lot and after parking, headed for the front door. Purple and red Bougainvillaea arched over the entry and hung down each side. Bees buzzed in the blossoms, and the westerly breeze tickled the ends of the vines, tossing them like kids at play. Creamy Plumeria in full bloom lined the front of the long, low building, scenting the air and inviting one and all to bend over and take in the heady fragrance that signaled the aloha spirit of the islands.

Once inside, she blinked in the dimness of the room. While a few of the red-and-white-checked tables were occupied, the noon rush was over and one waitress was refilling napkin holders and salt-and-pepper shakers to get ready for the evening crowd.

"One for lunch or . . ." The hostess tipped her head in the direction of the bar.

"Neither, thanks. I'd like to get an application for the job I heard was available."

"You had any experience?" The hostess tapped the edge of the plastic encased menu with one long red fingernail.

Maddy felt like hiding her fingers in her pockets. She hadn't checked to see if there was dirt under her nails, but she certainly wasn't sporting polish—let alone acrylics. She rambled off the names of the last three restaurants she'd worked at in Honolulu, knowing their solid reputation would help.

"Really? Right this way, then." The young woman's sarong-draped hips swayed as she made her way between the tables.

Fat chance I'd ever walk like that. If a swing that makes the hula look stationary is required here, I'll never get on. She tried to keep her boots from thudding on the wood plank floor as she walked. She'd found them in the closet the morning after she arrived and forgotten to change them before heading to town. But, then, she hadn't planned on stopping either. She'd make sure to wear more appropriate clothing when she returned for the interview. If she got one.

"All I wanted was an application."

If the hostess heard her, she didn't hesitate. She tapped on the door, which was rough framed to look like a barn door, and opened it. "Someone here to see about the job."

"Good, good. Send her on in." The voice had a faint accent, but not enough to denote nationality. Why had he assumed it was a woman?

"Thank you." Maddy nodded to the hostess and stepped through the door.

The man behind the oak desk rose as she entered and extended his hand. "I am John Yoshakara, manager of The Ranch House." He paused.

Maddy nodded and introduced herself. She took the seat he indicated to the side of the desk and observed him as he sat also. The man smacked of success from his designer floral shirt to the diamond on his right ring finger. The watch on his right wrist wore diamond chips around the face and a square cut gem in the center, anchoring the gold hands.

Maddy wanted to hide her hands—and her jeans and her plain white shirt, with long sleeves rolled up to her elbows. What had ever possessed her to leave without dressing for the occasion? She knew the value of appearance. And first impressions.

"You're looking for a job, Ms. Morton? And you have experience, Leilani said."

"Yes and yes." Again she listed the last three places she had worked.

"And what brought you to the Big Island?"

"I grew up here and decided Waimea was a better place to raise a boy than Honolulu."

"Ah." He nodded. "And can you work any shift? We open at seven A.M. and close the bar at two. Only pupus are served after ten on all but Friday and Saturday nights when we have entertainment in the Roundup Room."

Maddy nodded. She'd just have to work details out with her father. One more thing to ask of him. Being the last hire, she'd have to take the shifts no one else wanted. That's the way it went in service businesses.

"Can you start tonight?"

"Excuse me?" Maddy turned her head slightly to the side as if to hear him better.

"Tonight. We were down one already and someone else called in sick. Wednesday is usually a bit slower than the weekend so you could get into the swing of things here."

"I . . . I guess. I don't have a uniform, though."

"We dress Hawaiian-western here. What you have on would be fine. Aprons are in the supply closet. Friday and Saturday some of the girls wear skirts, but that's up to you. We have a family atmosphere here—karaoke is on Tuesdays and open mike's on Thursday. Even kids get in the act, especially on Thursday evening. You play an instrument by any chance—or sing, dance?"

Maddy shook her head.

"Well, then"—he pushed papers across the desk—"if you'll fill these out, I'll put your name on the schedule. Rosie will be training you, so be here by six for her to run through the basics." The phone rang and he punched a button.

"John, could you come to the kitchen, please?" crackled over the intercom set in the speaker phone.

"You just fill those out, and if I'm not back, leave them on the desk." He stood and came from behind the desk. "Glad you can come on board like this." He extended his hand, shook hers, and left the room.

Maddy felt like she'd just been flattened by a montrous wave.

6

Eavesdropping is not polite. Maddy ignored her mother's long-ago injunction as she stood with her full cart in the line at the grocery store, listening to the two Hawaiians in front of her.

"Some folks want the whole pig for the luau."

"There's no pigs around no more. Got to buy shoulders and hind quarters and wrap them up good, and they taste the same."

The first one shook his head. "No, they don't and you know it."

"You know it and I know it, but haoles, they don't know that. This way no one cries about the 'poor little pig.' From a package they don't know no better."

"Well, if I could find a good supplier, I'd buy them up at litter time and put 'em in the freezer till I need them."

Maddy suddenly felt like a person in a cartoon with a lightbulb flashing above her head. She could raise luau hogs! All she needed was a brood sow—and money. But the barn was there with even a couple of stalls left intact. If she could only find a bred gilt, she'd be in business.

Her head buzzed with ideas as she set her groceries up on the conveyor belt.

When the two men started to leave, she pushed her cart forward and stepped up behind them. "Excuse me."

The younger one turned. "Yes?"

"I . . . I heard you talking about luau pigs." She could feel the heat coloring her neck. "What are they going for now?"

The man shrugged and named a price per pound.

"Is that hanging weight or on the hoof?"

By the time she gathered up her grocery bags and paid the bill, she had a full-blown business plan in her mind and a ready market. The evidence lay tucked in her wallet, a business card with *Andy's Traditional Luaus* written in black ink. They'd said if she could raise good hogs, they'd take all she could provide.

Premium pigs would bring premium prices. Surely Pop would jump at a chance to diversify, especially if . . . She cut off the thought that they might have to destroy the cattle and he'd need something else. But first she had to tell both him and Nicholas that she had a job. She'd keep the other plan until she had a paycheck to buy a gilt with. And feed.

— — —

Simple gratitude didn't begin to describe Rosie's attitude after being with Maddy for only a few minutes that evening. "Thank God John found someone who knows how to post an order, let alone take it and deliver it."

Maddy smiled back at her. "That isn't usually the case, I take it."

"You ain't kiddin', honey. We had some real lulus here."

"Back before I went to Oahu, this place was near to impossible to get a job at." While they talked, Maddy checked out the coffee machine to make sure she knew how to run it. She did.

"Those were the good old days. Now the kids don't want to work, they only want to get paid, and any time we get a good waitress, she leaves for parts unknown. You wouldn't believe the stories I could tell you."

Maddy shook her head. "Yeah, I could. Seen plenty myself."

Rosie showed her the division of tables and which ones would be assigned to her for the evening. "But if you've got a free moment and the coffeepot, don't be shy about filling cups other than at your table. We believe in good service, along with good food, so the locals eat here a lot too."

Rosie tucked a pencil in the upswept bleached hair above her ear. "You got any more questions, you ask me or anyone. We work as a team." She nodded toward where the hostess was seating four people at one of Maddy's tables. "There you go."

And go she did. Her break time came and went as she and the two others did the work of four. Only when she took a moment to visit the ladies' room did she have time to think about the two surly men in her life, both of whom were probably parked, not speaking, in front of the television. Safe bet to say they didn't want to watch the same programs either.

The way Nicholas slouched down on his spine at the dinner table had been dramatic proof of his idea of the whole thing. But at least he wouldn't be out chasing on the streets with that gang of hoodlums—or hoods . . . or whatever it was they wanted to be called.

The straight-eyebrow look Pop had given his grandson at the groaning bode ill for all. She washed her hands, tucked a couple of stray hairs in her loose French braid, and headed back into the fray.

Since the last guests to leave were seated at one of her tables, she couldn't finish her clean-up. The door opening made her and Rosie swap rolled-eye looks. They'd have to be seated in the bar, since the dining room was closed.

The two men tipped their western hats to the girls and made their way on into the bar without pausing, continuing the conversation they'd come in with.

"That man makes my l'il heart go pitter-pat, that's for sure." Rosie stared after the larger of the two.

Maddy turned from filling napkin holders. "Who?"

"That Kam Waiano, the county extension agent. He has a voice that sounds richer than premium hot fudge sauce melting French vanilla ice cream."

"Oh."

"Do you know him?"

"Met him."

"You don't like him?" Rosie looked at her like she was two pineapples short of a case.

Maddy shrugged. "When a man comes telling you you might be forced to destroy your cattle, it doesn't make him too popular." She didn't tell the woman about Kam giving her and Nicholas a ride from the airport. What people didn't know couldn't hurt her.

"That's not his fault. He's done a mighty lot to help the farmers not only on this island but the others too. He says the way to stay ahead of the game is to diversify." Rosie shrugged one shoulder and licked her lips. "I'd like to try diversifying with him myself."

"I thought you were married."

"I am. What's good for the rooster is good for the hen. Hank looks, so do I."

Maddy didn't correct the saying. Ganders, roosters . . . what's the difference? They were the males of the species and thus worthy of staying away from.

"Look but don't touch, I always say."

Maddy muttered something under her breath that brought Rosie to her side.

"Hey, girl, you got something against men in general, or that specific one?"

If you only knew, Maddy thought. But she wasn't about to air her family laundry, so she just shrugged.

She said good-night to her departing guests and, bringing out a tub,

cleared off the table. The fifteen-dollar tip more than made up for staying the extra few minutes. Even with the percentage she had to throw
in the kitty for the busboys, she was sure she had close to a hundred
dollars. Not bad for a first night on the job.

At last she headed for the truck parked behind the restaurant with
the other employee rigs. Now that she thought about it, she wasn't sure
which hurt worse, her feet or her back. Her stomach growled, sounding
loud in the stillness. Should she go back and grab something to eat? A
meal came with the shift.

Instead, she climbed into the cab and leaned her head on her hands
propped along the top of the steering wheel. At least she wouldn't have
to ask her father for money again. She sighed. Goodness, she was tired.

As soon as she turned the ignition, she clicked the radio on to hear
Garth Brooks sing of love gone wrong.

"Ain't that the truth." Maddy shifted into gear, easing out of the
parking lot and onto the road heading home. *Funny*, she thought as the
truck headlights coned out the darkness, *it's like I never left here. I'm home,
and the years on Oahu never happened. Or if they did, it was another lifetime.
Maybe I was only a spectator.* But when she rubbed the bump on her nose
from where Gabe had broken it one of those times he was helping her
to "see the truth of things"—his truth, of course—she knew she'd lived
those years. And lived them the hard way.

She'd even thought of packing a gun, just in case. If he'd ever laid
a hand on Nicholas . . .

Amos welcomed her home to a house dark but for the light above
the kitchen stove. She dropped her purse on the counter and, heeling
off her sturdy but well-used working shoes, padded to the refrigerator.
Two pieces of chicken left from dinner and a piece of Hawaiian bread
made up her meal, along with an orange soda. She took them out to the
glider on the front lanai.

The night felt cool and soft, like flower petals on her skin. Birds
rustled and peeped in the eucalyptus tree that sheltered the roof from
southern sun. Long, slender leaves whispered secrets in the breeze. A

cow bellowed from up on the hill and another answered. Night sounds. Home sounds. She ate her meal and threw the bones to a patiently waiting Amos. He crunched them down as he'd been doing since a pup and leaned against her knee, making his ears convenient for her rubbing.

Maddy breathed deeply, the Plumeria by the step bathing her in its soft perfume. She leaned her head back against the cushion. Maybe if she stayed here, she would sleep. But habit made her push to her feet and she headed back inside, giving Amos a last pat. "You take good care of things now, dog."

He whimpered and lay down, nose on forefeet, his barely existent tail brushing the aged boards.

Maddy accepted another doggy kiss on her cheek and, after rubbing his belly for him, left the dog on the porch and tiptoed up the stairs to check on her son. Mr. Mops dangled precariously over the edge of the bed, so she restored him to his place under Nicholas's arm, dropped a kiss on her son's cheek, and left him, feeling a tug of longing in her heart. If only he would wake and smile up at her with sleep-filled eyes. He used to say "I love you, Mom" when she came home from work like this. She kept the sigh inside and headed for her room, unbuttoning her shirt on the way.

As usual, Maddy fell asleep instantly. And as usual, she woke before the dawn had even let the sky know it was on its way. She lay in the stillness wishing, praying for a return to the sleep she knew she needed. But her mind refused to shut down again, instead playing with thoughts of litters of piglets growing to luau size and being hauled off, leaving her pockets full of hundred-dollar bills. She made mental lists of the supplies she needed to turn the barn into a farrowing house. From there she jumped to what to do about Nicholas. His attitude left a lot to be desired, to say the least. What would it take to turn him back into the cheerful child he'd been?

She'd thought the animals would help, but he refused to even go look at the calves. Amos was doing his best, but Nicholas kept turning away. Just like he did with his mother.

And her father. Which loss was he still grieving, her mother or her brother? Mark had been shot down in the last days of the Vietnam war. His father had been so proud of his son, the pilot. Maddy had a hard time recalling his face, but she remembered his laugh and the way he slung her up on his shoulder. . . .

But like the proverbial elephant, her father never forgot anything, especially not the things anyone did wrong. She closed her mind on her past sins and sat up on the edge of the bed. No sense trying to go back to sleep. Pulling on her jeans and a shirt, she grabbed her boots and tiptoed down the stairs and out onto the porch. Still no light in the eastern sky.

She pulled on her boots and walked toward the barn while scruffing Amos's ears. Maybe she'd look at the tractor her father had been working on. Minutes later, she had the carburetor dunked in solvent to clean it and was taking it apart. Humming a tune, she stood at the work bench, the fluorescent light buzzing its own song, pliers and wrenches laid out according to how she would use them. Her father had taught her well. That's when they had gotten along, here in the barn tinkering with engines. His one compliment came the time she discovered the problem on an engine when he hadn't been able to figure it out.

Birds announced the dawn before the sunlight made it through the open, ten-foot-tall double doors. She was just checking the gap on the spark plugs when she heard Amos welcome someone. Turning, she nodded at her father. "Think the problem was in the carburetor. You want to crank her up?"

"Don't you never sleep, girl?"

"Good morning to you too. Well, you gonna turn her over for me or . . ."

Pop removed his grease-stained baseball hat with the John Deere logo, scrubbed a hand over thinning hair, and settled the hat back in place before climbing aboard the ancient machine. With the key turned, the engine coughed once, twice, and then turned over, settling into its customary chugging.

"You think the timing is okay?" she called above the tractor noise reverberating around the barn.

He revved the engine and let it settle back down. "Sounds good. You didn't lose your touch over there with all them city duds."

Maddy looked up from wiping the grease off her fingers. "Guess not." That was about as close to a compliment as her father might ever come again.

She watched him as he revved the engine again and cocked his head to listen for any sounds that shouldn't be there. "I'm going to wash and make some breakfast." She raised her voice to be heard over the rumbling.

He nodded without looking at her, his concentration still on the machine.

It sounded fine to her, but she knew him well enough to know that he'd want to tinker with one more thing, just to make sure he had the last word. Used to drive both her and her mother nuts. Now she'd be grateful for a final word from him, with the paucity of language going around.

Back at the house, she dipped her fingers in the can of grease solvent and massaged it into the crevices of her hands, then wiped it away on a paper towel. The bar of Lava soap still reigned in the soap dish at the kitchen sink, and she scrubbed till her hands felt raw. That's all she needed—dirty-looking hands for the restaurant crowd. Bad enough her fingernails looked like they'd been through a chopper. She scrubbed harder, digging down into the cuticles and under the nails. Whatever made her get in the grease anyway?

While she beat eggs and added buttermilk for pancakes, she tried to think of ways to ask Pop about raising luau hogs. She whisked in the flour and soda with no more ideas than she started with.

"Nicholas, breakfast's about ready," she called up the stairs.

"M-o-m, why can't I sleep in? It's summer, you know."

"I know that, but I thought maybe we could head for the beach this morning before I go to work." She heard his feet fumble on the floor.

"You coming or should I send Amos after you?"

She took his grumble as a negative.

Humming again, she laid strips of bacon in the pan. "Pop, how about raising luau hogs?" She shook her head. "You know that vacant barn? I got an idea how to make better use of it." Another head shake. No matter how she said it, his first reaction would be a solid no. That was his way.

She poured herself a cup of coffee, turned the bacon down to simmer, and wandered out on the lanai. What would her mother do? She had learned how to handle the man. Maddy answered her own question. "But Pop is different now. He used to laugh, and I haven't even seen a smile since I got home." She leaned against the post.

Amos sat in front of her, one paw on her knee. "Fetch Pop, Amos. Let's eat."

Nicholas stumbled into the kitchen as his grandfather turned on the water at the sink to wash his hands. They both took their seats without a word.

Maddy set plates of bacon, fried eggs, and pancakes before them and pulled out her own chair. Glancing at the clock, she noted it was only seven-thirty. No wonder Nicholas was grousing. Just because she'd been up before dawn didn't mean everyone else wanted to rise.

She passed the plate of sliced papaya and smiled at her son. The scowl she got in return took a bit of the brightness off her smile. So much for a happy day.

When the phone rang, she got up and went to answer it.

"Good morning, Maddy. Can I speak with your father?" the voice said. She knew immediately who it was. Her stomach clenched in a tangle of knots.

Y ou're sure about that?"

"Sure as I'll ever be. Your herd, like all those on this side of the island, tested clear. We were fairly certain, but with the feral pigs running all over the island, we had to check." Kam leaned back in his chair, the hinges squeaking in protest. He couldn't wipe the grin from his face, but then he hadn't tried very hard. Smiling felt good after the last few days of gloom. "I have the serum here and have to run up to Waimea anyway. I'll bring it by." He sat up straight. "How many head you got—including the calves?"

After hanging up the phone, Kam stretched and tapped the intercom button. "I have the list ready for you to call. I'll be out of the office for the next several hours."

Sue entered his office moments later and took the paper he handed her. "Anything else?"

He shook his head. "Just tell them the sooner they vaccinate the better, and they can pick up the vaccine at Dr. Sam's."

"There's enough?"

"I think so. A big shipment came in this morning."

"Where you goin'?"

"Out to play with a bunch of cows."

"Cows? You don't have any cattle." She gave him a look out of the side of her eye. "This wouldn't have anything to do with the Morton herd, by any chance?"

"Just being my friendly, neighborly extension agent self." Kam flipped his laptop closed, grabbed his cell phone out of the charger, and headed for the door. "Have a great day."

Sue shook her head and groaned. "I don't know what's gotten into you." But the twinkle in her eye said she knew far more than she was telling. "What shall I tell any callers?"

"To leave a message at the tone—what else?" Kam clapped his straw hat on his head and picked up a red-and-white cooler. "See ya."

"My, my, if we aren't in a good mood."

Kam paused in the doorway. "By the way, how did you guess the Morton herd?" He stared at his assistant.

Sue shook her head. "You think I don't know what goes on around here? You ask questions, we figure out why."

"Oh." Kam knew that if his face looked as confused as he felt, he was in trouble. He could stop and ask for an explanation or just beat it. He chose the latter of the two, which he figured was bound to be less costly in the long run.

"'This is the day, this is the day, that the Lord hath made, I will rejoice . . .'" Kam couldn't help but sing his adulation as he drove the curving road to Waimea. A mile before he reached the top of the pass, he turned right at a monstrous eucalyptus tree. He could hear cattle bawling before he stopped the truck.

The smile on Maddy's face when he got out of the truck with the cooler was worth driving all around the island ten times. As he walked toward her he nodded. Sure enough, her gray eyes changed with her mood. Today was pure sun and shimmering blue waves. "I thought I could stay and help if you could use another hand." He raised the cooler so she could see it. By the look on her face, he could tell the offer caught her by surprise.

"Oh. Well, Nicholas and I have to bring a few more down. I guess you and Pop could start with those already in the corral." She gestured to the three already in the chute. "He's pretty good with a needle."

"Okay, then I'll handle the lining them up. Your son ever done anything like this before?"

"Nope, but he learns quick."

"Might as well ear tag the calves as they come through," Jesse said after a warmer-than-before greeting. "Thanks for the help, though we could do just fine on our own."

"Never doubted that for an instant, but you ever been cramped up in an office all day?"

"Nope, but then I doubt you do this much either."

Kam set the cooler down by the squeeze chute. "You caught me on that one."

Once Maddy had all the stock in the corral, the pace picked up. Nicholas and Amos herded the cows to the narrow chute one at a time, Kam moved them into the squeeze chute and locked them in, Maddy gave the shots, and Jesse tagged the calves.

"Fine-looking herd you have here." Kam slapped one of the steers on the rump to get him moving forward.

Jesse clamped the tag in a calf's ear and let it loose to bawl its way over to its mother.

"You ever in 4-H when you were a kid?"

Maddy nodded. "I raised hogs."

"Young girl over below Kona had a steer getting ready for the fair. Had to be shot."

Maddy cringed. "Because of the anthrax?"

Kam nodded. "Heartbreaking." He glanced over in time to see one of the cows bowl Nicholas over in spite of Amos nipping at her heels.

Maddy started toward him, then stopped. Nicholas got up, brushed himself off, muttered something they couldn't hear, and went after the cow again, this time with a stick he picked up from under the fence.

Kam caught her gaze and smiled at her along with a slight nod. The boy needed to learn these things, and coddling him would both embarrass him and keep him from learning. Kam glanced to the side when he heard a throat-clearing from Jesse. From the look on the old man's face, Kam knew he'd seen it too. He could tell the grandfather didn't have a whole lot of respect for the boy—yet.

Kam was betting that by the end of the summer, however, they'd see a different boy inhabiting that skin.

"Don't you ever have to work?" Maddy asked when the last calf ran out of the corral and back up on the hilly pasture.

"You don't think this was work?" Kam wiped his forehead with the back of his tanned arm.

"Sure I do, but I don't guess helping with the Morton cattle is what most taxpayers would think was wise spending of their money."

"The job outline is pretty broad for an extension agent. That's one of the reasons I trained for this job. I do my share in the office too."

"I'm sure you do." Her voice sounded cool.

He noticed that she moved to touch the boy, but Nicholas would have none of it. Tough kid still had that eucalyptus log sitting on his shoulder, but at least he had helped them with the task.

"How come you put the tags in the calves' ears and made them bleed?" Nicholas asked his grandfather.

"Identification. Easier and more humane than branding them." Jesse handed the cooler back to Kam. "Thanks. How much do I owe you?"

"Sam will bill you. I don't know how much he's charging."

"You want to stay for lunch?" Maddy cleared her throat. "I'll have iced tea ready in a few minutes."

Kam schooled his face to cover the surprise. "Glad to—and thanks."

— — —

"So how do you like the island?" Kam directed his question at Nicholas once they'd settled at the table to eat.

Nicholas shrugged and took a bite out of his ham and cheese sandwich.

"He ain't seen nothing but the inside of that room." Jesse answered around a mouthful of bread.

Nicholas glared at his grandfather and shifted so he was looking away from the others. His back made a pretty effective barrier.

Hey, boy, you're sure pushing the bounds here. Kam glanced at Maddy to see what she was going to do. She appeared to be dissecting her sandwich with laser eyes. He could see a muscle twitching in her jaw.

"Maybe you'd like to come snorkeling sometime with me and my two nephews, Benny and James. They're about your age."

Nicholas shook his head. "Never been snorkeling."

Kam looked at Maddy, who shrugged and glared at the same time. *Uh-oh, not a good topic.* He was beginning to wonder if there was such a thing with these three.

"We have some good places for learning here on Hawaii. You know how to swim?"

When Nicholas didn't answer, Maddy said, "Nicholas swims well— I made sure of that, surrounded by water like we are." Her voice sounded apologetic, like he'd been accusing her of slacking off as a mother.

Kam finished his sandwich and got to his feet. "Thanks for the meal and the chance to push something besides paper." He set his plate on the low table. "I meant what I said about snorkeling. We have plenty of equipment, so you needn't worry about that." He glanced from son to mother. "I'll call you."

Maddy stood, her spine straight to the point of rigid. "Thank you for the help."

Her words and tone were an obvious dismissal. *Now* what had he said? Kam left after a couple of words with Jesse. Right about the time he thought he was making some progress, he managed to offend her.

Of course, she wasn't difficult to offend.

Wonder what's gone on that she wears a burr under her saddle all the time? Must be painful. He waved and honked as he drove away, but as far as he could see in the mirror, no one paid any attention.

"Well, Waiano, you could say you made the effort and call it quits or . . ." He knew himself well enough that he would go with the *or*. Both Nicholas and Maddy were hiding behind strong walls, and he'd always loved the challenge of wall bashing. Amazing the lovely gardens one found behind solid walls.

Don't push. Maddy narrowed her eyes watching the dust from the departing pickup. *He can't let well enough alone, can he?* Gratitude for Kam's help and resentment at what she decided was plain pushiness warred within her. Questions, always questions. She cleared away the lunch things and turned around to find both Nicholas and her father gone. The music upstairs told her where Nicholas was, and she guessed her father was either in the living room or on his way up to the cemetery.

"Why doesn't he just take his bed and sleep up there?"

Amos wagged his bit of a tail so hard he shivered all over.

"I don't know, dog, maybe coming here wasn't the smartest thing I ever did." Amos licked her chin. She wrapped her arms around him and hugged him close. Amos sighed and leaned into her, offering all the comfort he could. Maddy thought again of Kam. "Why does he have to be so darn nice?"

— — —

Maddy often strode the hills in the early morning hours when she should have been sleeping and couldn't. She didn't even try to sit at her mother's grave, for too often her father hunkered there, at any time of day or night. She kept hoping that if she walked fast enough or far enough she could outrun her mind, but the worries dug into her shoulders and took up root. *What should I do about Pop? How can I help him deal with his grief? Where will we get the money to survive if we have to leave the ranch? What if they release Gabe?* On and on the worries churned, over and over. The questions pounded within her brain, but there was never any answer.

— — —

"What's that cloud you got sittin' on your shoulders, girl?" Rosie asked one night. "You're walkin' like heavy doesn't begin to cover it."

Maddy just shook her head. "No time for a story this long." She grabbed the coffee carafes and spun away to offer refills to the many diners. At least they were full tonight and looked to stay that way with the backup at the door. Keeping too busy to think was about the only way she could deal with the mess of her life.

That, and dreaming of how soon she could buy her hogs. She kept ignoring the fact that she needed her father's okay first, since it was his land and his barn and truck and . . . The list continued.

You should be grateful for that herd of cows, her conscience reminded her. *Others have a lot less.* Guilt never rode easy.

Maddy groaned when the hostess showed a family to one of her tables.

"What's with you?" Teresa, one of the other waitresses, asked. She followed Maddy's gaze. "Oh, you lucky dog, you got Kam and his family at your table." She looked up at the scowl on Maddy's face. "You want to switch? He always tips good and that smile of his . . . why, he could make angels cry from the sheer joy of seeing it."

Maddy shook her head and snorted. "No, I'll handle it."

"What do you have against that man, anyway?" Rosie asked while dishing up salad plates for her table. "I don't know of anyone who doesn't like Kam Waiano."

"Now you do." Maddy tucked warm French rolls into a basket and folded over the corners of the red-and-white-checked napkin. Heading for a table near the laughing family, she passed around the salads and set the basket in the center. Pulling a long pepper grinder from its snug fit in her apron strings, she gestured with it as she asked, "Pepper, any-one?"

Concentrate on what you're doing. Her mind totally ignored her own instructions and waltzed over to watch Kam tease the flashing-eyed lit-tle girl to his right. *I thought he wasn't married. Isn't that what Rosie said a while ago? But if he isn't, why did she say "his family"?*

Teresa was right about his smile. Maddy felt the warmth of it when she stopped at their table, making sure she was across from him. Any closer was too close. Being in the same room was too close, she had to admit to herself. Honesty she prized above all things, having lived with so little in her years with Gabe.

"What'll you have, folks?" Pencil poised above her pad, she looked first to the older woman.

"Mother, this is Maddy Morton. She grew up here on the island." Kam smiled from his mother to Maddy and back again.

His voice, definitely warm butter over . . . She jerked herself back to the job at hand. "Glad to meet you."

"I am Marianna Waiano." She shook her head at her son, setting the dark strands of hair to swaying. Maddy could see where her son got his smile. Megawatts for sure.

"What can I get for you tonight? The mahi mahi came off the boat just this afternoon."

The woman nodded. "That sounds good. How is your father? I haven't seen him for quite some time."

Maddy felt her eyebrows go up. "You know my—?" She stopped herself. Of course they did. Most of the long timers knew each other.

"We used to talk at the coffee-growers meetings. He doesn't come anymore. Not since the bust got us."

"I know. He never replanted and went into cattle instead."

"Ah." Her tone said she understood it all. "I know it was hard for him when your mother died."

Maddy nodded, then took the rest of their orders, with Kam last. She held her pencil, waiting while he studied the menu one more time.

"I'll take the chicken stir fry." He closed his menu and handed it to her. "And bring us a double order of pupus, too, please."

"You want me to wait on ordering your dinners, then?" Maddy knew the appetizers would take a bit of time in themselves.

"That would be fine." He ruffled the hair of the laughing girl beside him. "But you better bring Maria's salad. She no like pupus."

"K-a-m." The girl batted his hand away, giggling all the while.

"Ignore my son," Marianna said. "He can't resist teasing the little ones."

Who love every minute of it, Maddy thought, nodding her head. *I wonder what it would be like to have those big hands of his run through my hair?* She nearly dropped her tray at the thought. What in heaven's name was the matter with her tonight?

Later that night on the drive home, she thought about the coffee trees she'd found up on the hill. Coffee was big again. She considered the rise of Starbucks in Seattle and how it had spread to the rest of the country, along with all the copycat companies. Coffee bars had sprung up in Honolulu like mushrooms after rain.

But it took years before a coffee planting would produce enough beans to sell.

Better stick to hogs. If she could get a bred gilt, the return would be only a few months. Now the issue was how to approach Pop. Maybe he had some savings he'd like to invest. She mentally counted the cash she'd stowed in the carved teak box in her top dresser drawer—all her tip money. Her paycheck she'd used to buy groceries and gas for the truck.

Living here certainly had simplified her life. When she'd offered to pay rent, her father had sent her a look that made sure she didn't suggest it again. Nicholas would need clothes for school, but that was still two months off.

What could she get for eight hundred dollars? It seemed an enormous amount to her. She who hadn't had bus fare to get to work at times in Honolulu. But now she didn't have a husband helping himself to her paycheck when he ran low either. The thought of Gabe made her stomach clench. She'd tried hiding her money, but he always found it or beat on her until she told him where it was.

If Pop was still up, she'd talk with him tonight. Nodding at her decision, she turned into the lane leading up to the house. The gate no longer hung like a drunken sailor. She'd fixed that, along with the screen doors and the porch light. Oiled hinges let the door open silently.

No lights, no sound. She'd have to talk with him in the morning.

Maybe she'd sleep more than three hours tonight. Now, wasn't *that* a novel idea?

The sound of someone clearing his throat made her jump. She stopped on her way to the kitchen and peeked in the living room. Her father sat in his chair.

"Why are you sitting in the dark?" She leaned against the door frame.

No answer.

She knelt by the chair. "Pop, what's wrong?"

"Nothing."

She waited. Moonlight carved angles on his face and shadowed his eyes to black holes. The urge to stroke his hand that lay so close to her own made her clench her teeth. He didn't like being touched any more than she did. Leastwise, not since her mother died.

Amelia had been the toucher in the family and taught her daughter so. Then Gabe had beat that out of her too. *Oh, Mom, if only you were here now.*

"Can I get you something? Coffee, glass of water? I brought you home a piece of pie."

His grunt obviously meant no.

Maddy got off her knees and sat on the ottoman facing him. She rested her elbows on her knees and her chin in her hands. *Was this a good time to ask about the hogs?* She studied him a moment longer and got to her feet. "Night, Pop."

Standing at the kitchen sink, looking out at the dark, she heard him go into his room and shut the door. She poured another glass of water and ambled over to the table. An official-looking paper lay open on top of the Sears catalog.

She held it under the lamp over the table, her heart falling further with every word she read. The farm would be put on the auction block for payment of back taxes. The sum listed at the bottom seemed bigger than the national debt.

Y ou look tired, my son." Marianna Waiano studied her eldest
child.

"Certifying that those three anthrax herds were destroyed and then
going around to make sure all the farmers and ranchers inoculated their
cattle would take the life out of anyone. It was bad enough giving them
the news in the beginning. If I never have another few weeks like the
last, it'll be too soon." Kam tipped his chair back to lean against the
house wall. The lanai welcomed him with open fronds of palm and banana scented with frangipani and Plumeria.

"It wasn't your fault."

"Tell that to the farmers. I even got a hate letter at work today."
Kam smoothed his dark hair back with both hands.

"But you believe it was your fault?" Her gentle voice joined with
the creak of the wooden rocker.

"To think that such a thing as digging for foundations for a barn
and machine shop could have caused all this grief." The chair legs

thumped back to the worn boards of the lanai floor. "Even with all our rules and care for quarantine, the stuff was already here. And look what it did." He looked out across their land. "Who knows what's under there."

"Kam, you can't be responsible for everybody and everything."

"According to that letter, I'd better be responsible for covering my back on a dark night."

"Have you told the sheriff?"

"Nah." He shook his head. "Just someone blowing off steam and I was the messenger." He thought back to the discussion with Sam. *"They kill the messenger."* Could that really happen? Surely not here on the Big Island.

"But if someone goes loco?" His mother caught the drift of his thoughts as she so often did.

Kam shook his head and tipped his chair back again. "Don't worry about it, okay?"

"I won't. I'll pray instead."

Kam knew that to be true. His mother was a staunch believer in the power of the Almighty to answer prayer. That belief was what had gotten her through the years of agony when her husband, George, came up missing in action in Vietnam. They never found his body, and the turmoil associated with the MIAs after the war had worn her thin but never to despair.

He sometimes wondered about himself, though.

Kam could still hear his father's words. *"Now, son, you're the man of this house until I come back, and I know you will take care of your mother and your brother and sisters."* Those words had been engraved on his heart and soul that day. Shortly after that, his father dressed in his army uniform and a duffle bag over his shoulder, climbed the steps to the aircraft, and with a wave, disappeared into the plane. Never to be seen again. Not even a body that was brought home to be buried.

Kam blinked away the past and turned to his mother. "I'm sorry, what was that you said?"

"I said Marlea and the boys will be coming over soon. Benny claims he hasn't seen you in forever."

Kam blinked again. Benny. If he'd taken better care like his father ordered, his brother, Ben, would be alive today. Kam scrubbed a broad hand over his face and shook his head. A sigh that carried the weight of the years caused his chair to thump back down again. "You need anything done around here?"

"No, not right now, thanks. But I do have a pitcher of papaya juice that needs drinking. I'll get you more." When he started to stand, she put a loving hand firmly on his shoulder and pressed downward. "Stay right there." Though her voice was soft and gentle, the order was unmistakable.

Kam closed his eyes and listened to the palm fronds rustling in the breeze. A chicken clucked to her peeping chicks under the raised lanai, birds twittered in the branches of the shiny-leaved guava tree, and two doves whirred their way to the lawn, their gentle *whoo-whoo*ing helping his shoulders to drop. He clasped his hands over his broad chest and tilted the chair back again.

The screen door slammed at the same time as a car turned in the lane. He took the papaya juice his mother offered him, and after a long swallow, he set the frosty, half-empty glass down on the round table beside the chair. A single spray of purple and white wild orchids in a heavy vase adorned the table that still sported a groove worn by one of his play trucks. For years he'd planned on sanding away that reminder of his brief boyhood, but his mother refused. He traced the gouge with a tanned finger. Amazing how such a simple thing could evoke the sorrows of yesteryear.

"Unca Kam, when we going snorkeling?" Benny and James bailed out of the car and hit the ground running for the main man in their young lives.

Kam spread his arms wide and gathered each wriggling brown body close. "Soon as I have a free moment." He looked up from the boys to study their mother, the eldest daughter and a month short of two years younger than he. He often wondered if she remembered their father, but he didn't dare ask.

"Aloha." Her voice carried much of the music of their mother's. Dark, almond-shaped eyes had the same gift of seeing under the skin. "Looks like you're carrying the whole island on your shoulders, big brother. Don't believe them."

"Sit, sit." Marianna came through the door with a tray of four more full glasses. She set it down and the boys flew to her like butterflies to a blossom. She hugged and kissed them both, at the same time listening to their tale of the first day of Vacation Bible School at their church.

"I have a poem for you." Marlea sat down on the cushions vacated by their mother. "Courtesy of . . ." She nodded at the boys.

"Shoot." Kam raised his eyebrows expectantly.

She laid a long-fingered hand on his arm, waited for his smile, and began. "If Noah really had been so wise, why didn't he swat those two old flies?"

Kam's deep laugh rang out and brought the two boys running. "So that's what they're teaching in Bible School these days."

"We need to build a boat, Unca Kam, like for the ark." Benny lifted his uncle's juice glass and drank. He set it down again at the raised right eyebrow and grinned at his uncle. "I was Noah today. Those nene just wouldn't go on the ark. I even tried using my crook." He made motions of snagging the endangered Hawaiian geese with a long, crooked pole.

"I was an elephant." James clasped his hands and pretended his arms extended toward the floor were a swinging trunk.

"And did you go on the ark?"

"Yeah, but Missy was the girl elephant." He made a face and shuddered.

"We need to make a model of the ark, and I told them you would help us."

"But Kam needs to work, you know." Their mother leaned forward and tousled Benny's hair.

"Not at night."

It's times like this I wish they had a father. Kam pulled back from the thought. While he'd not heard Marlea complain in the last few years, she had no compunction about asking for his help.

He heaved another sigh. What was the matter with him today?

But he knew what it was. The cattle thing had gotten him down like it had all the farmers he tried so hard to help.

"Mother, what do you know about Jesse Morton?" His own question caught him by surprise.

"Jesse—or his daughter?" Her question caught him off guard.

"Jesse. That's what I asked." He knew the instant the sharpened words left his mouth that he'd said too much.

"Ah." Marianna nodded and kept on nodding while she closed her eyes a bit in thought. "Jesse Morton never got over losing his son in the war, but he didn't really turn bitter until Amelia died. Let's see, that's about five years ago, maybe six. I've only seen glimpses of him since then. He dropped out of church . . . in fact, he about dropped out of life entirely. Edi and I, we tried calling on him but . . ." She shook her head. "Sad."

"His daughter's husband is in prison," declared Marlea.

"Her ex," corrected Marianna. "They got a divorce."

"How do you know all that?" Kam looked from his mother to his sister. The two boys had disappeared under the house to play with the dog and her puppies.

"We read the newspapers, my dear brother," Marlea added. "Something you might do—other than the sports page."

"I read the news too." He retreated behind his glass, swirling the ice cubes in the golden liquid. He set the glass down with a thump. "You got the boys enrolled in summer camp yet?"

"I will."

"You're going to be too late again at the rate you're going."

"Great, Kam, ruin a perfectly good afternoon with your big boss act." Marlea rose gracefully to her feet. "Come on, boys, we need to get going." She shot Kam a dirty look and shook her head.

"But, M-o-m."

"Now!" Kam knew his tone was too sharp again. He rubbed the back of his neck with one hand. "Sorry, guys. I'll come get you after work Friday. We'll hit the beach."

"Don't do us any favors." Marlea's turquoise muumuu with white orchids swirled around her legs as she descended the three steps.

But she blew them a kiss from the Bougainvillaea arched over the gate, letting him know she bore him no ill will. Or at least that's what he hoped she meant.

"I better get on the road too."

"You could stay for dinner."

"No, thanks. I'm not very good company tonight."

"Edi will be sad she missed you."

"Tell her aloha for me." Kam bent and kissed his mother's cheek. The two sisters lived together here on the Waiano homeplace, and right now he didn't feel the need to be ganged up on until he spilled all his woes.

"Just pray for me, all right? And all the families suffering on the island. Those with the cattle slaughtered are really being hit hard." He shook his head again. "I don't know what more to do." He stared at his hands. "And what if we didn't catch it all?" His whisper could barely be heard over the rustling banana leaves.

She was awakened by the hushed silence that tells the world the birds are about to begin heralding the sun. Maddy flopped around for a few minutes before throwing back the light blanket. What she wouldn't give for some extra sleep. She was running on caffeine and the engine was about empty.

So now instead of one thing, the question of raising luau hogs, there were two things to discuss. Where was her father going to get the money to pay the property taxes? She checked the carved box and counted her stash. Over eight hundred dollars, her pig money. She'd offer it to him, but with all the penalties, this would hardly make a dent.

In the kitchen she put the leftover coffee in the microwave and tapped the counter until it was hot, then blew on the steaming beverage and took it out to the lanai. The eastern sky had started to lighten, washing out the stars. The breeze smelled of the trees and the sea, alive and flowing. Too restless to sit, Maddy leaned against the post that held up the tin roof and sipped her coffee. Even warmed instead of fresh, she could feel it flowing out to her limbs and erasing the sludge.

So what's most important? She answered her own question quickly. Paying the taxes—or there won't be pasture for the cows, let alone a barn for the pigs.

Amos looked up at her and whimpered. Maddy put her now empty coffee cup on the low wicker table by the glider and headed for the plants along the back fence. It would be light enough any minute to be able to tell which were weeds and which were flowers. If only she could start cleaning again, but it wasn't fair to wake Pop and Nicholas like that—not that even vacuuming under his bed would wake Nicholas.

When she could smell fresh coffee she knew her father was up. Her knees creaked as she pushed herself to her feet. Time to attack the taxes.

Pop just came in the front door from picking up the paper as she came in the back. She glanced at the table, but the letter from the county assessor was no longer there. No matter. She poured two cups of coffee and handed him one when he sat down at his place and started to open the paper.

"Pop, we have to talk."

The paper rustled.

"I read that letter. It's been three years since you paid your taxes. Why?"

"Four, actually." The paper snapped.

She waited, but he sipped his coffee and read on like nothing was the matter.

"How are you going to pay them?"

She waited again.

"Pop!"

"None of your business!" He folded a section to see her better. "I've been taking care of myself for sixty years, missy, and don't you forget it." The paper flipped open all the way.

"I have money if you don't have enough. I was going to use it to buy—" She cut off her words. Better to breach one issue at a time.

"You spend your money the way you want, I'll take care of mine."

"All I want to know is if you have enough." His silence beat on her like Gabe's fists. When would she learn to keep her mouth shut, to stay out of other people's business like she wanted them to stay out of hers?

She took in a deep breath and let it all out. "And if you have enough, why haven't you paid them on time?"

The paper slammed to the table. "I didn't have the money then, I thought about letting the place go, and it's none of your business." He stood so fast his chair teetered and almost crashed over.

It is if I'm to stay here and make some kind of home for us, Maddy silently answered.

The door creaked to a close behind him and his boots thundered on the stoop as he headed out the back gate. She knew she'd find him up by her mother's grave if she wanted to go looking for him.

She didn't. "Stubborn old man. Why can't he just say yes or no? Answer a civil question with a civil answer?"

Why can't you? The question echoed in her mind.

Maddy headed back outside as if the ghost of her mother were beating her about the head and shoulders. When she tried to start the mower, it refused. Calling it several uncomplimentary names, she shoved it out to the shop in the barn and took it apart.

By the time she got it going, sweat was running down her back and under her arms. The day promised to be both hot and humid. Just like she felt.

— — —

By the time she got to the restaurant, she'd simmered about enough to be well done by any cook's standards. Putting on a smiling face for the diners took a measure of strength she wasn't sure she possessed.

"Uh-oh, thunder on the mountaintop." Ruby winked up at Maddy. "You want to talk about it or wait until something makes you erupt?"

"It's nothing."

"Right. And I look just like Dolly Parton."

Maddy glanced down at the short, well-padded, bleached-blond woman. "Well, you almost got the hair right."

"Sure, sure. Now, what's bothering you?"

"Anyone ever tell you you're nosier'n a hog after truffles?"

Ruby thought a moment. "Nope, that's a new one. Think I'll save it and tell my dear husband. He'll get a kick out of that."

Maddy felt a twinge of something—could it be jealousy?—at the casual way Ruby referred to her husband. They'd been married for twenty-eight years and Ruby insisted twenty-seven and a half of them were happy. The other half year constituted the fights they'd had and made up after.

"So come on, girl, give."

Maddy gave her a very abbreviated version to the shaking of Ruby's head.

"Oh, that poor man. He's been through so much, and now to have the government after him. I'll put him at the top of my prayer list."

Maddy rolled her eyes. "Yeah, thanks a lot."

"You know you and Nicholas are right up there too. Been there since the first day I met you. God's working something real special out for you, Maddy, my friend. You just wait and see."

Maddy took the bin of napkins and began folding. She hadn't the heart to tell Ruby what she thought of prayer and the One to whom she prayed. It just didn't work, that was all.

Ruby walked by and leaned over to speak only for Maddy's ears. "We'll just have to ask our Father to cash in a couple of those cattle that He has on a thousand hills."

"Well, He better make it a prime breeding bull, then. Taxes around here are astronomical."

Ruby's laugh as she set out the napkins Maddy folded made the other girls smile too.

Maddy had never realized she could indeed be funny. She'd been sarcastic. Didn't the woman understand?

— — —

"Kam, this is Dr. Sam. Sorry to call so early, but I thought you might like to ride along with me. Jesse Morton just called and said he has dead cows all over the hillside."

"I'll be ready by the time you get here."

"Father, please . . ." Kam didn't know what else to pray, so he repeated the two words over and over. He was just ready to open the door when he heard Sam's truck pull in the drive.

"You think it's anthrax?" Kam stumbled over the hated word.

Sam shook his head. "How can it be? You were out there when — three days ago? — and they were all healthy, right?"

Kam nodded. "Then what could it be?"

Sam shook his head again. "I just don't know, but poison of some kind would be my first thought. We'll know more when we see them."

When they arrived, Maddy met them at the corral. "They're up in the pasture. You can't drive any closer, but if you want we can take the tractor."

"No, this is fine." Sam dropped some syringes, disinfectant, and his rubber gloves in the stainless steel bucket. He pulled on his coveralls and galoshes just in case. If it was something contagious, he wanted to be prepared.

"How's your father?" Kam asked, looking up the hill. He could see several bodies of the cows from where he stood.

"Fatalistic. Frantic. You know him, he wouldn't tell you if he was bleeding to death."

As they drew closer to the scene, Kam wanted to close his eyes and will it all away. A calf nosed the dead cow, needing its morning feeding. Other cows and calves grazed the knee-deep grass. Jesse stood staring at a dead steer.

"I don't get it. They were fine last night. I checked on them all, like I always do."

Sam knelt to study one of the dead animals. "Only thing I can think of that would act this fast is a poison of some kind."

"Who would poison my cows? I never did anything to make someone hate me like that."

"Could be accidental. You had anything different up here or in the water?"

"I checked the water tank. It looked perfectly normal." Maddy stood next to Kam, her arms clamped around her middle.

"Heard anything strange lately?" Sam checked the eyes and the mouth.

Maddy and Jesse looked at each other, both of them shaking their heads.

"Less you call Amos barking in the middle of the night a couple of nights ago strange. I figure he heard the wild pigs up here." Jesse shrugged and shook his head again.

"You had much trouble with them?" Kam wished he could put an arm around Maddy and stop her shivering. While it was cool in the early morning sun, it wasn't cold.

Sam swabbed an oily substance from the steer's chin and held it up to sniff. "You better look around real good and see if you can find something foreign. This looks and smells like propylene glycol to me."

"Coolant?" Kam frowned and knelt down by Sam.

"How would that get up here?" Jesse knelt too.

"You sure they haven't been outside of the fence? Or maybe you had some in a can down by the barn?"

Jesse stood back up. "Now, look here, I don't go dumping something like that or leave it sitting around. Amos could get into it and it would kill him. No, no." He kept shaking his head in denial.

"You three go on and look. I'll check the others, but it looks the same. Maybe you should herd the rest of them down to the corral, where you know they are safe, until we get to the bottom of this."

Maddy and Jesse did as the vet said while Kam began walking the field. As soon as the remaining cows were safe, they joined in the search.

"You take the fence line on this side, and I'll go for that one." Kam waved them each to a section of the pasture.

Maddy shouted and waved at them when she found a pool of iridescent liquid cupped in a hollow of the rocks. She could see where it flowed from some rocks on the other side of the fence and pooled in the depression. Cow tracks around it showed what had happened.

Jesse and Kam hurried over, then climbed past the fence to investigate further. They could see truck tire tracks a hundred feet or so down the hill and the deeper tracks of a dolly. Whoever dumped the substance tried to make sure the contraband was hidden in the rocks.

Kam followed the rivulet that still seeped out of the original dumping.

"Had to be a service station owner or some such. No one else would have that much to dump." Kam stuck his finger in the rainbow-hewed liquid and sniffed it. "Or someone who owns a fleet of trucks or buses. Tour buses have theirs changed regularly. Anyone with a hauling business does."

"Just my luck to have it run over onto my property." Jesse sat against a waist-high boulder. He shook his head again and blew out his breath in a huff. "First the coffee, now the cows." He rubbed a hand across his eyes. "So how do I get rid of the carcasses? Bury them, burn them, what?"

"You better call Atkins. He picks up dead stock. The county health will be after you if you bury or burn them."

"Unless they had anthrax." Jesse pushed himself upright. "Can't sell 'em, and now I have to pay to dispose of 'em. Something sure is wrong with this country when we get regulated right out of business." He climbed back over the fence and stumbled down the hill.

Kam watched him, then turned to the woman beside him. "Maddy, I . . . I'm so sorry."

"Yeah, me too. I keep thinking of the stupid song. You know, 'If it weren't for bad luck, I'd have no luck at all.'" She shook her head. "That's my pop, huh?"

What could he say? He remained silent and walked beside her past the carcasses and down to the cows bellowing in the corral.

"I'll come back out later and help clean up that mess up there. We got to call the sheriff right now. He'll want to look into it."

"Why? They'll never catch the idiots that did that."

"Because that's the way we do things."

"Suit yourself." Maddy stared out over the ocean, her eyes returning to a vacant gray hue.

"W hy in tarnation would you want to bring pigs on this bad-luck place?"

Hang on to your cool. Maddy repeated the words three more times and sucked in a deep breath. Three days since the end of the cattle. She'd tried to wait longer, but getting something going felt more like a necessity than a dream. "Pop, I thought I explained myself fairly well. The luau outfits need luau pigs, and there is a scarcity of live hogs the right size. They are willing to pay premium price, we need money—"

His snort stopped her for a moment.

"Well, if you don't need money, I do and . . ." Did she dare mention the taxes? If he planned to use the money from the sale of the remaining cattle, was there enough? Why wouldn't he talk with her? She felt like she was banging her head against a granite wall.

"What for?"

She paused, wrinkled her forehead to help her think better, and shook her head. "Why, I need a car . . ."

"What's wrong with the truck?"

"Nothing, but . . . but that's yours and . . ."

"Did I say you couldn't use it?"

"No, but . . ." She rubbed her forehead. This was giving her a head-ache. Or something was—could be lack of sleep or anything. *How about I'm a grown woman and I can't live off my father for the rest of my life?*

The silence stretched while she tried to corral her thoughts, which had scattered like dandelion fuzzies in a breeze.

Her father never had liked talking about money, especially not with his daughter.

"Pop, I have to plan for Nicholas, school, sports, things like that. I think raising hogs is a good idea. I loved pigs when I had them in 4-H, remember? Those stalls in the barn are going to waste. . . ." She didn't add that everything around here was falling into ruin. "I thought maybe you'd like to go in with me. We'd get a couple bred gilts, a boar when we need him—with two or three farrowing stalls, we could run ten head real easy."

Her father snorted again. "Ain't you learned nothin' from what hap-pened? There's nothing about farming that's ever easy."

She couldn't argue that point, not after what they'd just been through. She often caught herself looking up to check on the cattle, wishing for the calves and their antics. Wishing Nicholas had taken a liking to the animals too. While Amos had adopted the boy and got in his licks whenever he could, the opportunities were rare.

Two stock trucks had come that very afternoon, one for the living and one for the dead. So far there was no word on the investigation.

She felt the sigh start deep within and work its way up. "I know it won't be easy, but if you don't want to go in with me, do you mind if I do it?"

As she waited for his response, her head felt like it weighed a hun-dred pounds, falling forward and pulling against the tight muscles in her neck and upper back. She blinked and sucked in a deep breath, rolling her head around on her shoulders.

"You can't fool me. You're so tired now, you're beginning to look like a scarecrow. What you want more to do for?"

"Someone once told me that hard work never hurt anybody."

"No, but lack of sleep does."

"Look who's talking."

"When you get old, you don't need so much sleep anymore."

"You're not *old*."

"Sixty-two tomorrow."

"Oh." What could she say? She'd forgotten her father's birthday.

"Maddy, if you're crazy enough to want to raise hogs, you do it — but don't expect any help from me." He heaved himself to his feet. "No help a'tall." He brushed by her and limped off to his bedroom.

Why is he limping? Maddy wondered. *And why hasn't he paid the taxes?* She shook her head and stood, arching her back and digging her fists into the tight muscles. He didn't have money. Land rich and dollar poor, like most of the other older people on the island. At least he didn't believe in farming on credit, or at least he didn't used to, so there shouldn't be feed bills and loans at the bank to be paid off.

She'd tried to talk her father into keeping a few head to start rebuilding a herd again, but he refused. He didn't want anything to do with them.

— — —

"You might look at this," Jesse said, tossing the newspaper across the table during breakfast the next morning.

Maddy looked at him, surprised that he'd said something without being spoken to first. She picked up the paper and glanced at the ads, then at her father. "What?"

"The livestock listings."

Maddy searched the ads. *Bred gilts and older hogs for sale. Call . . .* She looked across the table.

He refused to meet her gaze, studying his coffee cup like the secrets of the world lay within its depths.

"Thank you."

He grunted.

She glanced up at the clock. Seven. Too early to call yet. She'd give it an hour. Picking up her breakfast dishes, she set them in the sink and, whistling for Amos, headed out to the barn. What would it take to get a pen finished at the north end of the barn? If she ran hog wire behind the barn, she could leave the back door open and they could free range under the trees and to the meadow. How much did a roll of hog wire cost nowadays? And steel posts?

She took a hammer from the tool bench and a pry bar. Might as well get started right away. At least there was electricity and she could run a water line for an automatic waterer. She studied the layout. Where there had once been four stalls, two on either side of a wide center aisle, now there were only two on the east side of the barn. Looking up she could see toothpicks of daylight through a few places on the roof. Roof repair was added to her mental list. A pile of used lumber was haphazardly stacked against the wall. An old sink lay on its side, and various buckets and boxes, both wooden and cardboard, littered the floor. Used oil cans spilled out of one, paper and other junk out of another.

First step: Clean up the mess.

She put the hammer and pry bar back in their places on the tool bench and walked back to the house for the pickup. Loading the trash in the back meant a run to the dump before anything else.

When she entered the kitchen for a drink of water, the table was cleared and her father gone. Should she call Nicholas to come help her? Was it worth watching his scowl and listening to him grumble? Or would she rather work in peace? She checked the round clock above the window over the sink. Ten to eight. Time enough.

She picked up the paper and cradled the receiver on her shoulder, then punched in the numbers on the wall-mounted unit. She was about to hang up when a male voice answered.

"I was calling about your ad for pigs?"

"Yeah, we still got some."

"Any bred gilts or sows?"

"Some."

"Ah, can you tell me how to get there?"

He gave her directions to get there from Hilo, and she wrote them down, reading them back to him to verify.

"That's right."

"Can I come now?"

"I guess."

After she hung up, she realized she hadn't asked the prices. The man hadn't tried to sell her anything, that's for sure. It was more like he was doing her a favor by giving her the information. Oh well, he had hogs and that's all the counted. Now, if she could just afford to buy one.

She checked her father's bedroom, but he wasn't there. He'd said he didn't want anything to do with it anyway, but she still wished he wanted to go along. "Yeah, if wishes were fishes, we'd all be fed." She shook her head at the face in the bathroom mirror. What was the deal? Since she'd come home, she'd caught herself repeating her mother's sayings. She'd never done that before. With a hairbrush in one hand, she climbed the stairs to Nick's room.

"Hey, sleepyhead, you want to come with me to look at some pigs? I'll buy at McDonald's."

His head came off the pillow. One eye squinted up at her. He flopped back down.

She gave his rump a shove, then began braiding her hair. "Come on, lazy bones. This'll give you a chance to see some more of the island."

"Like I want to."

"Like I don't care if you want to or not." She let a touch of steel glint in her voice. "Get up, Nicholas, and come with me."

"Why do we want to go see *pigs*?" The twist he put on his final word revealed what he thought about those four-footed critters.

" 'Cause I plan to buy some."

"Why?" He looked up at her, his blinking eyes reminding her of a baby owl she'd seen one time when she looked down in a tree hole.

"I'll tell you on the way. Come on, I told the man I'd be there in half an hour, and ten minutes of that is already gone."

If she'd invited Nicholas along for the company, her plan failed—miserably. He'd started out slumped in the corner, glaring at her, but within a couple of miles, he'd nodded off. Maybe something was wrong with him that he slept so much. Then again, maybe he was absorbing all the sleep she was losing.

An hour later she was the proud owner of two bred gilts and a sow that the man said he'd breed again before she picked the old girl up. He agreed to hold the animals until she could find racks for the truck and get the pen ready. The older gilt was due to farrow in a month.

Nicholas had wrinkled his nose at the smell of the pig house, but she had a hard time dragging him away from watching a litter of five-week-old babies chasing each other around the pen.

"Their tails really do curl." He grinned up at her and pointed to a red-and-white-spotted piglet. "Look at that one. Why don't you buy that one?"

"He'll be weaner size in two more weeks."

"Weiner size?"

The man shook his head, a smile showing one missing front tooth. "Weaner as in weaning or taking it from the sow, not weiner like a hot dog."

"Oh." Nicholas's shoulders slumped in visible relief.

"Besides, we're getting bred gilts and a sow," added Maddy. "We don't need a boar yet and that one's too small anyway."

"A boar is a boy pig?"

"Uh-huh. And a gilt is a female who hasn't farrowed—had a litter of piglets—yet."

"And a sow is a mom like that one?" He pointed to the mother of the five. She lay in the corner sleeping.

"Right." Maddy paid the man and waited for a receipt. If she was going into business, she had to get in the habit of keeping receipts.

"Thanks, we'll be back in a couple of days. I'll call you first."

The farmer nodded. "I still got one more gilt, you know."

"I wish." Her money had actually gone further than she thought. Now if it would just work the same for feed and fencing.

She drove on into Hilo, and after a stop at McDonald's they headed for the Farmer's Co-op to price the supplies she'd need. After an hour dickering with the salesman, she owned only one roll of hog wire, ten steel posts, and two sacks of feed. The change left in her pocket would only buy her a cup of coffee.

Oh well, the pigs didn't want to dig around under the trees right now anyway. And she'd put Nicholas in charge of keeping the water trough filled. She'd cut that old water tank in two the long way with the cutting torch; half would be for water, half for feed. But how could she get all this done in two days—and work too? Good thing she didn't need much sleep. Or rather, she needed more and just didn't seem to get it.

"Get my sunglasses out of the glove compartment, would you please?"

When Nicholas didn't answer, she glanced over at him. "Nick."

"Huh?"

"Think I better find a doctor and get your hearing checked. I asked you to get my sunglasses out." She pointed at the glove compartment.

He handed them to her with a sigh.

She started to put them on, but they were so dirty she handed them back to him. "Use your napkin and see if you can't make it possible for me to see through them, okay?"

His sigh said she was asking an awful lot.

The sigh made her teeth clench. *What is the matter with him?*

But he did as she asked, and when she put them on, she nodded. "Thanks."

His grunt sounded just like that of his grandfather. How could the kid be picking that up? The two hardly spent three minutes together a day. Maybe it was genetic. Or maybe it was just male.

"When we get home, you can help me in the barn, okay?"

"Doing what?"

Maddy took a deep breath and wondered, *Why did I ever become a mother anyway?* She pushed aside the thought and replied, "Cleaning out the junk, setting fence posts, getting ready for the pigs."

Another grunt. *Perhaps he is related to the porcine family of creatures.* The thought made her smile. As did the sight of a Poinciana tree in full, fiery orange-red bloom. Nicholas used to be interested in everything with a curiosity that never quit. And that wasn't so long ago. Had they remained in Honolulu too long? Would the boy she so enjoyed ever return?

By the time she left for work, they had cleaned out the junk and fenced the plot off in back of the barn. "Don't you get lonesome up in your room?" she asked on one of their breathers.

"Nuh-uh." Nicholas held the cold soda can against his red face.

"Do you read?"

"Some."

She knew he didn't watch TV up there because there wasn't one. And she doubted her father let him watch the one in the living room, unless Nicholas enjoyed the soaps. Catching her father watching the soaps had been a real shocker. He'd switched to the history channel when she commented on it.

"So what do you do?"

He shook his head. "Nothin'."

To think she'd wished at times he wasn't such a chatterbox. As her mother had said more than once, "Be careful what you wish for—you just may get it." Maddy had, and she didn't like it one bit.

"The sides for the pickup are behind the cattle chute," Jesse said the next morning at breakfast. "When are you going to get them?"

Maddy poured him another cup of coffee and herself a third. "To-morrow. I have the day off, so I'll be here to make sure they stay where they're supposed to. I'm thinking maybe I should bend some rebar and pound it into the ground to anchor that hog wire."

"Or else run a line of electric fencing along the inside, 'bout eight inches above the ground."

"Umm." She didn't want to tell him she had no money for a charger, wire, and insulators. "It should take them a few days to plow up that patch back there before they go looking for trouble." Maddy remembered well how much pigs delighted in taking apart a fence. Just like kids, they needed to be entertained. Or else.

— — —

Nicholas didn't need nearly as much prompting to come along to pick up their pigs. But helping chase them up in the truck was another matter. They herded the two females toward the chute leading to the truck, where a line of grain led up the ramp and into the truck bed. The farmer's wife held one end of a sheet of plywood and Maddy the other. The man gave Nicholas a two-foot-square piece with a handle cut out.

"Now, if they come to you, just plant this board in front of one and she'll turn back."

Nicholas tried. The gilt ignored him and knocked him over with a shoulder maneuver.

He picked himself up and headed for the fence. The tough-guy look on his face said he wasn't hurt, or at least not going to admit it. When he wiped the sweat off his face, a smear of dirt remained.

"This isn't working. Son, hand me that bucket." The man pointed to a five-gallon bucket by the fence. "Ma'am, you take that little board and keep 'em from coming out again." Maddy did as he said, but as far as she could see, there was none to keep from coming out—yet.

As soon as she was in place, the man put the bucket over the head of the red-and-white gilt and turning, backed her right up the ramp and into the truck. Even though the pig tried to toss the bucket away, the man held on until she was in the truck.

He picked up the bucket the gilt sent spinning into the sideboards and winked at Maddy. "Now, you keep her in here, like I said. Just turn your board into the gate there."

Maddy nodded and looked over at Nicholas. His eyes took up half his face.

Within ten minutes the other was loaded and the tailgate snapped in place. "And that's how you load pigs without all the fancy chutes and stuff. Better'n a cattle prod anyday."

"Thank you, for both the pigs and the lesson."

"If'n they're young stock, just grab 'em by the hind legs and wheelbarrow them in. Easy as pie." He nodded to Nicholas. "Sorry you got dumped there, son, but I always try to herd them first, give 'em a chance to do it the easy way, you know. Sometimes they waltz right in, easy as you please." He winked. "But you got to be holding your mouth just right."

Nicholas smiled politely at the man's joke. On the way home he kept turning around in the seat so he could see the two gilts through the back window. "One's laying down," he reported.

Another check of the cargo. "The white one's sniffing the gate. Mom, she's pushing on it."

"She can't get the tailgate loose. It's bolted on both sides, remember?"

"She's walking right over the other one."

"Ouch, that would hurt." Maddy kept her eyes on the twists and turns of the road. She hadn't heard this many words out of her son since . . . since she couldn't remember when.

Nicholas actually let out a shriek. "She's got her snout right against the glass." He pushed his nose against the window. "See, pig, I can do that too."

Maddy rolled her lips together to keep from laughing out loud. Her son had actually laughed.

"How're we going to get them out of the truck? I'm not putting a bucket over their heads." Nicholas shook his head twice for emphasis.

"Me neither. I'd get banged around like that bucket."

"So?" His eyebrows disappeared in the hair that fell over his forehead.

"So you just watch. They'll be glad to get out."

She backed the truck into the barn and close to the pen's open gate. "We'll let down the tailgate and then the ramp, just like it was before. Then I'll guard the side and you herd them out."

"Can Amos herd pigs?"

"No doubt. Amos could herd elephants if he had to."

"Then he can get up in the truck."

Maddy shook her head. "They don't know Amos yet—he'd make them panic."

She set things up the way she'd planned and pointed for Nicholas to go up the ramp and into the truck. "Unless you'd rather crawl over the side?"

He nodded. Grabbing the side rails, he hoisted himself up and swung a leg over the top board. The two gilts edged toward the back, keeping an eye on the invader. When they saw the ramp open, they turned, snorted, and rattled down the ramp into their new home.

Nicholas walked out after them. "They're pretty smart, huh?"

"You'll see that pigs are some of the smartest animals alive. And they've got personality like you wouldn't believe." She swung the half door closed and dropped the bar in place. "We need to decide on names for them."

Nicholas climbed on a box so he could see over the sides of the stall.

"How about you take charge of the water trough? Pigs can't sweat, so they need lots of water and they need a mud hole to help keep them cool."

"Yuck."

"I'll feed them. You keep the water trough full, okay."

"Do I have to?"

"Yup, you have to."

What she would do if he didn't, she had no idea.

I'm feeling about as popular as a barracuda in a swimming pool."

"Kam, it's not your fault." Marianna Waiano shook her head, clicking her tongue in the sympathetic way she had.

"You know that, and I know that, and the farmers know that. But when people who used to joke with you and say, 'Come on, have a cup of coffee,' now only grunt and look anywhere but at you . . ." He raised his hands, palm up, and let them drop again.

"This too shall pass," his mother reminded him.

"I know. And I know God promises to bring good out of everything for those who love Him . . ."

"I hear a 'but' in there."

The song of a cardinal filled the silence. "But what about those whose cows were destroyed who *don't* believe in our heavenly Father?"

"He says that the rain falls on the just and the unjust. I hang on to that verse too. And leave the worrying to God. He's much better at it than I am."

Kam studied her. The love that seemed to flow from every pore of her being surrounded him like a fragrant cloud of Plumeria. He could breathe it in and welcome its fragrance deep into his soul. The thought that God was love—far more than his mother—brought a comfort he couldn't begin to express.

But what about Maddy and her family? So much had happened to them. First the anthrax scare and then their cows poisoned—not to mention what had gone on in Honolulu before she came home. If only they could find out who dumped the antifreeze, it might help.

He knew that's what the "but" was that his mother sensed. He'd always thought of anger as hot, like the volcanoes that ravaged the mountainsides, but somehow he knew that Maddy's emotions had turned to ice. Great walls of it that let him see her but not touch.

Knowing that, why couldn't he get her out of his mind?

Because you've always loved a challenge. Even his mind was talking back to him today. *You know she's been hurt, and you hope you can make things better for her. If only she would let you.*

"You want to talk about it?" His mother's voice invaded his reverie.

He shook his head. "No, not right now. I have to do some more thinking first."

"All right. But you know I'm always here."

He nodded, rose from the top step where he'd been sitting, and dropped a kiss on her broad forehead. "Think I'll go snorkeling."

"You taking Benny and James?" His two nephews loved to snorkel nearly as much as he did.

"Sure, why not?" He headed into the tin-roofed house to call his sister and ask if the boys could go. No sense driving clear over there if they weren't home.

Half an hour later he had an idea what a mother duck felt like, trying to keep her ducklings all in a row. Both boys swam like otters, splashing and playing in the waves gentled by the stretch of coral and rocks. "Okay, guys, this is the word." Kam spit in his snorkel mask, rubbed it around, and dipped the face mask in the water, sloshing it clean. The two eyed him from their back-paddling, fins churning the water and snorkel masks on top of their heads. "I want one of you on each side of me within reach, okay? If you want to stop, tap me and point."

"K-a-m." In unison, the boys gave his name the same inflection as if they were saying "M-o-m." You'd think they rehearsed. Rolling their eyes went along with it.

"I know, I say this every time. But the rule holds."

They nodded and splashed each other, making sure some of the sparkling water got on their uncle.

Kam stretched the rubber straps to place his snorkel and mask on his forehead, sat back in the water, and tugged on his fins. The three slipped their masks down over their faces, snorkel tubes in their mouths, and rolled face-down to scan the sandy bottom. Wave action made patterns on the sand and around worn beds of dead coral. Several small golden striped butterfly fish swam past. Flicking their fins sent the three into deeper water and bigger fish. They floated, the rippling water lifting them and letting them settle again, gently, like rocking in a mother's arms. The world below went on about its business as if they weren't watching.

Kam pointed at a hole below a small shelf. A red-and-white-spotted moray eel waited for prey. String coral sent long white arms over the coral ridges like a mop splayed out. A school of sea perch flashed silver sides at them and continued on their way.

Three black damsel fish with white spots zipped in and out of a rock cave, the larger one chasing the other two. Kam wanted to laugh but knew how easy it was to suck water that way. Brown sergeant fish with blue-and-yellow stripes from their open mouths to their eyes darted in and out.

Kam relaxed. The sun baking his shoulders, the water holding him up, the silence . . . it always brought him peace. One of the boys pointed at a sturgeon fish, lazing around a rock. Everywhere they looked, brilliant colors caught their attention, and the deeper they went, the bluer the world.

"This is my Father's world." Singing didn't work underwater, but Kam let the words of one of his favorite hymns float through his mind. How he wished he could come up with words and tune to begin to describe the world he was seeing now.

He felt a tap on his right side. Benny pointed farther off to the right. Two sea turtles were swimming parallel to the shore. The three turned to face them, grinning at one another through the glass. The turtles were in no hurry and neither were they as they kept their distance and watched. The sun gilded the turtle shells and caused their shadows to follow along on the bottom. One dove with powerful front legs propelling it downward, where it nibbled on some sea grass and then stroked onward.

How great it would be to show this to Maddy and Nicholas. If only his life on land could be this serene. He sometimes wondered why he cared when she barely gave him the time of day. He thought back to the night before at the restaurant, when Maddy had laughed at a joke told by another regular. That's the Maddy he wanted to be with more often.

When Kam and his cohorts finally staggered ashore, legs rubbered by the fins, they collapsed on the hot sand, the boys laughing and chattering about all they'd seen.

"We should have brought spear guns and gotten fresh fish for dinner," Benny, ever the practical one, said.

"Not today." *I've seen all the death and destruction I can handle for a long time.* Kam banished the thought and forced himself to stay in the moment. Sun and surf . . . sand hitting his back. He turned. The two boys were wrestling and showering everything within reach with sand. Kam grabbed a flailing leg and pulled.

"Knock it off, you two, or I might have to throw you back in the ocean." Their giggles showed abject terror at his threat.

"I'm hungry, how about you?" He put both hands over his ears at their chorus. "Good. How about the Ranch House? It's close." He almost grimaced at his stretching of the truth.

Other alternatives were immediately brought up. "Taco Bell." "Hamburgers at the Stop Awhile."

"Who's buying?"

"You!"

"Then I get to choose."

They groaned but gathered up their gear.

"You got shirts and shoes?"

"Uh-huh," they both responded.

"Then rinse off under the faucet and we're outa here."

Sun, sand, surf, snorkeling, and seeing Maddy. Kam knew he was grinning like a kid, and he didn't even care. She said she used to snorkel, and Nicholas was about the same age as the two puppies gamboling at his side. Maybe next time he could bring her and the boy along too. They both needed some laughter in their lives.

— — —

"Hey, Leilani, you got room for three hungry men?" Kam asked when they entered the Ranch House dining room.

"Sure do." She smiled at the boys. "You look like you've been in the ocean. Bet you're hungry."

Benny and James nodded. "And thirsty."

Leilani picked up three menus. "Right this way."

"Maddy in the kitchen?" Kam asked.

Leilani shook her head at Kam's question and shrugged. "Sorry, Kam. Maddy called a few minutes ago. A family emergency, she said."

"Come on, guys, we're outa here." Kam had the two boys out the door before they could sputter.

I *lost it because I was too tired to be patient,* Maddy told herself. She sat on the front steps, holding her head in her hands and her tears in check. Where was Nicholas? He'd run out of the house like it was on fire and the words he screamed over his shoulder had burned her ears. She'd hoped never to hear that kind of language again—from her son, at least.

Then she had to call work and tell them she had an emergency. Was a fight with her son a valid emergency?

It was if he'd run away. He didn't know the island, and while they called it paradise, there were vipers too. Even though they weren't of the poisonous snake variety. She looked up toward the trees. He was most likely hiding there, cussing her out for all her sins. According to him, they were many, the chief being her dragging him here to this totally boring place. And away from his friends.

What was her father going to say about this latest escapade?

Plenty, no doubt. And not one word would cross his tight lips.

Seemed he wore that tight-lipped look a lot, especially around Nicholas.

But then, what had Nicholas done to make friends with his grand-father? Not one thing. He'd gone out of his way to antagonize the old man and vice versa. The two were like dogs and cats in a barrel. No, that wasn't true. They didn't speak to each other at all. The animosity was silent—much worse than words, in her opinion.

But how could that be? Grandparents were supposed to love their grandkids. Of course, fathers were supposed to love their daughters too. On one hand she felt sure her father loved her . . . as much as he was able. Showing it, however, would be helpful.

She shook her head again. All this thinking wasn't helping the sit-uation at hand. All she had to do now was find her son . . . and get him talking. Better than half an hour had gone by—time enough for him to cool off.

She decided to check the house again, just in case Nicholas had sneaked in the back door, but found it empty. She then whistled for Amos and headed for the barn.

The sound of a pickup driving in the lane brought Amos barking from up on the hill and halted her from entering the barn. Maybe some-one had seen Nicholas and brought him home!

The imposing figure of Kam Waiano stepped out of the truck.

At the same time her stomach did a quick flip, she groaned. She definitely didn't feel like making polite conversation right now.

"What brings you here?" Maddy made no effort to season her tone with graciousness.

"I heard you had an emergency, and since we were heading by here, I thought I'd see if I could help." He had the kind of voice one could sink into and be . . .

Maddy clamped her teeth together. "Who told you my business?"

"Leilani. She's worried about you." He leaned his chin on arms crossed on the open vehicle door.

Maddy could see two boys in the cab of the truck, one of whom had been at the restaurant the night Kam brought his family in. They looked about Nicholas's age.

"May I help you?" His gaze never left her face.

She knew that because her face felt like she'd been lying in the sun for a month or so. All at once. *Not* can *but* may. *Someone taught him proper English, along with* ... Maddy stopped her thoughts. "Thanks anyway, but we'll manage."

"How's your father doing?"

Just leave! She felt like screaming the words.

"I thought Benny and James here might like to meet Nicholas. He anywhere around?"

"I wish." The words popped out before she could stop them.

"He off with your father?"

Oh, how she wished he were.

"Maddy."

She bit her lip and spun to look up at the treetops, rustling secrets in the breeze. Perhaps they knew where her son had gone. When she had her volcanic feelings back under control, she slid her hands into her back pockets and tried to appear like she had not a care in the world.

"You know, I'd really like to visit, but ... well, perhaps you could bring the boys back another time. We ... ah ..." She wished she could whistle or make a joke, but her mouth was dry as the windward side of the island. And like the arid land, she could feel her prickles growing like a cactus.

Kam watched her, wishing he could read her mind. Her eyes told one story, her mouth another. But both of them indicated one thing ... something was seriously wrong. And he'd bet his snorkel and mask it had to do with her son. Where was the boy?

"We're not in any hurry. We can wait until he comes back." He turned to the boys who'd made some remark.

"You might be waiting a ... long time." She edited out the harsh words that came so easily to her tongue.

"You don't know where he is?"

She shook her head and sighed in defeat. "He got mad and ran off. I was just going to look for him. The fool kid doesn't know his way around here other than up the hill, to the barn, and back." Like a dam had burst, the words poured out of her. "Even Amos disappeared for a while, and . . ."

"And your father?"

"Most likely up at Mother's grave. He might as well take his bed and live up there."

Amos whined at her feet. If only she had taken time to teach him to fetch Nicholas.

"You want me to call the sheriff?"

"No!"

"Okay." He kept his voice low and liquid. "Then we can fan out and search. These boys know the island like the backs of their hands."

"Look, why don't you go on home and let me deal with this? I'm sure he's up in the trees somewhere, probably watching us right now."

"Does he know about the feral pigs up on the slopes of Mauna Kea?"

She shook her head, guilt slashing at her like a boar's tusks would. "I . . . I haven't had time to . . ." She could feel her protective outer shell cracking, just a tiny bit but if she let it go any further, she might never get the pieces back together again. *Why do you have to be so . . . so nice?* Cruelty she could handle, but she knew *nice* and *gentle* would be her undoing.

"Look, we'll go up and over the hill. You go down and around." He pointed in the directions as he spoke. "I'll have the boys with me, and you take the dog."

Maddy nodded. "If you find him, there's an old triangle hanging by the back door. Clang on that—the sound carries well."

"So does my car horn." Kam motioned the boys out the door and started out. "Come on, guys, we've got a boy to find."

Maddy and Amos followed a track that curved down and around the hill, the dog using his nose as if he were a hound on a rescue mission. Every once in a while, he'd stop and look up the hill.

Half an hour later, Maddy wished she'd brought a water jug along. While the sun was going down behind the mountain, the heat hung over the grassy slopes. Farther down she could see the fields of the Smythe farm, home of her best friend when she was younger. She wondered if they still lived there. Of course, Alison was married by now and probably had five kids. The place next to them had been broken up into duplexes—she could count four. A swingset behind one spoke of the family dwelling there.

Her throat hurt from calling her son. Her heart hurt that he would pull a stunt like this. If he thought he had it rough before, when she did find him she was going to ground him until he was twenty-one . . . or married. Whichever came first.

"Nicholas!" She put her hands to her mouth and called again.

Amos pricked his ears and turned toward home.

She stopped and held her breath. Was that a horn honking? And a triangle clanging?

"Come on, fella." She turned and broke into a run. Over the hills was shorter but the path would still be faster. She could run on it. "They found him, boy, they found him."

By the time she got back to the house, she had a stitch in her side and a thirst big enough to drain a lake. Nicholas ran to meet her, throwing his arms around her waist and burying his face in her shirt.

"I . . . I tried to come home." Hiccups cut him off. "B-but . . . they wouldn't let me."

She hugged him close, murmuring comforting words as she stroked his hair back. He was as sweaty as she was, his face bright red. "They?"

"The . . . the pigs."

She looked up as Kam joined them. "The feral pigs. He must have gotten between a sow and her piglets or a boar with a meaner than usual streak. He was up a tree."

"Thank God you're all right." She ran her hands over his arms, shoulders, his clothing, feeling for any injuries. *Thank you, God, thank you.* The words rolled through her mind, like the tears down her cheeks.

"I . . . I . . . c-climbed up and they wouldn't go away. I called for Amos, but he didn't come." He looked up at her, terror still darkening his eyes.

"Too far away, probably." She hugged him again. "Oh, Nicholas, why did you take off like that?" He dropped his gaze and wiped his eyes and nose on her shirt front.

"I was mad at you."

She sucked in a deep breath. "I was mad, too, son, but running never solves anything. We've got to learn to talk things over."

Benny and James stood behind their uncle. "He did good, gettin' up in the tree and all."

"Or he'd a been a goner."

"I h-hate pigs."

"Wild pigs and our pigs are not the same at all." She hugged him again and, keeping one hand around his shoulders, started to the house. "If the rest of you are as thirsty as I am . . ."

Within minutes she had poured tall glasses of iced tea, but only after first drinking three glasses of straight water herself. She took the glasses on a tray to the porch and passed them around. "There's sugar there if you want. I already sweetened it a bit."

"Thanks." Kam tipped his head back and chugged half the glass. "That hits the spot. It was hot up there."

"Not where I was," Nicholas said.

"Bet you could see clear to the mainland from that big tree." Benny drank again.

Nicholas shook his head. "Most of what I could see was that monster pig. He had teeth that curved up clear over his snout. The little ones were cute, but I never run so fast in my whole life."

He turned to his mother. "Whose pigs are they?"

Kam chuckled. "God's pigs, I guess, or maybe the devil's, with all the trouble they cause. Years ago some hogs got away from the farmers and ran wild. They've multiplied enough that now they are both dangerous and they're tearing up the land. Over on Maui, they've about killed off all the Silver Sword plant—it's on the endangered list. They can tear up an acre of planting in no time."

"Why don't we catch them and raise *them* for luaus? They'd be free." Nicholas looked up at his mother.

"Thanks but no thanks. They'd tear the fences down and try to kill anyone who had to get in the pen with them. I'll take these nice old domestic pigs any day." *Why did he have to bring her new venture up in front of company?*

"When did you get the pigs?" Kam asked.

"The other day. Two bred gilts and I'll pick up an older sow as soon as she's bred again."

"We're going to raise pigs for the luaus." Nicholas swiped his hand under his nose and wiped it on his shorts.

Maddy flinched but looked to Benny, who asked, "Can we see the pigs?"

"Well . . . um, I guess so. Nicholas, you want to show them the girls? And fill the water trough while you're there."

Nicholas gave her a do-I-have-to look, but at her nod, signaled the boys to follow him.

That left her in another quandary. Now *she* had to talk with Kam. She sipped her tea, wishing she were anywhere else but right there. Since Nicholas was found, maybe she should call work and ask if they need her. No, there were still some of the *D* things to do. Like discipline and discuss. But she really couldn't afford to take a day off like this. She'd spent all her money on the pigs.

"You've made some improvements here. Looks good."

"Oh, ah . . . thank you." She tried to think of something to say. "Thank you, too, for finding Nicholas. Seems I owe you another big one." She hated owing anyone anything.

"It could have been bad, but his guardian angels were watching out for him for sure."

Maddy ignored the angel comment. "Were the pigs still around?"

"We made lots of noise and they took off up the hill. We didn't see them, just heard grunts and saw the grass waving." Kam leaned back against the post holding up the tin roof. "You better convince him he can't go off by himself—or take Amos along, if nothing else."

"Well, he didn't ask my permission." She got to her feet, hoping that he'd get the hint and hit the road. Keeping the bitterness out of her voice took more effort than she had energy at the moment.

"Boys can be a real handful at times. He can come play with James and Benny one of these days. The three of them will get along well." He looked up at her without moving from his place against the post. "I'd love to take him snorkeling."

She shook her head, feeling neglectful. Most kids on the island took such an activity for granted, but they hadn't been able to afford the mask and fins, and Gabe had never had time, or so he said. Of course, Gabe never had time for anything with his family. She rubbed the tender spot on her arm.

Kam watched her, his eyes warm, smile ready. "How long since you did any snorkeling?"

Again she shook her head. "Not since I was a kid." She shrugged. "Soon as I can get some gear, we'll go."

The boys raced up the hill from the barn, Amos barking at their heels.

"For an old dog, he sure is lively."

Maddy nodded. *Good thing someone around here is lively.* She felt like Mauna Lea had settled on her shoulders and had no intention of getting off.

Kam got to his feet. "We'll see you later, then. Thanks for the tea."

Heading toward the barn, he yelled, "Come on, boys, we gotta hit the road." As he heard their groans in response, he shook his head and flashed Maddy a smile that curled around her heart and fluttered her belly.

"See ya."

"Thanks again."

"You're welcome. I'll be back to collect one day."

"Right," Maddy said, thinking there was nothing right about it. She waved once in response to the horn honking, then turned to Nicholas. "I think we have some talking to do, Nicholas Adam Morton. Now!"

The clock bonged down in the living room, and without thinking about it, Maddy counted. Two o'clock. She wished she could add "and all's well," but it wasn't. Nicholas was complying with her restrictions as far as she knew. No television, no boom box for two days. There hadn't been much else she could take away. How she yearned to find that kid with the happy smile, but all that remained was a sullen boy who did as she asked but no more.

Her father had retreated even more since the cattle had been sold. She didn't know how to reach him either. At least the taxes were paid now, but from a mutter or two that she translated, she realized her father no longer had much money.

She shook her head in the darkness. Tired as she was, she had thought she'd drop right off to sleep as soon as she hit the bed.

The breeze billowed the sheer curtains on her bedroom window, and moonlight etched a rectangle on the wood floor silvered by age. What she'd give to be able to hear the surf at night. But up here on the mountain, she heard leaves gossiping and birds twittering instead . . . and a car passing by on the highway, a Beamer just like Gabe's. . . . With alarm she jerked her mind back to the present, but fear left a metallic taste in her mouth. What if Gabe. . . ?

That brought up another subject, one of those that preyed at the back of her mind continually. She needed a car. The truck exchanged one weird sound for another, and none of them good. Saying it had seen better days was like saying the ocean was blue—neither went far enough. If she was any judge, it not only needed a new or rebuilt engine, but the transmission was in trouble too. Hardly worth putting that kind of money into a vehicle so old.

It was money she didn't have anyway. And her father didn't seem to care. Long as it ran, it was fine with him, but then, he never went anywhere anyway. Since she took over the grocery shopping and any of the other errands, he never left the place.

Something else to worry about.

She flipped over on her right side, then her left. Seeking a cooler place for her cheek, she turned the pillow over. Finally, thinking a drink would help, she padded down the stairs toward the kitchen. Amos came out of Nicholas's room to accompany her down the stairs. It pleased her to see how the two of them were often together—a definite step in the right direction.

Amos's cold nose bumped the back of her knee, sending goose bumps up her spine. Maddy thought of taking her glass of water out on the front porch but instead headed back up the stairs. She *had* to get some sleep.

If only she could turn off the worries. *What if Nicholas runs away again? What if the truck breaks down? What if Gabe finds me? What if. . . ?* She held the glass to her cheek, feeling like she was drowning in uncertainty.

"Oh, Mom, I need you so. You were always the one with the answers."

Let the day's own troubles be sufficient for the day.

Where had *that* come from?

Be not afraid.

"It's not that I'm afraid, you know." Maddy stopped, realizing the absurdity of her response. If she wasn't afraid of what might happen, she wouldn't have to worry about it. "But, Mother, you know all this stuff could ruin my hopes for the future." She held the glass to her mouth and took another long swallow. "Mom, how did you get so wise?"

Immediately a picture of her mother sitting on the porch swing with her Bible in her lap came to her mind.

Maddy shook her head. "No way, I'm not going there, so don't even get any ideas." She crawled between the sheets and sucked in a deep breath, letting it out slowly. "I wish you were here."

The breeze whispered again and with a billowing curtain came the scent of Plumeria, her mother's favorite flower.

Maddy slept right through the sunrise.

— — —

"What you gonna do on your day off tomorrow?" Ruby stood next to Maddy at the salad station, dishing up salad plates.

"I think I'm going to the coffee-growers meeting. How about you?"

"Whatever for?" Ruby asked, obviously surprised.

"I . . . well, I've got to get more money coming in, and coffee is doing great right now—doesn't seem to be slacking off any."

"You got coffee trees on that place?"

"A bunch of seedlings left over from when Pop had coffee years ago."

"You talked to Kam yet about it?" Ruby slid her hand under the tray and hoisted it to her shoulder.

Maddy walked away to serve her table, pretending she didn't hear Ruby's question. All the while she smiled at her customers, poured coffee, refilled soda glasses, and tried to come up with a good answer for Ruby. *Just because coffee is his specialty . . .* But until Ruby asked her the question, she hadn't really planned on going to the meeting. It just popped out.

"Well?" Ruby was determined to get an answer when they met back at the salad station.

"Well, what?" Teresa asked, filling a basket with warm rolls.

"Maddy's thinking about raising coffee. Like she ain't got enough to do."

Teresa looked up at Maddy. "You talked to Kam Waiano about it yet?"

"For Pete's sake, quit ganging up on me." Maddy tried to keep from smiling, but she could tell they knew they had her on the run.

The two swapped raised-eyebrow glances and rolled their eyes. Teresa's giggle carried back over her shoulder as she crossed the noisy room.

"Yes, sir?" Maddy turned to answer a question from one of their customers. A tall man, his salt-and-pepper hair caught back in a clip, toothpick in his mouth, grinned down at her.

"I asked if you might like to go out for coffee—you know, after you finish here."

"Thanks, Harv, but I don't think so." Maddy didn't know his real name, since everyone called him Harv because he'd graduated from Harvard sometime in the long, distant past.

He nodded. "Another night, then?"

" 'Scuse me, I got someone calling." Maddy shot him a smile that was supposed to be apologetic and hurried off, breathing a sigh of relief. That was the second time he'd asked her to go for coffee. How could she tell him she wasn't interested in any man. Any time.

"So why'd you tell old Harv no?" Ruby and her eternal questions.

"Listen, Ruby, I'm only going to say this once. I learned my lesson well: After you get burned, stay away from the fire."

"All men aren't like Gabe."

"How do you know what Gabe was like?"

Ruby studied the placement of lettuce on a salad plate.

"And how do you know his name?"

She set a cherry tomato precisely next to the slice of cucumber. "I . . . ah . . ." Deep sigh. "I asked around."

"Asked around? Who'd you ask?"

Ruby named the assistant editor at the Hilo newspaper. "He's my brother-in-law. He looked stuff up for me. Said Gabe's trial was in all the newspapers. Found a little piece about you and one of the times the police made a house call 'cause you were beat up."

"Oh, how naïve can I be?" Maddy leaned on the counter, her elbows locked to help hold her up. "If you could find information so easily, so can he."

"The Internet makes stuff pretty available, if you know how to use it. I don't, but Al does. 'Sides, he's a newspaper man and knows where to look."

Maddy should have headed for the mainland like she originally thought. But she didn't have the money. It always came back to the money. She *had* to get enough money together to be able to run if she needed to. Gabe had threatened to kill her, and his threats were as good as if the deed were done. *If* he ever got out of prison. Maddy looked up to see tears brimming in Ruby's washed blue eyes.

"I'm sorry. Me and my curiosity, always gets me in trouble. Please, Maddy, don't go all cold on me. I really like you, and you know I just want to help."

"You can help the most by leaving me alone."

"Sorry, honey, I can't do that. You're my friend now and like it or not, we're gonna stay friends."

Maddy wanted to slam the back door and drive the hills until she could cool off, but she had customers waiting. Like the hand of death, she could feel Gabe's cold fingers reaching for her. And Nicholas. "Just . . . please don't mention this to anyone else. I've got to keep Nicholas safe."

"I won't, Maddy, really I won't." Ruby nodded at someone across the tables. "Be right there."

"You guys all right?" Teresa reached between the two of them to snag the coffee carafes.

"Yeah, we're fine." Ruby flashed Maddy a smile that was meant to be reassuring.

And to think I'd begun to feel the least bit safe. What a joke. She finished her shift with relief, dropped her percentage of tips in the kitty for the busboys, and headed out the door.

Her father had left the lamp above the table on in the kitchen, and when she walked over to switch it off, she saw a letter with familiar handwriting. While it was addressed to her father, she knew he'd left it for her to read. Apprehension and fear left her trembling.

She drew the lined tablet paper out of the envelope and unfolded it, wishing she could wash her hands after even touching the same paper his hands had touched.

The scrawl leaped out at her. *Tell her I'm comin' for her! Gabe.*

Maddy swallowed a scream. Her hands shook so much she could barely turn the envelope back over. As she suspected, it was addressed to her father. Gabe didn't know where she was, he was simply guessing. She'd left no trail. Besides, her name was now Morton, not Hernandez. He didn't know that either. Unless court records were available over the computer. But then, how could he use a computer? He didn't know how to read very well, let alone type.

But he could get someone else to do it for him, just like Ruby did.

Run! Run! Hide! The words tied her stomach in knots and set her injured arm to twitching. She sucked in a deep breath, held it, and released it slowly, dropping her shoulders at the same time. She had to relax so she could think.

Gabe didn't know where they were. He was shooting ducks in the dark.

She looked down at the letter, lying in the pool of light from the lamp. Shivers chased each other up and down her back.

"You don't know where we are, and you won't find us." She started to crush the letter and throw it in the garbage before anyone else saw it, then stopped, smoothed it out again, and refolded it. A lawyer would want to see it. After the divorce, there was a court restraining order that said Gabe could in no way contact his former wife. He wasn't to call or write, and prison kept him from attempting a visit.

She stuck the letter in the envelope, switched out the light, and headed for her room. She'd ask her father in the morning if he knew of a good lawyer. *There goes the money I've saved plus a whole lot more. And they wonder why I'm so obsessed about money.*

— — —

"He won't get you here," Jesse Morton announced when she came in the door to make breakfast. She'd greeted the rising sun with gritty eyes. Sleep never had dropped in, even for a visit.

"I know."

"I'd kill him before I'd let him take you and Nicholas."

"You'd have to race me for the gun."

"I mean it." Jesse caught her eye and held his gaze steadily.

"I know you do and so do I." She poured coffee beans in the grinder and pushed down the lid. The grinding of beans sounded loud in the morning stillness. After filling the filter with the fine grounds, she added the water and watched the darkening liquid drip into the glass pot.

A myna bird flitted by the window, his harsh cry sounding like a warning. The cry sent a shiver up Maddy's neck.

"Any ideas what you're going to do?"

Maddy carried him his cup of coffee and took her place at the table. "I'm calling a lawyer to check on some things for me. You know any good lawyers?"

"Is that a joke?"

She half smiled and nodded. "Let me rephrase that. An attorney who is good at what he or she does."

Jesse sipped his coffee, and his eyes narrowed in concentration. Finally he nodded. "I did some business with Harcourt and Harcourt. They seemed to care about the client, not just the money." He studied her over the rim of his cup. "You got enough money?"

"I hope so. If not, maybe they'll take payments. I have to find out if the court can put a restraining order on Gabe's mail rights in prison. Since he turned in state evidence to lessen his sentence, I don't think he has any friends or cohorts left on the outside. No one trusts him, thank God."

"How long is he in for?"

"Ten years with no early release, no matter how he behaves. But . . ." She shook her head. "He has a temper that ignites like a firecracker. I don't think there's much chance he could get early release anyway. He doesn't know I changed my name and he was told I was leaving for the mainland."

"Anyone know you didn't go there?"

"Only Rita, and she'd never tell."

Maddy got up and refilled their coffee cups. "You want bacon and eggs?"

He shook his head. "Just toast."

"Mashed avocado and bacon bits on it?"

"Sounds good."

Maddy halved an avocado and scooped out the soft green flesh. Her father had said more to her in this last half hour than all the time since she'd returned. What made the difference?

I guess I'll take what I can get, no matter what. She spread mashed avocado on the whole wheat toast and sprinkled bacon bits on the surface. Setting the plate before him, she finished making one for herself and returned to the table, bringing along another plate with papaya halves ready to be spooned out.

They finished their breakfast in a quiet kind of peace, not merely silence.

"Think I'll build a gate across the driveway, down by the big eucalyptus." Jesse licked his fingertip and used it to pick up the bacon bits. "You want to pick me up some hardware while you're in town?"

Maddy nodded. "Just write down what you want." She made her

way upstairs for a change of clothes and then to head for the shower. Maybe between that and the caffeine, she'd get her mind back. She thought back to her discussion with Pop. She'd had a glimpse of the man he used to be and she liked it.

Sitting on the bed to remove her boots, she reminded herself that she needed to call the attorneys' office to make sure one of them was in and would take on a new client. She fell back on the bed. *Perhaps if I close my eyes for just a minute, it'll help.*

Run, run . . . faster, faster. Air tearing in and out of her lungs. But always Gabe was behind her. Gaining. Screaming out what he would do to her. . . .

She shrieked. He had her arm. Maddy sat straight up in bed. Sweat poured down her neck and back.

"Mom? Are you sick?" Nicholas took a step backward.

She shook her head, still feeling like Gabe would grab her at any moment.

"Grandpa said you're going to be late for work if you don't get going."

"Oh." She wanted to say something else but pushed back her hair and said, "Thanks, Nicky, but it's my day off." So much to do, and she'd crashed instead. *Can't I get anything right?*

14

"What is the matter with you?"

"Matter?" Maddy's response was snappy, but the tone of Ruby's voice grated on her nerves.

"You look like you seen a ghost."

"Thanks. I could be home lolling in bed, but instead I come in on my day off to make your life easier and look at the welcome you give me." She knew what Ruby meant. Her mirror didn't disguise the black circles under her eyes, nor the red rims.

"Well, leastways you're talking. You looked right through me for a minute, as if I wasn't even there. Something's got you spooked."

"You a mind reader or something?"

"Don't have to be a mind reader. Your face says it all."

"If you girls have so much time to chat, maybe we could get by with one less waitress, hmm?" John Yoshakara said for their ears alone. He raised one dark eyebrow at them and continued his stroll around the dining room.

Ruby rolled her eyes. But she didn't say anything further, just hustled off to care for her tables.

Maddy could feel the fire ignite in her midsection. They all worked hard and he never had a good word to say. In fact, he was rarely in the dining room at all, spending most of his time in the bar. And here he made a remark like that. *Men! They say you can't live with 'em, can't live without 'em. Ha! I sure can. And I plan to do just that!*

She was still having trouble controlling her anger when Kam and his mother were seated in her section.

"Lucky dog." Teresa nudged her as they picked up plates of food to take to their customers.

"I don't care how great a smile he has, he's a *man*." Maddy's emphasis on the last word brought a wide-eyed look of surprise to the younger woman's face.

"You're not a man hater, Maddy, are you?"

"Getting there." Maddy set her last order on the oval tray and hoisted it to her shoulder. *Now to just get through this shift.* She'd just set the tray down when she heard a man laugh, the sound sending waves of adrenaline through her. She spun around, searching for Gabe, knowing at the same time it was impossible. But it had sounded so like him.

"Are you all right, miss?" The man at her table looked up at her.

Maddy took in a deep breath, her heart pounding so loud she was sure everyone in the room could hear it. "I . . ." She choked on the word, cleared her throat, and tried again. "I'm fine, thank you." She ordered her lips to smile, but they were so dry they couldn't stretch that far. While she bent to pick up a plate, she licked her lips, pasted on a smile, and set the filled plate in front of the woman. "Scampi, right?"

"Yes. Is there anything we can do to help?" She smiled up at Maddy, a smile so warm and genuine that Maddy now had to fight the burning at the back of her eyes. Mean she could handle, but nice . . . that was her undoing.

"Th . . . thank you, but no. I'm fine." The lie didn't come easy. Lying never did.

"You looked so stricken, terrified even." The woman wouldn't let it go.

Maddy set the plate in front of the man. "Can I get you anything else?" *Guess I better learn to keep my face under control,* she thought, noticing that now her hands shook. She hid them at her sides, wishing she could run out the door and keep right on running. "I just heard a laugh that reminded me of someone. Caught me off guard."

The man nodded, the light silvering his hair. "Memories can play havoc with us at times." He looked at his plate and inhaled the steam. "This looks delicious. Thank you, Maddy."

It was later, when she cleared their table, that she found a business card tucked under the generous tip. Reverend Andrew Kamaki, Kamuelo Community Church. A note on the back said, *If you ever need someone to talk to, I'm available.*

One part of Maddy wanted to rip it up. The other, the winning side, had her tuck it in her pocket. One of the icicles that fearful laugh had frozen around her heart tinkled to the floor. She sniffed. One thing she didn't need was someone preaching at her. So why save the card? She had no reply to the insistent voice in her head as she stuck the card in her jeans' pocket.

"I see you met our pastor," Marianna Waiano said with her warm smile when Maddy reached their table. "He and his wife are such fine people."

"I'm sure they are." Maddy was still fighting to get her smile under control. "What can I get you for dinner?" She looked up to feel Kam's eyes studying her.

"What happened?"

"Wh-what do you mean?" *Please, someone call me so I can hide for a few moments.*

"A few minutes ago. You were fine when we came in and then . . ." His eyes narrowed. "No one bothered you, did they?" He glanced around the room at all the men.

Maddy shook her head. "Kam, I am fine." The clipped words

dropped into the pool of silence surrounding this particular table.

"Now, dear, don't go nosing in other people's business." Marianna laid a hand on her son's arm, then looked up at Maddy. "Kam believes it is his job to save the world. He forgets Jesus already did that." Her musical laugh held not one iota of malice, and Kam chuckled along with her.

"Guilty." But when he looked at Maddy again, his eyes had that piercing stare she'd seen earlier.

She kept herself from shivering. "Well, I'm just real glad I'm not on your bad side, then, but if I don't take your dinner order, someone's going to complain about my lousy service." She wanted to bite her tongue but the two of them had a gift for getting her to confess more than she had planned. Or thought of.

"Not us." Marianna smiled up at her. "I'll take the special."

"Me too."

They left as soon as they'd finished eating, and Maddy breathed a sigh of relief. Why was it that whenever Kam Waiano was in the restaurant, she felt like she was a bug under a microscope?

Business crawled to a stop about half an hour before they closed the dining room. Even the bar had only a couple of patrons. Maddy refilled all the salt-and-pepper shakers, added sweetener packets to the rectangular holders, and made sure there was steak sauce in the bottles. Ruby and Teresa took care of the salad and coffee stations. She could feel them looking over at her, waiting for her to say something.

It would be a cold day in Havana before she said anything after Yoshakara read them the riot act like that. What bee had gotten in his bonnet? Concentrating on her resentment of the manager helped her forget the laugh. How could anyone sound so much like Gabe and not be him?

You're just freakin' out, she scolded herself. All over a laugh. How silly.

But the letter to her father wasn't silly, and after sleeping so much of the day, she hadn't seen an attorney. At least she'd called one and had an appointment in the morning.

Ruby managed to be going out the door at the same time as her. "So what happened that made you look like someone scared the socks off you?"

Maddy looked at Ruby in the parking lot light. She saw a kind woman who'd done nothing but try to be her friend. A friend Maddy knew she needed like she needed air. She sucked in a deep breath and began. "Crazy coincidence, that's all. You know how we were talking about Gabe last night?" Ruby nodded. "Well, low and behold there was a letter from him on the table when I got home."

"He found you?"

"No, it was addressed to my father but the message was for me. I'm seeing an attorney in the morning to see what kind of teeth the restraining orders have." She felt like someone had put a quarter in her and she couldn't stop talking until it was all used up. "And then tonight, everything was going fine until some guy laughed. Ruby, I swear it sounded just like Gabe. I totally freaked."

"You want to go to the all-night place for a cup of coffee? We could talk there." Ruby laid a gentle hand on Maddy's arm.

Maddy moved away just enough for Ruby to drop her hand. The tears she'd turned to steam with her anger now boiled up at any gentle word or touch. She gathered her wall around her and shored up her defenses.

"I better get on home. Thanks anyway." She turned toward the pickup. She'd just opened the door when she paused. "Sorry I got you in trouble tonight."

"Oh foo, John just needed to spout off. He gets that way sometimes, so don't pay him no never mind."

"Yeah? Well, since he's paying my wages I think I better listen."

"You'll learn. You're a great waitress—you have nothing to worry about."

"Easy for you to say." Maddy slammed the truck door as she muttered. She turned the ignition but nothing happened. She turned it again and got a clicking sound, much like cards slapping against each other during shuffling.

She bit off the string of words that threatened to roll past her control and slammed the palm of her hand on the steering wheel. Bailing out, she called, "Ruby, you got any jumper cables?" At the same time, she pushed the seat forward to see if there were any behind it. An old coat, a gunny sack, a roll of paper towels, two cans of oil, some odds and ends, but no jumper cables.

Her father *always* carried jumper cables.

Ruby pulled her car head-to-head with the truck, popped the hood, and got out to open her trunk. "Here, hon. My Tom always makes sure he has whatever we might need." She held out the jumper cables. "I'm not good at putting them on, though."

"Thanks, Ruby, no problem there." Maddy untangled the cables and clamped the jaws on the battery terminals, first of the truck, then Ruby's Buick. "Okay, rev her up." She got back in the truck and turned the key. The truck roared to life. She let it idle while she disconnected the cables and put them back in the trunk of Ruby's car.

"You want me to follow you home?"

"It's out of your way." Maddy stopped by the driver's window.

"Not that far. Get going, I'll be right behind you."

Maddy figured the bright lights must be causing her eyes to water as she wiped them with the back of her hand. She honked her gratitude when she turned off at the giant eucalyptus and continued up the lane. What in thunder was draining the battery? She knew she hadn't left anything on.

One more thing. When would it end?

— — —

She had her head under the hood when her father came down shortly after sunrise.

"What happened?"

"Stupid thing needed a jump last night. How long since you cleaned these spark plugs?"

Jesse shrugged. "Probably the alternator. Got a lot of miles on that one."

Maddy stood straight and wiped her hands on a rag. "I'll go get one as soon as the parts store opens." She plugged the cable from the battery into the charger and turned to her father. "That should hold it long enough to get me there and back. I've got tonight off since I worked last night. If that new girl is okay, that is."

"The coffee's hot."

"Thanks."

After breakfast he handed her five twenty dollar bills. "For the new alternator."

"That's more than enough." *I thought he didn't have any money. What's he doing, printing it out back?*

He waved her away and headed out the door.

Maddy climbed the stairs to Nicholas's room. "Hey, Nick, you want to go to town with me?"

He buried his head under the pillow.

She tweaked his heel. "Come on, I'll buy at McDonalds."

He shook his head, fluffing the pillow.

"Your loss." She paused at the door and studied the sheet-covered body. *What's it going to take to get through to you, son of mine?*

She had the alternator in and the truck running again just in time for a shower and a fast drive back to Hilo. Harcourt and Harcourt had offices right across from the courthouse.

They made her wait.

"I'm sorry," the secretary said. "Ms. Harcourt said she'd be back as soon as possible. She asked you to please wait."

"Fine." Maddy leaned back in the chair, crossing one ankle across the opposite knee. She flicked a bit of red clay off the heel of her boot. Perhaps she should have dressed up more.

Too late now. She checked her watch. Half an hour had passed. Her foot wouldn't stop jiggling. She set it back on the floor and picked up a magazine. She put it down, then glanced at her watch again.

The door opened and Ms. Harcourt emerged, the perfect stereotype of everyone's granny: comfortably padded, gray hair, a smile that set Maddy instantly at ease. At ease, that is, until in a sergeant's voice the elderly lawyer snapped, "Come, then, let's get on with this."

Maddy leaped to her feet, immediately aware of the grease beneath her fingernails. Her gaze darted to the door that had closed behind the human dynamo crossing the room toward another door. Too late.

What had her father gotten her into this time?

She's at a lawyer's? What happened?"

"Now, I'm not so sure I should be tellin' you her business." Jesse crossed his arms over his chest.

"No, I don't suppose you should." Kam copied the older man's posture. The silence between the two lengthened. Amos sniffed at Kam's shoes, then sat down at the man's knee, raising one foot to shake hands. Kam leaned down and ruffled the dog's ears, then took the proffered paw. "Amos, old son, you one kine dog."

Amos leaned closer, then closed his eyes in bliss as Kam scratched his ears, a low whine saying thank you.

"Where's Nicholas?"

"That one." Jesse shook his head. "He's playing with one of those idiot battery-operated games, I s'pose. He spends too much time in his room." He shook his head. "Not good."

"How about he comes with me? I'll drop him off at my sister's so he can get to know Benny and James better. They'll get him off his duff, that's for sure."

Jesse squinted, the motion adding more lines to a road map face. "I don't know. Not my place to make decisions for that boy. He got chores to do here."

"You mind if I ask him if he wants to go?"

Jesse sighed, this time one of defeat. "Ah, why not? She can't do more than yell at me. You'll know which room is his; the noise box will tell you. He keeps the door shut, but I tell you, he won't have any hearing left by the time he's thirty."

Kam started up the stairs and paused. "Maddy's trip to the attorney didn't have anything to do with Gabe Hernandez, did it?"

Jesse spun on the balls of his feet and clenched his fists. "What'dya know about that lowlife?"

"Come on, Jesse, you know the coconut telegraph is faster than any telephone. People here knew and liked your daughter years ago. You, too, for that matter. My mother asks about you all the time." When Jesse only grunted, Kam continued. "They aren't going to hurt her, you know. The Hernandez clan is gone now with Gabe in prison, and that brings a sigh of relief to all who knew him or them. But, Maddy . . . we protect our own." He waited, one foot on the step, one on the lanai. *Come on, Morton, you must remember how it is, now matter how hard you've tried to keep us all out. You're going to come back to the land of the living, whether you want to or not.*

Jesse stared up at the big Hawaiian. "Just see that you do." His eyes narrowed. "Just see that you do."

Kam nodded. He didn't need to promise, for protecting the people he cared about was as ingrained as his love of the island. "Who did she go see?"

"Harcourt and Harcourt."

"Husband or wife?"

Jesse shrugged.

"Good choice. I hope it's the missus, though. She's got more teeth in her bite than a shark. If I ever had need of an attorney, I'd want her on my side." When Jesse failed to respond, Kam made his way through the house and up the stairs. He felt like an intruder. Would Maddy mind that he'd come for her son? Actually, he'd come for her, but since God knew what He was doing, this was the way it was supposed to be. Kam had learned and relearned that principle many times, starting at his mother's knee.

"God is in control of everything—nothing happens to even that little ant on the ground without Him knowing it. He says He knows even the number of hairs on your head." She'd reached over and brush one off his shoulder. *"See, now He knows you have one less. If He knows so much, don't you think it a good idea we trust Him, no?"*

Kam had a sad feeling deep within that Maddy would not agree.

He knocked on the closed door that barely muffled the boom box from within. At least it wasn't as loud as the first time he'd heard it. Someone had been on the boy's case.

No answer.

He knocked harder. "Nicholas, you in there, buddy?"

No answer.

He cracked the door open and peeked inside. The boy lay on the bed, earphones in place, eyes closed. If it weren't for one leg crossed over the other, swinging out the rhythm, Kam would have thought him asleep. Stepping through the door, he crossed the floor and snagged the waving foot.

Nicholas jerked and surged to his feet. "What ya doin'?"

"Just trying to get your attention. I knocked."

"Oh." Nicholas sat back down on the edge of the bed. He took a deep breath and let it out before looking up at the intruder. "So?"

"You want to go with me to my sister's? You could pl—hang out with Benny and James." His nephews repeatedly tried to teach him the right lingo, but he failed more often than not.

"I guess." Nicholas shrugged, the kind of shrug that said, *I'm cool and don't you forget it.* "What'd my mom say?" He tried to act like he didn't care, but the glint of interest peeked out of his eyes.

"She's not here, but your grandpa said it was all right."

"He's not my boss."

Lord, save me from ten-year-old boys trying to be twenty. "Stay here, then. I just thought you might enjoy yourself." Kam turned to leave.

Nicholas slouched to his feet and followed him out the door.

"You better turn that thing off."

"Oh yeah." The boy did as he was told and caught up with Kam at the front door. Amos greeted them at the doorway, and in spite of himself Nicholas bent over and scrubbed the dog's ears, getting a clean nose out of the bargain.

Jesse was nowhere in sight.

"You want to find your grandfather and tell him you are leaving?"

Nicholas shook his head. "He don't care."

"Then you better leave a note."

"He said I could go, didn't he?"

"Just go write a note. I'll wait for you in the pickup."

Nicholas rolled his eyes and sighed like he was being asked to paint the house in five minutes or something equally unlikely. But he turned back to the house, his shoulders angled in opposition.

Kam watched the body language. "You know, son, I think your mother got you out of Honolulu just in time. Let's just pray it wasn't too late." Kam crossed his arms over the steering wheel. Visiting Benny and James at his sister's house would be a very good thing. And he really wasn't that disappointed that Maddy wasn't home—was he?

— — —

"What do you mean, you let him go with Kam Waiano?"

"Kam came looking for you and asked if he could take the boy—"

"His name is Nicholas."

Her father ignored her and finished his sentence. ". . . over to play with his nephews."

"Oh." Now she knew what a flattened balloon felt like. She glanced at the clock, then remembered she didn't have to go to work today. She could have taken Nicholas to the beach. Why did that man have to keep butting in where it was none of his business? "Did he water the pigs first?"

"How should I know?" With that, he headed outside, presumably to the cemetery.

Maddy shook her head and strode toward the barn to water the pigs. Having one obnoxious child was bad enough without a second one. *And he should know better*, she grumbled silently as she returned to the house.

Maddy tried to hold on to her irritation, but with both rain clouds out of the house, she felt freer than she had in a long time. Until now she hadn't realized how thin the egg shells were she'd been tiptoeing on.

With time to complete a big project, she tore into the living room, hauling out to the lanai everything she could carry and shoving the heavier pieces out to clean under and behind them. Dust rose from the ancient hide-a-bed so she took the cushions out to air in the sun and vacuumed every nook and cranny. Rolling up the old rug, she carried it outside and slung it over the clothesline. The colors used to be vibrant.

"And you will again," she promised the Oriental tapestry. Once she had the walls washed, she realized that a coat of paint was two steps beyond necessary.

When her father came back in the house, she had moved the remaining pieces of large furniture to the center of the room and covered them with drop cloths she found in the pantry. "Good, you're just in time. We need to go pick out some paint."

"Paint!"

"Yeah, you know that stuff you apply to walls to make a room look clean and fresh again? I think a creamy white would look good, how about you?"

"I don't have money for paint. Next thing you'll want is new curtains and furniture."

"No worry, I'll just use the change from this morning." She planted both fists on her hips. "And now that you mention it . . ." She grinned at the look he shot her. "You want to come with me? I'll buy lunch."

"Plenty of fine food here."

She nodded. "Must be my deodorant, can't get either of the men in my life to go out for a meal. See you in a while and don't you disappear. You roll and I'll edge, and we'll be done in no time." Taking her cue from his past actions, she ignored the muttered response and trotted out to the pickup. At least it started right up again after her morning's ministrations.

She was finishing painting the last window sash when Kam brought Nicholas home. She watched through the window as Nicholas bounced out of the truck, waved good-bye to the driver and his two nephews, then assumed the slouch and sullen expression she'd come to know too well.

"That little rat." Maddy went back to her painting, irritated by Nicholas's boomerang attitude.

"Did you have a good time?" She stopped him on his way toward the stairs.

"Umm."

"What did you do?"

"Nothing."

"Well, I got nothing for you to do here too. Remember those pigs you are to keep watered?"

He groaned. "I forgot."

Maddy could feel her blood begin to boil. "Would you like to go without water?"

"Stupid animals, they just tip it over."

"I seem to recall telling you to give them a mud hole too. Sound familiar?" She could hear his feet hit the stairs. "Nicholas Adam Morton, I'm talking to you." *With* would have been so much better. She sucked in a deep breath, redolent of paint fumes.

He reappeared in the doorway, glaring at her.

"I'll remember from now on. Did you do it?"

"Yes, I watered the pigs. I can't let animals suffer because you're too lazy or selfish to do what you've been asked." She studied the top of his head since he seemed to be counting the holes for the laces in his tennis shoes. "So what are we going to do about this?"

"I said I'd remember."

"And I said that next time your boom box goes up on the shelf. Bring it down. If you've kept your end of the bargain for a week, you can choose whether you want the boom box or the Game Boy back." Despite her words, she ached to put her arms around him, swap hugs and a tickle or two, like they used to.

A scary thought flipped into her head. "Nicky, are you on anything? What with all this sleeping and all."

He shook his head. "I'm not stupid."

She could feel her shoulders slump in relief. Nicholas never had been a liar. "Look at me." She tipped his chin up with a gentle finger. "Now tell me that again."

"No, I am not doing drugs." His eyes flashed lightning bolts. "Dad did drugs and look where it got him. I'm not that stupid!"

"Good, then I won't mention it again." She could feel her knees copy her shoulders.

He started up the stairs, then came back. "They want me to come back tomorrow. I promise I'll take care of the pigs first." When he glanced up at her out of the side of his eye, she caught a glimpse of the boy he used to be.

"I could drop you off on the way to work."

"Kam said he'd come for me early in the morning. He has a project for us to do."

Stuffing down the questions that boiled up, she nodded. "I guess so, if it is all right with Mrs.—" She didn't know Kam's sister's last name.

"Mrs. Langston. She said I should call her Marlea." He turned away again. "Thanks, Mom," he said over his shoulder as he started back to the stairs. Before she could say a word, he reversed and headed out the kitchen door. "Just checking on the water trough."

Maybe there was hope after all.

By the time he came back, she was at the clothesline, whapping the hung rug with the flat of the broom. Dust billowed, making her sneeze. "How about taking the other side? I'll bat, then you."

"With what?"

She thought a moment. "Why don't you use the back of the grass rake."

"Is the vacuum broken?"

"No, but the sun helps get rid of any mildew. You can take the hose to it after we beat the dust out."

"Harder," she called when he returned and tapped lightly at the rug. "This is the way they used to clean rugs all the time." She whacked the rug a good one.

The bamboo tines on the rake rattled when struck against the hanging rug. With each swing, Nicholas hit harder.

"That's right, put some muscle into it." Maddy pictured Gabe's face on the rug and thwacked a mighty one.

Dust rose as the two hit harder and faster. Nicholas grunted with the force of his swing.

Maddy wiped her nose and eyes. Dust was making her cry, even. She hit Gabe again and yet again, swinging with all the fury she possessed. His friends' faces came to mind and she struck them, too, grunting with the effort.

Soon water streamed down her face, from both her eyes and pure sweat. Her shoulders ached and the palms of her hands burned from gripping the broom handle.

She could hear Nicholas muttering, once even his father's name, as he swung and struck.

"G-get the hose." Maddy wiped her forehead with the back of her hand. She headed for the house, sobs still choking her throat. What had gotten into her? "I'll be right back. Go ahead and spray the fool thing."

She sucked down a glass of water, wiped her eyes and nose with a paper towel, and headed back outside to pick up her broom again and whack away.

Water sprayed over the top of the rug. "Careful over there. The object is to clean the rug." She whacked again.

"Nicholas, watch the spray."

"I am."

She turned just in time to catch the full force of the spray right in the chest. "Nicholas Adam Morton!" She dove for the hose but he kept blasting her, backing up and darting around, laughing all the while.

She snagged the rubber hose closer to the faucet and reeled him in. "Now it's my turn."

He dropped the hose and leaped away from her avenging arm. She directed the full force of the blast on his back, charging after him until the end of the hose brought her up short. "Cheater!"

She could hear her son's laughter, then silence. She watched the edge of the house, and when he peeked out, she blasted him with the water again.

Her hair hung in her eyes. Plastered to her body, her shirt showed every freckle.

"Sorry I missed out."

Kam Waiano stood beside the sagging clothesline pole.

As heat blazed up her neck, turning her wet shirt to steam, she leveled the gushing hose right at his broad chest, a bit on the high side so his laughing face dripped like hers had a moment before.

I think I'm going to die. She dropped the hose like a snake about to bite. "Nicholas, turn off the hose." She took a step forward. "I . . . I'm sorry. I don't know what go into me."

"I think it's not what got into you but what got *on* you." Kam threw his head back and laughed. "I know it's warm, but I hadn't planned on cooling off this quickly." He brushed water off his face and shirt.

Nicholas's eyes were as big as the rims of two teacups. "M-o-m."

His voice held the same awe as his eyes.

"I . . . don't know what came over me." Her face felt like it was sizzling, making it difficult to see through the steam.

"Looks like water to me." Kam laughed with her this time. His smile deepened the creases by his mouth. "You need to laugh more often."

Maddy fanned her face with one hand. *Maybe I should just turn the water on me. One minute I'm crying, the next I'm laughing like some crazy person.* She put her hand on Nicholas's shoulder where he stood right beside her. "Anyone care for iced tea? And cookies?"

"I am if you're serving it in a glass." He looked down at the front of his soaking hibiscus shirt. "My flowers already got enough water."

Nicholas actually giggled.

"You ready to put the furniture back in?" Kam asked after they drank their tea and cleaned up the cookie plate.

Maddy shook her head. "The rug isn't dry and I think I'll paint the floor too. Could be sanded and finished, but this will be faster." She leaned back in her father's recliner, which sat on the lanai along with almost everything else from the living room. "Things should be all right out here."

"Okay, but don't say I never offered."

She looked up from studying the rim of her glass, feeling the warmth of his gaze on her face. "Thank you."

"For what? I haven't done anything yet." He raised an eyebrow.

Yes, you have. You've made my son smile. And you took a drubbing and came up laughing. I'll never forget this.

Kam rose and handed her the glass. "I gotta get going. Thanks for the drink—both kinds." He turned to Nicholas. "See you in the morning, buddy. And bring your swimsuit just in case."

— — —

Maddy lay in bed early that night, thinking of the big man who moved with a dancer's grace. And had a smile that warmed her like . . .

Shame he was a man. And she had sworn off men—forever. Hadn't she?

She let her thoughts continue. She needed another friend besides Ruby. Having Kam as a friend would be a good thing—after all, Ruby and Teresa considered him a friend. As did half the residents of the island.

Maddy closed her eyes in contented resolution. They would be friends . . . just friends.

I f she thought the water fight would make a difference, she was wrong.

Or so it seemed.

Nicholas would much rather be over at Benny and James's house than at home now. She hoped that he was more pleasant there than at the ranch with her and his grandfather. While she took him over there sometimes, she hadn't taken Marlea up on her invitation to stay awhile. Her excuse of "too little time" was wearing pretty thin, even to her ears.

Kam dropped into the Ranch House on a regular basis, sometimes with other guys, sometimes with family, sometimes alone. He never brought a date.

She knew he wasn't married, and according to Ruby, Kam Waiano had no steady woman friend.

"He likes you," Teresa said one evening after Kam took a seat at a table in Maddy's station.

Ruby grinned mischeviously. "You can see it in his eyes, the way he

looks at you. You watch, he sit back and keep an eye on you alla time."
Ruby let the island lingo slip into her speech at times.

Maddy just shook her head and continued serving her customers.

"Aloha," he said when she got to him.

"Aloha to you too. What'll you have tonight?" A person could simply drown in his smile. She jerked herself back to the matter at hand, took the pencil out of her hair above her right ear, and with pad in hand, waited.

"Are you on break soon?"

" 'Scuse me? That's not on the menu."

He chuckled, the smile crinkling the edges of his eyes. "Well?"

Maddy looked at the man looking up at her. Then she glanced around the dining room. "Doesn't look like there'll be break time, at least not for a while. We still have a line at the desk."

"Then how about going for coffee with me after you get off?"

"Thanks, but no thanks." She switched directions. "The special is good tonight."

He sighed. "All right, I'll take that. You're a hard nut to crack, Maddy Morton, but my mother taught me to never, never give up."

"Your mother and mine must have gone to the same school." She talked as she wrote. "The honey mustard dressing is fresh—real good on your salad."

"You talked me into it." He handed her his menu. "But then, I have a feeling you could talk me into most anything."

Maddy felt the flush as it raced up her neck. "What can I get you to drink?"

She glanced up when he didn't answer. Candlelight from the center of the table threw his eyes into shadow, highlighting his cheekbones and broad, straight nose. He looked like a carving of one of the ancient Polynesian kings. The way he looked took her breath away.

"Drink. . . ." She motioned, willing him to answer.

"Is that as in 'Coffee, tea, or me'?"

She groaned at the old line. "Sorry, I'm not a stewardess."

"Flight attendant."

"Not that either." She turned away. "I'll get your salad." She fanned herself with her order pad on her way back to post the paper.

"He got to you, huh?" Teresa winked at Maddy over the bun warmer. "Here, I have this ready for you." She handed Maddy a basket and put two others on a tray.

"You take it to him."

"Uh-uh. He's your customer tonight."

And every night lately. How does he get my station every night?" Maddy fixed salads for two tables, and with her loaded tray she navigated the narrow spaces between chairs. She had at least cooled off by the time she got back to Kam.

"Mahalo." His Hawaiian 'thank-you' was so much more musical than the English.

"You're welcome." She set his salad down and scurried off like a mouse being stalked by a cat.

"How are your hogs coming?" he asked when she brought his dinner.

"The one gilt is due to farrow any time. I've got her in the farrowing stall just in case."

"Good. You have a good idea there, providing luau pigs. I wish I could get more farmers to diversify. You think your dad will do cattle again?"

"No chance. He's not interested in doing any kind of agriculture."

"What's he going to live on?"

"He applied for Social Security since he turned sixty-two not long ago."

"Oh, miss." A customer waved at her from another table.

Maddy responded, still feeling like that stalked mouse. *What on earth possessed me to tell him that? Pop will have my head on a platter for discussing his business with someone else. Why didn't I just tell him it was none of his business?* She took the bread basket the man handed her and went to refill it. Since the rolls, chock-full of sunflower and other seeds, were made right there in the Ranch House kitchen, most tables ordered re-fills. When the nights were busy like this one, frequently that's all Maddy had for dinner.

"He likes you, I tell you." Teresa tossed her long, dark hair over her shoulder some time later. "See you tomorrow."

Maddy glanced into the bar, where she knew Kam waited. She'd heard his laugh more than once. Why couldn't he take no for an answer? This thing needed to be nipped in the bud, and tonight was as good a time as any to do just that.

When her tables were finally set up for the morning crowd and all the other chores were finished, she headed for the back door and free-dom.

He stood leaning against the side of her truck.

Not surprised, she gritted her teeth and clenched her fists. *Well, if you can't take a polite no, here comes the real stuff*. She marched up to him, planting her heels in the gravel and her hands on her hips. "Okay, Waiano, let's get something straight. I told you no, I didn't want to go for coffee. Now I'm telling you no, I don't want to go tonight. No, I don't want to go at all. You got that straight?"

"You don't like coffee?" The moon was so bright she could see the twinkle in his eyes.

She stifled the groan behind her clenched teeth. "I am not interested in dating anyone."

"Ah, but this isn't a date. Just coffee between two friends."

She shook her head. How confusing could this get? "Forget it, okay?" She shoved past him to get to the truck door. *But didn't you say you wanted to be friends?* Telling her little voice to be quiet, Maddy felt like she hit a wall of solid ironwood. Only this wall made her arm tingle, and that tingle set her heart to pounding and . . .

"You don't like friends, either, is that it?" His voice, much too close to her ear, fell softly like the kiss of the first trade wind. "Your walls so high and dark, there's no room for anyone else, eh?"

"Right. But they are *my* walls, and I like it this way." She stopped and sucked in a deep breath. "Look, Kam, I think I'd like us to be friends but—" His hand came at her and she ducked away, her heart thundering in her ears.

"Maddy, what's wrong?"

"I . . . I . . . " She licked her dry lips and gulped air.

"You thought I was going to hit you." The horror in his tone matched the bleak light in his eyes. "Why, I . . . I would never . . ."

Maddy got her self back into some kind of control. "I know that." She gulped again. "Sorry, force of habit." She threw open the truck door and herself inside. "I . . . I'm sorry. Really I am."

"Me too." Kam stepped back, took hold of the door, and gently closed it behind her. "Remember, my mother said never give up. One of these days you come talk with my mother—she'll be good for you." He started to raise a hand in farewell but dropped it to his side. "Good night, my friend."

"It's better this way," Maddy said to herself as she clenched the steering wheel till her fingers cramped. "So now he knows probably more than he ever wanted to. Probably the last I'll see of him." But if that's what she wanted, why, then, were her eyes burning, the oncoming cars blinding her with their headlights?

Getting out of the truck took almost more energy than she had to spare.

She dragged her feet up the stairs, stopped in the kitchen for a drink, and shut off the light over the stove that her father had left on for her. The stairs to the second floor looked about as tall as Mauna Kea. One foot at a time.

Halfway up she wrinkled her nose at an odor—a stink, actually, one that belonged in the barn—that seemed to come from upstairs. She topped the stairs and flicked on the light. A pile of Nicholas's clothes lay in a heap beside his door.

"Mom!"

His voice sounded so much like Gabe's she felt rooted to the spot. Mom! Maddy! How could they sound so much the same? She pushed open the door to see Nicholas sitting up in bed, his arms crossed, his eyes shooting sparks.

"What's up?"

"I *hate* those pigs of yours. If I had a gun, I'd shoot them."

Maddy groaned. "Nicholas, if you're not hurt or sick, can we talk about this in the morning? I am really beat."

"I'm not watering them ever again. They can die for all I care."

Maddy sank down on the edge of the bed. "What happened?"

"They knocked me over, right in their mud hole. I was trying to turn the water trough back over and . . . " He narrowed his eyes and gritted his teeth. "I'm never going out there again."

"Did they hurt you?" Visions of one of the gilts chewing on her son flashed through her head.

"No! I told you! Don't you ever listen?" Gabe in miniature form.

An adrenaline surge caused Maddy to square her shoulders as words began to tumble out of her mouth. "Don't you *ever* talk to me like that again, Nicholas Adam Morton." She could feel the anger pouring out with every word. "I will not allow you to talk to me that way." She reached for him, grabbing his shoulders with both hands and shaking. "Do you hear?" Each consonant clipped, every word fire hot. "Do you hear me?" She tried to keep her voice from a scream and almost succeeded.

Nicholas edged backward against the headboard.

"Never!" She dropped her hands before she could shake him again. "You got that? You are not your father, and God help me, you never will be." She pounded her fist on the sheet, wishing she had Gabe to pound on instead. "Nicholas, answer me!"

"Yeah, I hear you." His lip quivered. "But I hate those pigs and I hate you."

"Too bad, kiddo, 'cause you're stuck with me." She surged to her feet. "And you better wash those clothes in the morning, right after you water the pigs." She headed for the door before she gave in to the temptation to whack her son right across the mouthy part of him.

She resisted the urge to slam the bedroom door and instead pulled it shut with a sharp click. Likewise her own. Throwing herself across the bed, she let the tears flow, drowning out the voice that accused, *You really blew it big time. If he runs away again, it is all your fault. What kind of a mother are you?* And finally, the ultimate insult of all. *You're no better than Gabe.*

— — —

The next morning greeted Maddy with swollen red eyes and a pounding headache. She reached inside the medicine cabinet for one of the samples of pain killers she'd gotten in the mail, hoping she could numb the pain. Chasing the pills with an entire glass of water made her stomach roll.

She called herself every name she could think of and repeated some with each step down the staircase. Going back to bed, pulling the covers over her head, and forgetting the world existed sounded like the best thing in the entire world. Maybe the only viable idea. Her head pounded so hard she saw white whirling dots before her eyes. She closed them and sank down on the bottom step. Maybe a wet cloth on her forehead would help.

Using the wall as a support, she pushed herself to her feet and shuffled into the kitchen and across the floor to the sink. The sound of the running water hurt her ears. She let the coolness run over her wrists, soaked a dish towel, and after shutting off the faucet, made her way out the front door to sink down on the glider.

The movement made her nauseous.

She, who never had headaches, lay back, put the cloth on her head, and closed her eyes.

Her feet were burning hot from running, running after Nicholas being dragged away by a dark-haired man. She screamed at them to stop. Nicholas cried for her but the man dragged him on. Her blistered feet were on fire.

She jerked awake to find the sun heating her bare feet.

Amos whimpered beside her. Had she been screaming to cause the dog such concern?

Just a dream. She pulled her feet back into the shade and rested her neck against the rolled teak back. At least her headache was gone — along with every bit of energy she possessed. By the looks of the sun, it was past nine. Surely her father was up, but she hadn't even heard him. Nicholas, of course, would be sound asleep.

Leaning forward, resting her elbows on her nightshirt that covered her knees, she patted the dog and stared at the overgrown grass between the house and the fence. Could she get the mower started again? Last time had been a fight. One more thing that needed fixing.

What a night she'd been through. Told Kam to get lost. Shook her son so hard his teeth rattled. Bawled herself into the mother of all headaches. All after promising herself no more tears . . .

Where do mothers go when they need to run away from home?

T he thought refused to go away.

Where else could she run to? She'd already run from one place, and look what it got her. The only problem with running was that she had to take herself with her.

The only way she'd ever heard to run without taking yourself was with drugs—and you always had to come down. Besides being too expensive, she knew she'd never turn to that panacea. She'd had up-close-and-personal experience with druggies, Gabe being one, even though he'd always sworn he wasn't hooked. She shook her head. Swearing was one thing he'd done well.

She ambled into the cool of the barn and leaned over the half wall to check her gilt. "How you doing, girl? No piggies yet, I see."

The gilt grunted and got to her feet. She made her ponderous way to the bars and looked up at Maddy, one ear flopping over her eye. She oofed, as if to say, "This is the pits."

"I know . . . been there, done that. Best thing is to just get it over with; then you'll feel better." She scratched the red ears and along the pig's back. "Bet you're hungry, huh? Be right back." She knew she was taking the coward's way out by doing Nicholas's chores, but right now she just didn't want to face him.

After pouring hog pellets in both feeders, she refilled the water troughs and thought of Nicholas being dumped on his rump by the white gilt, definitely the wilder of the two. She'd have to spend more time gentling the animal so they could be in the pen safely with her when she farrowed. Since the sow had already been through two far-rowings, she'd be easy to handle.

"Sheesh, getting dumped in the mud on your keester isn't the worst thing in the world." Talking with the pigs was about as productive as talking with her son. At least they answered her, though she hadn't learned to talk pig yet.

She hadn't learned to talk boy, either, it seemed. His "I hate you" rang in her ears. Her head knew he didn't really mean it, he was just angry. But her heart ached. Nicholas seemed further away again, and here she'd hoped things were starting to work out.

Intent on making the morning productive, she turned on the hose to make a better wallow, then trundled the lawn mower into the lighted work area and started working on the engine. Why couldn't her father fix the stupid thing? After all, it *was* his lawn mower, just like this was his place—and he wasn't taking any better care of it than he did of himself.

He wants to die. The thought made her stomach clench. Other people got over their losses, but Pop couldn't seem to. Losing a son to the Vietnam War knocked him down once, but losing his wife so early de-livered a knock-out punch. His body lived on in spite of him.

"So all you have to do is . . ." She focused on the nut that refused to respond to the wrench. ". . . is get your father to want to live again, bring your son out of his shell, earn enough money to keep food on the table and . . ." She felt like kicking the thing. She pushed harder and the bolt released, scraping her knuckles in the process.

She greeted the reddening scrape with a few choice words and threw the wrench on the wooden floor. "That's it! I've had it! I don't care if the lawn grows ten feet deep, old pile of junk." She gave one of the wheels a kick and stomped out of the barn.

Halfway to the house she remembered the hose she left running and returned to turn it off. With her luck, she'd drain the well. *Money. We've got to have more money.* The thoughts chased each other around in her head. Glancing up the hill, she could see it terraced on the steepest places and planted with coffee trees. The shiny green foliage would look great against the red soil and once established, the upkeep was far less labor intensive than raising hogs. The two enterprises would almost run themselves.

"And if you believe that, girl, there's land down south by the lava flows that's going cheap!"

The phone was ringing when she got to the porch. She took the steps at a leap and managed to get to it before it stopped ringing. You'd think the kid upstairs could at least answer the phone.

"Hi, is Nicholas there?"

"Benny?"

"No, James. If we come get him, can he go to the movie with us? My mom said to invite you, too, if you'd like to come."

Maddy stifled a groan. After last night she felt like grounding Nicholas until school started. But maybe if she did something like this with him, with them, it would help ease the tension.

"What time are you going?"

When he said the first showing, she computed the time. They'd be done in plenty of time for her to get to the coffee grower's meeting tonight. And if they brought Nicholas home, she wouldn't have to make two trips.

"How about if we meet you there? No wait, James, let me talk to your mother." Within a few minutes the details were all worked out, including that they would meet at the Ice Creamery for lunch first."

They had an hour to get ready.

"Nicholas, get a move on." The stink from his dirty clothes re-minded her of their fight. Now she needed to say she was sorry for losing her temper.

She tapped on his closed door, then opened it and stuck her head in the room. A fleet motion told her Nicholas had just covered his head with the pillow. "I know you're awake. Come on, I got a surprise for you."

"More pigs?" The pillow muffled his voice.

Maddy sat down on the edge of the bed and laid her hand on one of his legs covered by the sheet.

Nicholas moved his leg over.

"No, they aren't born yet. You would have heard me whooping it up if they were."

"I hate the stupid things."

"Oh, they're not stupid; in fact, pigs are one of the smarter animals." His grunt sounded much like the ones she'd heard in the barn. Maybe pigs and boys were related. Looking around his room, that could be so, except the pigs were neater. If her father saw this mess . . . but then, he might not care enough anymore to react.

"Nicholas, please remove that pillow because I have something very important to say to you." She waited.

The pillow came off and Nicholas rolled over. "What."

"I'm sorry I lost my temper with you last night and I'm asking you to forgive me." The words came in a rush, as if she'd memorized them and had to talk fast before she forgot. "Please?"

He dropped his gaze and then looked back up at her. "All right." He appeared to be choking on something. "I . . . I'm sorry too."

She barely heard the words but his eyes said far more.

"I'm sorry you got knocked on your . . . umm . . ."

"Butt?"

She grinned at him, rejoicing in the dimples she could see trying to come out. Nicholas had a dimple in each cheek, and she'd told him they were the marks of angel kisses from when he was born.

"I still hate the pigs."

"That's your choice. I fed and watered them this morning, but watering is still your charge."

"I know."

"Good. Now that that's all out of the way, you want to go to a movie?"

"What?"

"You heard me. James called, and we've been invited to lunch and a movie."

"We?"

She nodded. "As in you and me. So hustle. You've still got some mighty stinky clothes to put in the wash."

"Did you get the lawn mower fixed?"

"How did you know?" Her gaze traveled to the window. "Could hear me, huh?"

Nicholas nodded, the dimples playing hide and seek again. "You said some, ah . . ."

"Bad words?"

His nod was big this time, his eyes twinkling. "What movie we going to?"

"Something about monsters." She got up from the bed. "If you have a couple of extra minutes, you might . . ." She nodded to the mess.

" 'Kay. If I hafta." The dimples stayed in sight.

Was her son back or was this a short-term imposter? "You hafta." She ruffled his hair and headed for the shower.

— — —

After enduring the monster movie, Maddy figured she had two hours until the meeting and about six hours worth of errands. First she planned to stop at the co-op to look at information on coffee growing and prices for plants. Maybe if she had all the information in hand and presented it to her father as a well-thought-out plan of action, he'd respond with a yes.

When she finally arrived at the meeting, she slipped in the door and took a seat in the rear, only to find Kam Waiano at the podium. Why hadn't she thought of that? *He must think I'm an idiot after the parking lot debacle.* The thought sent heat roaring up her neck. Thoughts of leaving tugged her attention toward the door, but she forced herself to stay in her seat. She needed the information if she really wanted to raise coffee.

After taking notes on the lecture, watching the slides, and listening to the growers discuss everything from seedlings to selling, green versus roasted, and flavored versus non, Maddy wondered if she really wanted to do this.

Kam was fielding another question when she got up, stopped by the table with stacks of literature to pick up one of everything, and headed out the door.

He caught up with her in the parking lot. "What's your rush?"

"I need to get home to check on my gilt." Any excuse sounded good at the moment.

"You thinking of raising coffee on your father's ranch?"

"Thinking."

"It won't work there. Those hills are great for ranging cattle, but coffee? Not a good idea."

"Thank you, Mr. County Extension Agent. I'll have you know there are several coffee trees left over from when Pop grew coffee there ten years ago, and even without cultivation, they are doing fine. I'm going to use some of the seedlings to get started."

"Sorry. I thought you'd want an honest opinion. Maybe I should rephrase that to say you can't grow premium Kona coffee there."

"Maybe you should step back so I don't accidently run over your foot." She slammed the truck door. "And thank you for your encouragement."

She kicked the vehicle into first gear and roared out of the parking lot. Against her will, she looked in the rearview mirror. He stood under the light post, watching her go. She could feel his eyes on the back of her neck all the way home.

Whatever is the matter with you, girl, acting that way? Stupid, stupid, stupid. If that's the way you treat your friends, you'd make a great enemy.

But why did he have to be so . . . so . . . bossy? Know it all? Condescending? No, the last one didn't fit; she'd go with the first two.

The lights were on at the barn when she returned. Amos announced her arrival, and Nicholas came tearing out of the open double barn doors.

"Mom, Mom, she's having them right now!"

"Where's Pop?" She bailed out of the truck and took off running for the barn.

"With the mama pig." Nicholas ran right beside her. "I went out to check on her like you do and there were two already. Now she has six!"

Maddy dropped to a walk when she hit the barn door. The animals didn't need any scaring at this point. A light hung over the corner she'd boarded off with room for the piglets to go under and be safe. Her father knelt beside the sow, moving another baby to a nipple.

"Makes eight." He glanced up at Maddy. "If she don't roll on 'em and has enough milk. Don't you go counting your pigs until they go out the door."

"I know." But Maddy could feel the dollar signs ringing up in the cash register of her mind. She quietly opened the gate and knelt down by her father. "They look good, don't they?"

"Are they still alive?" Nicholas, right beside her, motioned to three piglets by the mother's front leg.

"Yup." Jesse nodded. "If you watch close, you can see them breathing. All of them have nursed so far, so here's hoping her colostrum is good."

Oh, Pop, do you have to be so negative? Of course her colostrum is good. And if I have to sleep right here beside her, I'll make sure every one of these little piglets live.

She glanced at Nicholas to see his eyes shining, a smile playing with the corners of his mouth. She remembered the first time she'd seen an animal born. She must have looked about the same, awe and delight vying for top billing.

"You had any sense, you'da been here, close as she was, 'stead of running around all over the place. Not for Nicholas, you mighta lost the whole shebang."

Words, hot and hurting, broiled up within. *You mean old man! The one time I went somewhere that wasn't work or to get the groceries . . .* She nearly choked on her thoughts. *I should have known better. He's right, I should've been here. No matter how hard I try, it just isn't enough.*

The eleventh, and last, piglet was half the size of the others.

"She's got ten healthy ones and only ten good teats. Knock this one on the head now and get it over with," Jesse said.

"No! You can't do that." Nicholas scrambled to his feet and reached for the piglet. "Let me get him to suck. He'll be okay."

At the sudden commotion the sow raised her head and started to get up. Piglets flopped every direction. "Mom, she's going to step on them."

I don't know, Mother, I'm beginning to think this is a waste of time."

"You mean Maddy Morton is a waste of time?" Marianna Waiano arched an eyebrow that spoke a language all its own.

"One day I think we are getting to be friends and then . . ." He shook his head. "I'm absolutely sure she doesn't like me."

"Is it you or men in general?"

"Oh." Kam rubbed the bridge of his nose with one finger.

"You know her husband was an abuser."

"Gossip says that, but she hasn't told me herself and you know what kind of store I put in hearsay. Until the other night." He told his mother how Maddy had flinched away from him.

"Come on, Kam. Don't be so surprised." His mother rolled her eyes. "You knew the Hernandez clan. Might be some of them still alive if they'd been more . . . more . . ."

"Kind, gentle, loving?" His sarcasm brought a smile that creased the lines at her eyes, so much like his own. The Waiano family knew

how to laugh—and love. And his mother spread love around to everyone she met like the sun spread warmth.

"You care for this woman?"

"Don't seem to have any choice in the matter."

"Ah."

"You're using *that* tone of voice."

"Are you in lust or love?"

"Mother!" He shook his head, gave a self-conscious laugh, then
thought for a minute before answering. "Neither at this point. I just
can't get her out of my mind." He half closed his eyes, remembering. "I
want to make her laugh more. She's so serious all the time but when
she does smile . . . well, let's just say it's worth waiting for. She's trying
so hard to be a good mother to Nicholas, who is being a real brat, and
you know as well as I do that living with Jesse Morton isn't any picnic."

"The boys sure get along well." She took a few more stitches in the
orchid quilt block in her lap. Marianna was a master at quiltmaking the
ancient's way. "Jesse Morton has suffered a great deal in his life. Going
on is not easy."

"I know, but seems to me some make it harder than others. I'd
hoped the boys would be my in. She won't even go snorkeling with us."

"Kam, my son, you know so little about abuse. Maybe you need to
talk with Pastor Andrew about it. He has counseled many women,
many families in abuse situations. He could give you good advice on
how to help her. And Jesse too."

"Mother, you are one of the wisest people I know. I'll do that. Any
other good advice?"

She thought a bit. "Yes. Do not rush her. Be a friend—she needs to
learn that men can be friends also. You are a fine man, my son, and if
this is the woman God has in mind for you, He will work things out . . .
in His time."

"But *His* time can be even slower than Hawaiian time."

Her chuckle floated behind him as he left her on the lanai and
headed for his pickup. He'd call Andrew in the morning.

He thought of swinging by the Morton ranch but changed his mind before he'd driven onto the main road. Why give Maddy anther chance to get mad at him? His Saturday stretched before him, the first one he'd had free in some time. He could take Maddy and Nicholas snorkeling. He could work in his yard. He could take Maddy to the new movie in town. He could weed his garden. He could drop by the Ranch House, but if Maddy wasn't working, why bother? He could fix better coffee at home.

"Waiano, you are going coconuts for sure."

Something made him turn west on Highway 19, back toward Waimea. Just driving the roads of his island always calmed him and gave him time alone to think. As usual, he took great pleasure in the beauty of both ocean blues and jungle greens. The palette of vibrant colors always brought him back to gratitude to his Maker for the richness of this island tapestry. He switched to a tape and sang along with the gospel singers, his voice rich and as alive as the colors surrounding him. He slowed, passing through the scattered town, glancing at the Ranch House parking lot to make sure Maddy's truck wasn't there.

He drove past the turnoff to the Parker ranch and nearly through the twists and turns before the highway straightened out on the Kona side. Flashing red-and-blue lights had traffic stopped. Most likely another accident. This stretch was notorious. Too many people in a hurry and one Sunday driver could cause a backup within minutes. He breathed a prayer for any victims, mentally checking the whereabouts of his own family.

He tapped out the rhythm of the tune, his fingers adding complicated patterns on the steering wheel. When he got up to the patrolman directing traffic, he asked, "How bad, Juan?"

"Hi, Kam. One DOA and another that will be airlifted to Honolulu, most likely, if she makes it that long. Drink a few beers at the picnic, then hurry along this stretch . . . " He shook his head. "Won't ever learn, these kids. Thank God I don't have to be the notifying officer this time."

"Did you know them?"

"No. Two on vacation from somewhere mainland."

As the cars passed from the other direction, Juan's hand-held radio crackled to life and he waved the waiting line forward. "See you, man."

"Mahalo." Kam averted his eyes when he saw the crumpled car. At least it had been a single-car accident so no others were injured. Why couldn't people believe the signs that showed curves at thirty-five miles per hour? By the glimpse he'd had of the car, it had been going double that. And they'd probably not had their seat belts on. As if death took a vacation even here in paradise. As a volunteer fireman, he'd had to take first aid and emergency medical treatment and so had learned first-hand the fragility of life. The tenacity too.

Following an afternoon spent with his cousins and their families, he took the twists and turns more cautiously than usual, only to earn the angry honk of a car when it was finally able to pass him.

He didn't return the one-finger salute of the driver, not even with the "hang loose" sign of Hawaii.

Angry people. He shook his head. Life was too short for such ugly feelings.

Deep down, he'd bet Maddy was real angry too.

Now, why couldn't he keep from thinking of her?

— — —

After being up most of the night with the farrowing sow, even Maddy slept in—if you could call six A.M. sleeping in. She padded through the house on silent feet, making sure she skipped the stair that squeaked and headed for the barn. Amos trotted beside her, sticking his nose in her hand every other step, reminding her that she could walk and scratch his ears at the same time.

The sow lay on her side, piglets nursing contentedly, some drowsing off until another climbed over. They were still in the which-teat-is-mine stage. The runt lay sleeping just in front of the sow's back feet.

Maddy opened the gate and the sow opened one eye. When that was all the reaction she got, Maddy went on into the stall. She knelt by the sow's rear end and picked up the runt, moving him over to one of the teats and holding him until he latched on. When the one next to him woke up and tried to push the runt away, she intervened. If Nicholas wanted this pig, she'd do her best to keep it alive. He'd have to come out often and do the same thing. Otherwise it would be bottle feeding for sure.

"Hi, Mom."

She looked up to find her sleep-until-noon son leaning over the gate. "Well, good morning to you too." She bit off the smart remark that threatened to spill out.

"How's he doing?"

Maddy shrugged. "We'll know more in a couple of days. You'll have to come out here every hour or two and make sure he gets a chance to nurse. The others are already pushing him out."

"How come they're so mean?"

"No one taught them to share?" She glanced up in time to catch the shadow of a smile. She shrugged again. "That's just the way with nature. Survival of the fittest. Some sows have more teats and then they can raise more piglets. If we can get enough colostrum into him, then if you have to bottle feed, he'll be more inclined to make it."

"I'll make sure he gets enough." Nicholas came into the stall. "Would Grandpa really have knocked the baby on the head?"

"Most likely. Sometimes the runts make it out of sheer guts, but why take milk away from the others if the runt is just gonna die anyway?" She glanced to the boy beside her. The rapt look on his face as he watched the pile of sleeping piglets made her want to reach out and hug him. She contented herself with a pat on his shoulder. For a change he didn't pull away.

"Come on, let's feed these guys so we can go make breakfast." She got to her feet and left the stall. "You fill the water troughs and I'll get the feed."

At the sound of the feed buckets, the sow surged to her feet, piglets flopping over one another.

"Mom, she stepped on one." Nicholas shrieked and dove for the babies.

"Push them under the heat lamp so they get used to going there. That's why we made them a safe corner." Maddy poured the pellets in the sow's feeder and watched as Nicholas did as she said.

When they were all under the board, he glared at the sow. "Why can't she be more careful? She's such a mean mother."

"No, not mean—it's just the way of pigs. Some sows are more cautious than others. I've seen one who I swear could count. She'd check for her babies before lying down. Others just flop over. Sort of like human mothers, I guess. Some are good, some not."

Nicholas let himself out of the stall and went to turn on the water. At least all the troughs were in the right place so he could just pour the water over the fence and not have to go inside.

Mother and son headed for the house together, Amos prancing in front of them. He'd dart back, nip at Nicholas's shoe, and dance off. When the boy feigned as if to grab him, the dog ran barking in circles.

"I think Amos has gotten younger since we came. Look how he plays again, like he did as a pup."

"Grandpa said Amos is thirteen years old. That's old for a dog."

"Getting up there all right. Leastwise he's healthy so far." Maddy made a grab for the dog and Amos rewarded her with a crescendo of barks. "What do you want for breakfast?"

"Pancakes?"

Maddy groaned. "I should have know better than to ask." She motioned toward the garden of sorts up behind the house. "You go pick that ripe papaya and check the bananas. I think that stalk of apple bananas is about ready to pick." The wide banana fronds waved in the breeze, while underneath, the tiny bananas fingered all the way down the stem to the huge purple flower hanging upside down at the end.

Her father always used to have a big garden, but the bananas had taken over much of it, along with other brush. The tropical jungle reclaimed its ground as soon as the land was allowed to go fallow. It grew so fast you could almost watch it happen.

The fragrance of fresh coffee met her at the back door and invited her into the kitchen.

"Hi, Pop, thanks for making this." She poured herself a cup and at her questioning look, he raised his cup with a nod. Taking the carafe to the table, she refilled his before taking a sip of her own. She sighed with her first swallow. "You know, growing our own beans again might be kinda fun." She watched her father closely at this first hint of her plans.

"Too much work. Easier to buy it."

"True, but there's money to be made in coffee again." She opened the cupboard doors and began removing the pancake fixings. She never had been one to use a mix, figuring it took only a minute longer to make them from scratch. Breaking an egg into the bowl and whisking it, she tried to plot out what to say next. This hadn't been her idea of when to broach the subject, but since she'd started, why not go for it?

The newspaper rustled behind her.

"You know, that hill above the barn would be real easy to terrace and set some plants out."

No answer.

She looked over her shoulder. The upright newspaper shrouded all but his hands. "What do you think?" Pause. "Pop?"

"Huh?" He let the left side flop in so he could see her around it. "What'd you say?"

"I said I thought the hill above the barn would be easy to terrace and set some coffee plants out."

"Now, why in thunder would you want to do that?" The paper now lay flat on the table.

"To earn some money. Growers are making a good living now. It's not like when you raised coffee before." At his frown, she winced. She shouldn't have added that last line.

He picked up the newspaper again, the rustle telling her in no uncertain terms to not bother him, especially with any wild schemes like hers.

She sifted in the flour, soda, and salt. "So what's wrong with the idea?"

The paper snapped together. "What's wrong is I'm not gonna raise coffee or cows or anything else. I learned my lesson and that's that." He shoved his chair back. "Raising coffee again on this place is a fool idea, and I won't have any part of it. You'd think that waitressing, taking care of your son, and those pigs would be enough for any sane woman."

"So I'm crazy—I don't care. And I don't want to be a waitress for the rest of my life either."

"You add coffee plants to all you already do and you won't have to worry about nothing. You'll work yourself into any early grave and that ain't fair to the boy."

"His name is Nicholas!"

Jesse slammed the paper down and headed for the door.

"Breakfast is almost ready."

"I lost my appetite."

"If I want to work that hard, what is it to you?"

The slamming of the screen door was her only answer. She took in a deep breath and let it all out. At least he hadn't said *she* couldn't do it.

"What's the matter with *him*?" Nicholas put a sneer on the "him."

"His name is Grandpa to you and don't you forget it." She slammed the skillet on the stove and turned on the burner. *Men!* Just when things seemed to be going better. When would she ever learn to keep her mouth shut?

19

All eleven piglets were three days old.

"He's gonna make it, huh, Mom?" Nicholas squatted in the corner of the box stall and made sure the runt got his share at the breakfast bar.

"Let's hope. You've done good with him."

"Hector. His name is Hector." Nicholas scratched the sow on her neck and behind her ears, earning a grunt of satisfaction. "She likes me."

"She might like you but if one of her babies is in trouble, she can go for you anyway. You be careful."

"Mom, you worry about everything."

"Well, keeping you alive and healthy is at the top of my worry list." She reached over and ruffled his hair.

He tossed his head to make the hair go back.

"You need a haircut. I better find the scissors."

"M-o-m. No one else's mothers cut their hair. Besides, you always make it too short."

"Only too short for a week. That way I don't have to cut it so often."

"Can't we go to Super Cuts or something? It's only ten dollars."

"Ten dollars that I don't have. And if I did, why spend it on something we can do for ourselves? Tell ya what, you want to earn the money for the haircut, you ask Pop if there is anything you can do around here to earn some money."

"Fat chance." He moved Hector to another teat.

"Why do you say that?"

" 'Cause he don't like me, and I don't like him." The words rushed out as if dammed up too long.

"How do you know?"

He rolled his eyes and shook his head as if she were as dumb as a box of rocks. " 'Cause he never talks to me and when he does, he growls. And looks meaner'n . . ." He paused, waiting for something brilliant. Instead, he just shook his head again. "You should know, he acts the same way with you." Tossed his hair back. "I hate his guts."

She refrained from answering, knowing that anything she said would be used against her.

How does one explain to a ten-year-old boy that life can make one bitter at times? Of course, her mother had always said you have a choice. You can be bitter or better from life's hard knocks.

Suddenly she felt as if a huge hand grabbed her insides and squeezed. The pain of it brought tears to her eyes, a runny nose, and the urge to scream. *I want my mother! God, why did you take the one person in this family who could handle Pop and . . . and things? We need her here right now.*

She laid her cheek on her knees and turned her face away so Nicholas wouldn't see her. *You will not cry! You will not cry!* Rolling her eyes upward, a trick she'd learned back in the early days when if she cried, Gabe struck her again, she took a deep breath and blinked several times. Another deep breath and she'd made it through. What in the world brought *that* on?

"If you don't cry, it don't hurt so much." Nicholas continued to scratch the sow and kept his gaze averted.

Maddy stared at him. *What goes on in that boy's head? How much does he know of what went on between his father and me? No matter how I tried to keep it a secret, he was there. But he never says anything.*

"Why did you say that?" She kept her voice to just above a whisper, like sharing secrets in the dark.

He shrugged and shuffled Hector again, who by now had gone to sleep and had no intentions of more nursing. He patted the sow, but most importantly, he refused to look at her.

"Nicholas?"

He shook his head, got up, and left.

Had there been a little chink in his wall?

As usual, breakfast was a silent affair. Jesse read his paper. Nicholas ate fast and left. Maddy struggled with deciding if this was a good time to try talking to Pop again about the coffee planting. She refilled their coffee cups and returned to her chair again, doodling numbers on a pad of paper beside her plate.

Five years was a long time to wait for a harvest. Could she afford to invest the kind of money needed and wait five years for a return? Especially if she bought seedlings rather than five-gallon-sized plants. One gallon versus five gallons. She needed to go up and see how many seedlings and young plants she could transplant from the trees up on the hill. It would take a backhoe to move the established trees. They sent roots down clear to Africa. And then there'd be no guarantee they'd make it. Besides, she needed money for PVC pipe for a drip system to irrigate.

And time. It was overwhelming.

Between the hogs and the Ranch House and trying to get some work done on this place, she felt like the rope in a tug-of-war. All the stretch had gone out of it.

They'd been talking of government agriculture loans at the meeting. Now, that would be the day when a Morton applied for "a government handout," as her father used to call them. That's all she needed — to have to worry about making payments.

No, it was pay as you go and if you work yourself to death, at least you died honorably.

She glanced across the table at the newspaper that shielded her father from the rest of the world. *He must read every word of the fool thing. Including the ads.* She felt the sigh coming and didn't try to stop it.

He heard. The newspaper rattled.

She sucked in a breath of courage and squared her paper and pencil. "Pop?"

The newspaper rattled again.

"I need to talk."

His sigh nearly matched her own. He flipped one edge so a corner folded down and bent his neck so he could see over his reading glasses from the local drug store. The other half of the paper remained upright and rigid. Message: This better not take too long.

"I've been thinking some more about raising coffee."

He harrumphed and flipped the paper upright. "I already said it wouldn't work."

"But it could. There's some seedlings up around two mature plants and if we —"

"There's no 'we' about it. I am not going to raise coffee or anything else again." Each word was pronounced separately. "Period."

"I'm not asking you to help. I'll do it. I just need your permission to use the land."

"And my machinery."

She nodded. He'd been listening all right. "That too. But I'll keep it in repair." She didn't add, "better than you have been," but she might as well have for the unspoken words laid before them on the table like a coiled snake.

"Where you gonna get money for something like this? You know you got to have money to make money in farming. That shoestring stuff will kill you."

"But there is real money in coffee now. Everywhere you go, there are coffee bars and even drive-up places. Starbucks started it in Seattle and it is sweeping the world. And Kona coffee is some of the best. I've tried lots of them—I know."

"It'll last about until your plants are bearing and then the bottom will drop out again, mark my words."

She sighed. "Guess that's just the chance I'll have to take."

He shook his head and kept on shaking it while he talked. "You want to do this, that's your business. Just don't count on anything from me." He folded his paper on all the creases and laid it beside his plate. "Not nothing."

Were his shoulders bent even more so than usual? Maddy wondered as she watched him leave the room.

She sat, caught in a state of shock. He'd said she could use his land and equipment. So what if he didn't want to help? Hard work paid off in the end, and she was willing to put everything into it. She stared at her hands, turned them over, and flinched at the grime beneath her fingernails. Long fingers, strong, square palm, calluses already in place. Working hands. She was as strong as most men, and she already knew how to run the tractor. First thing would be to terrace the hill. She could cut that with the tractor blade. It wasn't like the original ones had totally disappeared. But Pop never had laid an irrigation system.

She studied her hands. They looked more like a man's hands than a woman's. And planting coffee would only make them worse. She squelched any thoughts of what might have been and used her very capable hands to scrape the plates. If she really wished for soft hands and nail polish, she'd just have to ignore the desire. Just like a lot of other things she ignored.

She pushed back her chair and gathered the dishes to put in the dishwasher. They'd have to stretch hoses and water with buckets for a while. Maybe the rain would be enough after they were growing.

Could the well handle all that?

The phone rang, making her jump she was so deep in coffee planting.

"Ms. Morton? This is Ms. Harcourt. I've contacted the judge and the prison officials, and there will be no more threats from Gabe Hernandez allowed to be sent to any address, addressed to anyone. All mail in and out is censored and the warden apologized that this threat letter came through. The judge said the injunction will be enforced and you are to notify me if anything else occurs."

"I have to keep him from knowing where we are." Maddy felt hope flutter in her heart like the first butterfly wings out of the chrysalis.

"I understand that and so does the judge." A bit of warmth crept into the sargent tone. "Will there be anything else I can do for you?"

Just keep him away from us. "No, not that I can think of. Thank you. Do I owe you any more money?"

"No, we're fine. I will mail you a copy of the letter and the injunction so you have them."

"Thank you very much." Relief felt remarkably like hope.

"You're welcome." The phone clicked off.

Maddy set the receiver back on its hook and leaned her forehead against the newly painted woodwork. One major worry to lock away for now. As if she ever could get entirely free of Gabe. Only death would accomplish that, either his or hers.

These thoughts followed one another like ducks in a row and always ended with her awash in a sea of guilt. The divorce lawyer had explained to her that men who abused their wives used any excuse to get angry. There was nothing she could have done to change that, other than leave. But while he'd promised her freedom in a divorce, he was unable to promise her protection from Gabe's threats.

She shook herself, shaking the images out of her head and the weights from her shoulders. Digging terraces for coffee plants beat thinking about Gabe, hands down. Hard work could always banish thoughts and worries, at least much of the time.

"Hey, Nicholas, want to come ride the tractor?"

No answer. What else was new? She took the stairs two at a time but when she stuck her head in Nicholas's room, it was empty.

Where was he? She headed back down the stairs. She had seven hours before she had to leave for work at the restaurant, enough time to make a serious dent in that hillside.

She grabbed a pair of leather gloves out of the box by the back door and leaped over the two steps from the lanai to the path. Trotting to the tractor, she caught herself whistling and grinning like a kid on a picnic.

"Nicholas?"

"In here, with the pigs."

For a boy who hated pigs, he sure was having fun with Hector. And at the same time, the sow and her other babies. If she believed in the God of her mother, this would be one of those times she would have asked for special privileges. *Please keep that little pig safe.*

"You want to ride the tractor up the hill?"

Nicholas came bolting out of the barn door. "Yeah, can I steer?"

"No, but you can help me hook up the scraper." She pointed to the blade lined up with the other tractor implements.

"What are you going to do?"

"Renew the terracing up the hill and then plant coffee starts."

"How come?"

"So we can grow coffee and maybe make some extra money. I don't want to be a waitress all my life." She turned the key on the tractor and it roared to life, settling down into the rhythm that spoke of a good tune-up. At the time she fixed it to impress her father, but now she was grateful. If she'd had to take time to work on the tractor, her planting would have been set back even more.

Now that she had permission, she couldn't get started soon enough.

Nicholas hung around for a while, then worked his way up the hill, Amos at his side.

"Watch out for the wild pigs," she shouted. When he waved back, she knew he heard. But he didn't really need reminding. She knew he still had nightmares about them.

She'd cleaned out several of the terraces when Amos came streaking down the hill, barking his warning bark. She looked out to see Kam and his two nephews striding up the hill. Nicholas shouted from the eucalyptus grove up the hill and the boys charged past her, waving as they went. She set the blade again and kept on going.

Kam waited for her at the end of the rows where she turned the tractor.

The temptation to ignore him and keep on clearing the run-off dirt and weeds away kept her looking back at the blade. Until she had to raise it and turn.

"Aloha."

Sometimes she wished her mother hadn't forced manners on her. "Aloha." She shifted into neutral and let the engine idle.

"I take it you're going ahead with the coffee idea?" He stopped just ahead of the rear tractor wheel, raising his voice to be heard over the tractor.

She nodded. "You know I'm not the only one on this side of the mountain. I met some other farmers at the meeting from around here. They seem to be doing all right."

"I wish you luck." He studied the work she'd done. "You laying PVC pipe first?"

He would hit the sore point right on the head. "Can't afford it."

"You thought of applying for a farm loan?"

She shook her head. "No way. My father—"

"Say no more. Credit is out." Kam picked up a handful of the red dirt and squeezed it before letting it fall again. "This stuff will grow anything, given *enough* water but not too much. But I'd be remiss in my job if I didn't say again that there are other things that will do better on this side of the island than coffee." He enunciated precisely and dusted off his hands.

"So you've done your job!" Maddy clutched and shifted gears.

"Thanks for the advice." He now had to step back or get run over by the tractor. The grin he shot her let her know that he understood what she was doing.

"Is it all right if the boys stay here for an hour or so? I've got another place to stop before I take them to lunch."

Maddy nodded and focused her attention on the blade leveling the dirt as it pushed clumps of grass out of the way. It hadn't taken any time for the grass to grow knee-deep again since the cows were no longer there to keep it grazed down. She looked up when he was half-way down the hill. Why couldn't she take his advice? And why did she feel in the wrong again?

All three boys had had a ride on the tractor by the time Kam returned. Maddy checked her watch. He'd been gone well over an hour. Her stomach rumbled, reminding her it was time to eat.

"Can Nicholas come with us?" Benny asked of Kam. His khaki shorts now sported streaks of red dirt. His mother would have a terrible time getting the stains out.

"If his mother says it is okay. Perhaps she would like to come too." Kam raised his voice so Maddy could hear and smiled up at her.

"Thanks but no thanks. Nicholas can go, though. I need to get as much done as possible before I leave for work." She waved at the red gashes in the hillside. "I'd like to go, too, but another time maybe."

"You need to eat."

She stared at him, feeling her face don its inscrutable mask. "Is that more *free* advice?" Her stomach rumbled again. It would be so easy to shut off the tractor and go. She knew they'd have fun too. She clenched both her teeth and her mind.

"Take it for what it's worth."

"I will." *Why do men think they have all the answers—know what I need before I do?* She had to double clutch because her timing was off and the transmission sounded like it stripped a couple of gears. Oh good, let her father hear that kind of treatment and he'd forbid her to use the tractor. *Thank you, Mr. County Extension Agent.*

Nicholas ran back to the tractor. "Thanks, Mom. See ya."

"Have fun." She watched them go down the hill, the three boys like puppies running beside their leader. Amos got his barks and licks in wherever possible. Nicholas was so tan he could fit right in as a member of the Waiano clan.

Was that jealousy she felt? Maddy shook her head and went back to her field work. So much for friendship.

— — —

By the time she got home that night, she had worked eighteen hours total for the day and was feeling every one of them. She checked on the pigs before stumbling her way up the stairs and peeking in on Nicholas, who slept curled on his side. She leaned down to kiss him and smoothed a lock of hair back from his forehead. She contented herself with simply touching his hair, then stealing from the room. At least she could do that while he was asleep. Anything to stave off a return to the sullenness of the last weeks. The boy she'd been with today was the real Nicholas, the one she'd begun to think was gone forever.

She fell into bed and for a change didn't try to right the entire day's wrongs before sleeping.

— — —

"M-o-t-h-e-r!"

She shot upright. "What's wrong?" Her feet hit the floor before he burst into her room.

"I hate that sow." Nicholas cradled a dead piglet. "I hate pigs. It's all your fault!" He fought back tears that welled up and threatened to wash over.

The sow had lain on Hector.

"Hey, Kam, good to see you."

"Thanks, Andrew, I'm just glad you had some free time when I did." Kam took the seat the pastor pointed to and crossed one ankle over the other knee. The two played the small-talk game for a couple of minutes, catching up on family things since Andrew was married to Marianna's cousin.

"So what's the problem?" Andrew leaned back, his hands clasped behind his neck.

Kam tapped his fingers on his worn boot. He took in a deep breath, sighed it out, and looked up at the man who'd been his friend, let alone pastor, for many years. "I . . . I need some help for and with a friend of mine."

Andrew waited. Kam sighed again. "I'm not sure how much of this story is mine to tell."

"You know it will go no further than these walls." Andrew motioned to the book-lined shelves surrounding them.

"I know." Kam nodded.

"Can you tell me who this person is?"

"You've met her, I'm sure, up at the Ranch House restaurant. She's one of the waitresses there. Maddy Morton."

"Ah." Andrew nodded. "The woman with the terror-filled eyes." He nodded again. "Winnie and I had dinner up there the other night and she waited on us. She was charming and friendly and then something happened that spooked her. Like a deer caught in the headlights."

Kam nodded again. "That's her. And she thinks she has to handle it all by herself."

"Can you give me some background?"

"She's the ex-wife of Gabe Hernandez."

"Oh, my friend, say no more. If he is anything like his father, I know what that poor young woman has been going through." Andrew tented his fingers and studied Kam. "How do you fit in this story?"

"I . . . I'd like to be her friend."

"And?"

"She has a hard time accepting friendship."

"Meaning help."

Kam nodded and tipped his head slightly to the side. "Not just from me, but everybody. Her father, Jesse Morton . . ."

"I know him. I conducted the funeral service for his wife."

"I was away at school then, so I don't know a lot of what went on. He's had a bad time."

"And blamed it all on God."

"Could be. There's also her son, who is Benny and James's age. The three of them hit it off real good."

Andrew blew across his fingertips and set his chair to rocking. "Back to my original question. How can I help you?"

"My mother said you have worked with families in abuse situations."

"Yes."

"And you would give me some advice on how to help." He went on to describe the way that Maddy flinched from his hand. Kam's foot thumped on the floor and he leaned forward, propping his elbows on his knees. He studied the floor for a long moment before looking up again. "I wanted to kill the scum that made her react that way."

His words hung in the still air.

"Are you in love with her?"

"Funny, Mother asked me the same thing. I don't think so, but I do care about her. . . ."

"Kam, you *care* about every living thing and try to take care of them all. Now, how is this different?"

Kam stared across the desk. "I . . . I've never felt like killing anyone before." He stared down at his hands, now clenched together. "If he'd been here or anywhere I could get to him, I . . . I don't know what would have happened. I saw the fear in her eyes. No one should ever have to feel that way."

"I agree. What's God been telling you?"

"I'm not sure. That's why I'm here."

Andrew nodded. "I can give you some general advice. Things like take it easy, don't rush her. Be there for her, but don't try to be more than a friend. Since she's been in a controlling relationship, she'll probably rear back at everything you say."

"Ain't that the truth."

"Better than being a door mouse that will fall right back into that kind of relationship since that's what she's known."

"She isn't big on trust, that's for sure."

"Why should she be?"

"And she has an independent streak two miles wide and ten deep."

"Good, that's one of the things that will keep her both sane and healthy." Andrew reached behind him and pulled a couple of books off his shelf. "I can give you these; there's lots of good information there about how those who've been abused feel. And what it takes to help them regain wholeness again." He handed them across the desk. "Any idea where she is spiritually?"

"On the run, I think. Mother says Maddy was raised in the church, so there's that."

Andrew nodded again. "Not unusual. God uses whatever means He needs to bring us back to himself. So, my friend, I suggest you read those, be real careful in how you come across to this young woman, and if she is the one God has chosen for you, then we can count on Him to work things out."

Kam could feel his neck get warm. Is that what he wanted? "Time will tell, huh?"

"Right. And for you, I pray that you will learn to turn things over to our Father first, rather than carrying them around on your broad shoulders until the load gets too heavy. God didn't assign you to be savior of this island. He already did that."

Kam got to his feet. "I'll remember that." He picked up the books. "Thanks."

— ~ —

"Don't you talk to your mother that way!"

The roar came from the bottom of the stairs.

"I don't care! Hector's dead." Nicholas cradled the baby pig in his arms and ran into his own room, slamming the door.

"Don't let him get away with that! You're too soft on the boy." All from the base of the staircase.

Maddy rolled her head around on her shoulders. She felt like she'd been dragged out of a swamp or something.

"Maddy? Are you listening?"

"Yeah, Pop, I hear you." *And Nicholas and all those others who take up residence in my head and yell at me. I hear them too.*

"So . . . what are you going to do?"

Why did he have to choose now to get involved—the one who hasn't said ten words in a row since we moved here? "I'll take care of it, okay?" She heard him walk away, then fell back on the bed, relief making her feel light-headed. Poor Nicholas. She pulled her nightshirt over her head and stepped into her work jeans. As she dressed, she kept an ear cocked for any noise from Nicholas's room. What could she say to him? How could she comfort him?

As soon as she braided her hair, she tapped on Nicholas's door. When there was no answer, she poked her head in. Her son lay on his belly across the bed, his face buried in one crooked elbow, his other hand around the still form of Hector.

Her throat tightened at the sight. She sat down on the edge of the bed and laid a hand on her son's bare calf. Scratches on it showed the tree climbing of yesterday with Benny and James. "I'll help you bury him."

"But why did he have to die? He wasn't hurting anyone. That stupid sow, I hate her."

"I don't blame you a bit, but this is just the way of pigs. Hector might not have gone under the lamp when he was supposed to. All kinds of things go wrong when you are raising animals."

"But Hector was mine."

"You could choose another."

He turned his face to the side and glared at her. "Just go away. I'll take care of him." The rock-hard tone was back in his voice, the fury in his eyes.

She sorted through the words that came to mind, searching for just the right ones. None fit. Life and death were part of farming, part of being human . . . but how did you explain that to a boy suffering from a broken heart? A boy who just lost his first pet.

"We could invite James and Benny over for a funeral." She took his growl for a no.

If only he would let her comfort him. She thought of the times her mother had held her close and let her cry out whatever had caused the hurt. That's what mothers were for—to bandage scrapes, kiss away bruises, and whisper love words in a child's ear when the rest of the world seemed out to get her. Or him. *Oh, Nicholas, I love you so and you won't let me show you.*

"I'll help you bury him right after breakfast and then we've got to go work up on the hill. You can help me flag the coffee plants we are going to transplant."

"They'll probably all die too." He turned over on his back, one bony wrist across his forehead.

"I sure hope not. That would be a lot of hard work for nothing." A shiver ran down her back. She got to her feet. "Breakfast will be ready in a few minutes."

"I'll eat after Grandpa leaves. He hates me."

"It only seems that way. He's concerned about you growing up right." She stopped at the door and looked back. Nicholas was sitting up and stroking Hector's soft little ear.

Nicholas needed something all his own to love.

They buried Hector under the Plumeria bush at the north corner of the lanai. Maddy was glad he didn't ask if pigs went to heaven. She hated questions when she had no answers. Right now she wasn't too sure there was a heaven. After all, if there was no God, how could there be a heaven?

But if there was a God, why did He allow things like husbands who beat their wives, children who die before they'd had time to live, and even seemingly inconsequential things, like baby pigs that are squashed beneath a careless mother? At one time she'd believed in a loving and merciful God who sent His Son to die for mankind, but no longer. Or at least that's what she tried to convince herself of.

Together she and Nicholas dug up ten seedlings, some of which were several years old and had a deep root system already. After laying them on the trailer bed, she covered the root balls with wet gunny sacks and drove back down the hill to the terraces. An hour later, they had them planted and staked against the wind.

Maddy looked up to see the dark clouds hovering on the western sky above the mountain. "I guess now it will rain and our plants will grow. Good timing, huh?" She turned to look at Nicholas, who wore a smear of red dirt across his cheek. "Thanks for helping me."

"You're welcome." He looked up at her, his eyes serious. "Now can I drive the tractor back down to the barn?"

She rolled her eyes and shook her head. "An ulterior motive. And here I thought you were helping me because you knew I needed help."

"Uh, that too but . . ."

She ruffled his dark hair, leaving behind a smudge of dirt from her gloves. "Okay, fair's fair. I'll give you a lesson in tractor driving but I got news for you. You are never to touch that tractor unless I am right there with you. Got it?"

He nodded.

As they carried the shovels and post-hole digger back to the trailer, she glanced out across the slope to the Pacific, frosted by whitecaps courtesy of the approaching storm. If she had cut the terraces correctly, the rain should soak in and the runoff angle toward the north side of her growing field, where she'd trenched a drainage ditch. She looked back at their day's labor. Ten saplings didn't look like an awful lot, but since the hoses weren't long enough and they had to carry water, too, she felt proud of their accomplishment.

"We ought to celebrate." She climbed up to the tractor seat, scooting back to allow Nicholas in front of her.

"For what?" He had both hands on the wheel, waiting for her commands.

"That." She waved toward the terraces. "That's the beginning of our new life. How about hot fudge sundaes down at the house?"

"Sure." He turned the wheel from side to side. "How do you start this?"

Shaking her head, Maddy talked him through the process. "Now, you have to remember to push in the clutch when you are going to shift. Start in neutral, right here." She jiggled the gear shift back and forth to show the play in it.

They made it back to the barn in one piece and didn't even lose anything off the trailer. She was glad Pop was nowhere in sight. He'd taught Mark and then her to drive the tractor. Why was he treating Nicholas so differently?

After taking care of the pigs, they headed for the house. On the table lay a stack of books and pamphlets on coffee raising.

Had Kam brought them by? She picked up the first one and glanced inside. The release date showed fifteen years earlier. They were from her father.

Guess he must approve after all. She laid the booklet back in the pile and scooped them together. They would make good bedtime reading. She'd just started for the stairs when the phone rang. Juggling the stack, she picked up the receiver.

A woman's musical voice answered her greeting. "This is Edi Waiano, Kam's aunt."

"Yes." Maddy felt like taking a step backward. What was wrong now?

"I'm planning a luau for Sunday afternoon and I would like you, your father, and Nicholas to come. It will be mostly family, but I thought you might enjoy getting to know some others of the area. Help get you back into island life."

"Ah." A luau, Kam there, a bunch of people . . . the last thing in the world she wanted to do.

But Nicholas would love it.

Her father would hate it. How could she possibly get him to go?

Nicholas needed more companionship.

She'd have to see Kam.

"I'll have my son pick you all up about one. Make sure you bring swimsuits and snorkling gear."

"Ah, can I bring anything?"

"No, that is all taken care of. I look forward to seeing you."

Maddy stared at a silent receiver. She should call her back and say no, thank you. But she didn't know the woman's phone number.

"Looks like we're going to a luau."

Nicholas turned from dishing out ice cream. "When?" He poured hot fudge sauce on the two bowls of ice cream and sprinkled on chopped macadamia nuts.

"Umm, that looks good." She picked up one dish and, dipping out a spoon of warmed fudge sauce, opened the door to the lanai with one hip. "Come on, let's eat on the glider so we catch the breeze."

"Who's having a luau?"

Maddy filled him in on the details and as soon as she said Benny's and James's names, he let out a whoop.

Later on the way in to work, windshield wipers slicing away the sheeting rain, she replayed the conversation in her mind. Why in the world hadn't she said no? Simple and direct. No, thank you.

Wait until her father heard about this. Maybe that would be her excuse if her father refused to go. She nodded. That would do it. But Nicholas's excited face flashed across her memory. How could she disappoint him?

She pounded on the steering wheel. "How do I get myself into such situations? No way can I make everybody happy. Never, ever." She peered through the downfall, hardly able to see the turn off to The Ranch House. *I wonder what made her call me? Or rather, us?*

As usual, in spite of the rain, or maybe because of it, they were beyond busy and the new girl hadn't showed—again.

"That's the end of her," Ruby said in passing. "John doesn't believe in his waitresses getting sick or having to stay home with sick kids. You can tell he was never a mother."

"Was she sick again?"

"That's what she said."

"I think it's more than that." *Stay out of it, dummy*, she told herself. *You know better than to get involved in other people's business. Just take her at face value.*

But her face was what caught Maddy's attention. Diana Jones wore far too much makeup some nights and on others hardly any at all. Plus, she always had on long sleeves buttoned to the wrist, and on some of the hottest nights she wore a turtleneck. Altogether, the signs pointed to a heavy-handed husband, in Maddy's estimation.

Now the quandary. Should she say anything? Let Diana know what she suspected?

Stay away! Don't get involved! She felt like there was a terrified little girl in her head, screaming the words.

"You thinking what I'm thinking?" Ruby stood beside Maddy at the salad station.

"I don't know, mind reading has never been my specialty." Maddy added a dollop of ranch dressing to the salad she'd been fixing and reached for another cold plate.

"Come on, girl, you've been there. I know you recognize the signs."

Guilt welled up like bubbling lava pots. *Leave me alone*, her insides screamed.

"We could help her, you know. She doesn't have to put up with that kind of life."

"Your husband ever knock you around?" The words leaped out before she could stop them.

Ruby shook her head. "No, thank God. I mighta just taken a gun to him myself if he did." She shuddered. "I can't even comprehend something like that."

"You got lucky." Maddy hoisted the tray to her shoulder.

"Not luck, my dear, the grace of God."

Maddy pondered those words as she served her salads, smiled, took another table's orders, smiled, and promised to bring the drinks right back. *Grace of God, huh. He sure didn't send much my way.*

You're alive, aren't you? You have a fine son, a good home, and friends who care about you. The gentle voice continued, reminding her of the things she had to be thankful for. She could add more without a great deal of thought. A job, out of the city, Gabe in prison . . . She called a halt to the thinking when the picture of a tall, broad-shouldered Hawaiian with a heart-squeezing smile took over. Kam wasn't hers to be thankful for and never would be, if she had anything to say about it.

She heard a man laugh and shivers ran up and down her spine as she realized it was Kam. She was beginning to look forward to that marvelous laugh, and that wouldn't do at all.

Sure enough, he sat in her station area. That was no surprise. No surprise, either, that her heart speeded up just a bit. She could feel the warmth coming up her neck and into her face. What would it be like to quit fighting and let her real feelings emerge?

She nearly dropped her tray at that thought. *You know better. Just don't feel, it's safer. After all, you don't know what you feel anymore.*

"You okay, miss?" one of the customers asked, concern written across his sunburned face.

"I'm fine, thanks." She knew she sounded abrupt, so she paused and smiled. "Can I get you anything else? Our macadamia nut cream pie will make you glad you came to Hawaii. There's chopped nuts in the crust and a thin layer of chocolate between the crust and the cream filling, then more nuts and whipped cream on top."

The man and woman looked at each other and groaned. "Did you have to tempt us?"

"Can't have you going home missing out on our Hawaiian specialties." She looked from one to the other. "One for each?" At their nods and more groans, she headed for the refrigerated pie shelf.

Knowing she had to pass Kam's table on her way, she slowed her pace to say, "I'll be right with you."

"No hurry."

Maybe the heart palpitations were caused by stress. And rushing around the restaurant brought on flushed cheeks. Sure, and maybe they were building a bridge between Oahu and the mainland.

C an you go out for coffee with me tonight?" Ruby asked. "I've got to celebrate."

"The coffee's better here."

"I want to be waited on, thank you very much."

Maddy thought a minute. There really was no reason she had to go right home, other than her feet hurt, her head ached, and she wondered if she could make it home as it was. "Okay, but not for long." Ruby's husband let her sleep as late as she wanted in the morning, but then, Ruby didn't have hogs to feed.

As they were picking up their things in the locker room, Ruby said, "Oh, by the way, I invited Kam too. Ken is going to meet us there."

Maddy groaned.

"Now, don't you go thinking you can back out on me. We are going to celebrate."

"What are we celebrating?"

"Tell you when we get there."

"Maddy, would you like to ride with me?" Kam appeared at her side while she was talking with Ruby.

"No, thanks, I'll take my truck." *So I can leave when I want or need to.* She glanced up at him. "But you can ride with me if you like." She felt like looking around to see who said those strange words. *Please, please, say no.*

"Fine with me." The way he smiled at her let her know he knew exactly what she was thinking.

"So what is it we are celebrating?" Kam asked after they got in the truck.

"Got me. Ruby just insisted that I had to help her celebrate."

"Same here." Kam put his arm across the back of the seat.

Maddy could feel the heat from his fingers even though he never touched her. "You finally got all the cattle fracas straightened out?"

"All but the girl who lost her steer. I'm going to ask Hampton up at the Parker ranch if they will donate a calf for her next year."

"What a good idea." Maddy checked traffic both ways on the highway before easing out. "You really care about the people you serve, don't you?"

"Especially the kids. That was one of the reasons I went into County Extension work. I truly believe in the value of 4-H, and keeping kids on the farm is absolutely necessary if we are to continue to have food to eat. And if I can get the farmers to diversify, our economy will be stronger and more stable." He shrugged and chuckled at the same time. "Those are just two of my soap boxes. Bet you didn't plan on hearing all that with a simple yes or no question."

"Maybe not, but I appreciate it just the same. I watch you with the boys; you are really good with kids." *Nicholas thinks you can walk on water.* But she didn't tell him that as she turned into the parking lot of the all-night cafe.

He was around her side of the truck to open the door before she could turn the ignition off and set the brake.

"Ah, thanks." The shock of it made her catch her boot heel on the door frame.

He caught her before she stumbled farther and set her on her feet. Her arms burned where his hands had been and her face burst into flame. Since when had she become clumsy?

Ken and Ruby were already sitting on one side of a booth when they entered the room.

"Come on, we saved you a place." Ruby waved them over. "We already ordered since I wanted a gigantic hot fudge sundae for all of us to share. The waitress left here laughing." Ruby leaned over the table and lowered her voice. "I think they're trying to figure out what to make it in."

After Ruby introduced Maddy to her husband, she leaned back and sighed. "How nice. I've been wanting to do this for so long."

"Okay, so what are we celebrating?" Kam propped his elbows on the table.

"We are celebrating . . . " Ruby turned to her husband.

He winked at her and continued. "The payoff of our mortgage. After we eat a mountain of ice cream, we are going to burn that sucker right out there in the parking lot."

"You mean to say people really do pay off their mortgages?" Maddy made her eyes and mouth both round in disbelief.

"Congratulations." Kam shook both Ruby's and Ken's hands. "It'll be a long while until I have that privilege."

"Since I don't even *have* a mortgage, it'll be even longer for me." Maddy leaned back and let her shoulders relax. With this group of people, she didn't have to be on guard. Strange feeling, it was.

"Oh my!" Ruby laughed at the tray the waitress brought. A mountain of ice cream topped by a lava flow of hot fudge and crowned by a snowdrift of whipped cream, along with nuts and four cherries on top, brought chuckles from them all.

"We should have brought the boys." Maddy looked up at Kam.

He nodded and the smile he gave her went straight to her heart—and took up residence.

"I brought you four spoons and here are extra napkins." The waitress giggled at the looks on their faces. "You said you wanted a big one."

"I didn't plan on feeding all the kids on the island, let alone four adults." Ken picked up one of the spoons. "Here's to many more happy years in our *own* house." They all touched spoons and dug in.

"I think I'm going to pop," Ruby said a while later. The mountain had shrunk but by no means disappeared.

"Me too." Maddy leaned back against the cushion. "And if I don't head home, I'm going to fall asleep right here."

The four of them wandered outside and stood near the flower beds. Ruby pulled the paper out of her purse, Ken lit a match, and they watched the paper curl and turn black in the flame. When it got near his fingers, Ken let it drift and finish burning on the gravel.

"I never thought I'd see the day." He dusted off his hands and put an arm around Ruby's shoulders. "We were going to throw a luau but decided this would be more fun. Thanks for helping us eat Mount Mortgage." He shook Kam's hand and took Maddy's in both of his. "My Ruby has told me so much about you, and I am sure looking forward to more times together. You are one gutsy lady and I really admire you."

Maddy swallowed the lump in her throat enough to say "thank you" and return the hug that Ruby gave her before she moved on to hug Kam.

"You two go on now and let us old folks go home and get some rest."

"Yeah, right." Maddy figured she'd be out faster than any of them.

"Thanks for the ride," Kam said when they returned to his pickup.

"You're welcome." Maddy smiled and propped her wrists on the steering wheel.

"I'd like to do something like this again."

"What? Eat a mountain of ice cream?"

"Not necessarily, but with Ruby and Ken, or maybe just us or maybe us and the three boys or maybe . . . ."

"Or maybe I better get on home while I can still see."

She waited while Kam came around the truck. "Good night."

"Good night, friend. I'll be right behind you all the way to your turnoff."

"That oughta keep me awake." Maddy waited until Kam started his car and turned on his lights before she turned around and headed for home. Never before had she realized how comforting it could be to see familiar headlights in the rearview mirror and have a horn beeped twice to say good-night.

"Good night, friend," she whispered as she turned into the driveway.

— — —

Later, in bed after crashing asleep like she'd been hit with a sledgehammer, the nightmares attacked. Gabe screaming at her, throwing her across the room, down the stairs. She woke with her arm throbbing.

She sat up in bed and used the sheet to wipe away the sweat streaming down her face and neck. Gabe, always back to Gabe. Would it never end? She padded downstairs for a glass of water at the kitchen sink and stared across the yard, gilded by moonlight that deepened velvet shadows. So peaceful out there, as if violence didn't even exist.

The third time she awoke with the same dream she gave up, pulled on her jeans and shirt, and grabbed her boots. Maybe seeing the sunrise over the lava fields would bring a measure of peace.

But the light on in the kitchen said she wasn't the only one up before sunrise.

"You couldn't sleep, either, huh?" She leaned against the wall of the arch to the kitchen and watched her father measuring coffee grounds for his morning cup.

"Na, sometimes my hip gets to acting up and the only thing I can do is get up and move around." He nodded to the clock. "Too early to get up and too late to go back to sleep."

"Four-thirty is too late to sleep?" She shook her head. "What do you have going that you need to be up so early for?"

He ducked his head and filled the carafe with water. "I like to see the sunrise with Amelia. She liked the sunrises as much as I do, so I can't see no reason to stop."

"Oh, Pop." What would he do if she crossed the room and gave him big hug? The need was so strong it set her feet in motion, but by the time she got there, she'd thought the better of it and poured herself a glass of water instead.

He limped past her and took his place at the table. "Paper's not here yet." His fingers twitched as if they needed the reassuring feel of the daily news to keep steady.

"Soon." If she didn't leave now, the sun would be up by the time she got to her special place. Seeing the sky change from indigo to pearl was part of the pleasure. Out the kitchen window she could see the horizon already lightening.

Oh well. She'd do that another day.

When she poured his coffee and set it in front of him, she heard Amos bark and the sound of a car in the drive. The paper thunked on the porch. "How come you get porch delivery instead of having to walk down to the road?"

He shrugged. "I pay extra. Back after I had this hip replaced, I couldn't get down there. They started dropping it off here and we've kept it that way."

"When did you have that done?" She cupped her hands around the coffee mug, more for consolation than warmth. He could have died and Maddy wouldn't have known. After taking a sip, she pushed herself to her feet again and retrieved the paper. Amos greeted her with a wiggle and a yip, licking her hand and trying for her face as she bent over.

Tucking the paper under her arm, she framed the dog's head with her hands. "I could probably find out what's gone on here as easily from you as from that old man in there." She rubbed his ears. "What do you think?"

From his contortions, Amos obviously thought she should sit down and give him a good petting, but he only whined when she went back in the house.

Handing her father the paper, she paused a moment, waiting for a thank-you. When nothing came, she shook her head and continued over to her own chair. Looked like his manners had been buried in the casket with her mother.

She looked up at the calendar. Today was Friday, the luau Sunday. Edi was expecting all three of them. Maddy cleared her throat. Might as well get this over with. "Edi Waiano invited us all for a luau on Sunday. I have the day off."

No answer, but the paper rustled.

"I said we'd go."

The paper hit the table like it was lead.

"Not me."

"All of us. She especially asked for you."

He shook his head. His eyebrows drew together, forming a hard line across his forehead. "No."

"Fine. You call her and tell her you won't come. I got the feeling she'd come over here and lasso you if she had to. Said it was about time you got back in the world."

She thought she heard him mutter something about busybody women as she strolled out the back door to go feed the pigs. Stubborn old man. If only she dared to hug him.

"Maddy, lookit here!" Her father met her on the porch, waving the paper.

"What?" If she didn't know better, she'd think he was smiling.

"Read!" He pointed to a small article near the bottom of the page.

Maddy scanned the words, then read them again more slowly, shaking her head. "Well, I'll be." She handed her father back the paper. "Guess there is some justice in this world after all." A local auto repair place had been indicted for illegal dumping of coolant. In return for not being prosecuted, the local EPA had fined them heavily and imposed a restitution program on them for any harm done by the dumping.

She looked up at her father on the step above her. "You'll get paid for the dead cattle."

He shrugged. "Maybe, maybe not, but it won't happen again."

Leave it to him to ignore the possibilities. "But at least you'll apply."

Nodding, he tucked the paper under his arm. "Yep, that I will do."

With that good news, maybe he'd relent and go to the luau too. Maddy decided not to hold her breath on that score.

Rain drumming on the tin roof woke her Sunday morning.

Good, now maybe they'll cancel the luau. Maddy stretched and rolled over on her side. Her father still refused to go. But if the party was canceled, Nicholas would be beyond just a little sad. He'd talked of nothing else since he heard of the invitation.

And her? She was beginning to feel like a piece of frayed rope. Too hard a tug, and she'd come apart with ends flying both ways.

She glanced at the clock and groaned. Not yet seven, and she'd worked until nearly two o'clock because John needed additional help with the Robertson party. She'd called the taxi for several of the guests who couldn't be allowed to drive in their condition. Her ears still burned from the invectives one man hurled at her. While some of them had been rather creative, others she'd heard from Gabe many times. Perhaps that was another reason she'd had the nightmares again.

That and the news that John had indeed fired the new girl. And she'd done nothing to help her.

I'm having enough trouble caring for myself, she told herself repeatedly, trying to still the voice inside that called her to duty. After all, it wasn't *her* fault the woman was allowing the beating to continue or had gotten into the relationship in the first place.

But since it wasn't her fault, why did she feel like it was?

In her dream the judge had pounded his gavel and shouted for the entire world to hear, "Guilty! Guilty as charged!" And, pointing directly at her, he began to read a three-foot list of her crimes. She could still hear the thundering of the gavel, feel it deep inside where the thought of freedom was a tiny flame that flickered and died repeatedly. There was no freedom for one as guilty as she.

She rolled to the edge of the bed and sat up. Her head pounded like she'd been the one imbibing. Could she get a hangover from the fumes of those she waited on?

The tempo on the roof picked up. Looking out the window, Maddy craned her neck to see the terraces that were home to her fledgling coffee plants. How long had it been raining? Headache or no, she pulled on her clothes, stopping only long enough to use the bathroom, and tossed down a couple of pain tablets before heading out the door.

She was drenched to the skin before she got to the gate. Grabbing a shovel from the tool bar, Maddy strode up the hill to the red slashes in the green hillside. She deepened the entrances of the horizontal drainage ditches to the one that carried the runoff down the hill, then walked the terraces to check on her plants. One thing for sure, they weren't lacking for water. Puddles of red circled every plant since she'd created saucers for water retention. The huge drops hitting the shiny green leaves slid down and plopped into widening pools. After checking them all, she heaved a sigh of relief and brushed her hair back off her forehead so the water didn't run quite so quickly into her eyes.

The clouds showed no cracks of blue, only shades of gray that ranged from gunmetal to dirty sheep. She thought of drain tiles, which would help keep her hill in place until the coffee trees took solid root.

All she needed was a year or so of fairly mild weather. Something one took for granted in the islands.

She wiped her hair back again and whistled for Amos. His barking from up in the trees told her he wasn't happy at whatever was there. Shovel over her shoulder, she headed back down the hill to feed the pigs and then to the shower. As if she wasn't wet enough.

Amos caught up with her halfway back, but he kept looking over his shoulder.

"Pigs up there, fella, or is someone's cow out?" How she wished their own cows were up there. Never a day went by that she didn't look up the hills to check on them.

Amos licked her hand before looking back up the hill, growling low in his throat.

The thunderclouds were worse inside than out when she entered the kitchen after cleaning up. She thought of heading outside again. Rain clouds were easier to deal with than temper clouds any day.

"They canceled the party." Nicholas dumped his cereal bowl in the sink and turned to leave.

"Since when did a little rain make a difference for a luau?" Jesse shook his head. "This generation, so . . ." He flipped his paper back up and went back to reading.

"I . . . I thought you weren't going?"

"Not now."

"Oh." What more could she say? When had he changed his mind? Men! She followed Nicholas as he pulled himself upstairs by the handrail. Each foot thudded on a step like it was too heavy to lift to the next.

"Sorry, son."

He spun around. "No, you're not! You didn't want to go anyway." He pointed back down the stairs. "And *he* really wasn't going to go. Nothing ever goes the way I want."

Only by exerting supreme effort could Maddy refrain from patting his shoulder, let alone a brief hug. She kept her voice even and gentle.

"Sure seems that way, doesn't it? I don't blame you one bit for being angry."

He glared at her from under his eyelashes.

"You want to call Benny and James and ask if they can go to a movie?"

"Can't. They're at Sunday school."

"Oh. Maybe later, then."

He eyed her. "How come we don't go to church?"

Maddy could think of no rational answer. *Because I don't believe God exists anymore?* If that were the case, why did she catch herself praying again? She'd never done that in Honolulu. *So if I believe God is real, why don't we go to church? I used to. Pop used to.* Not a good thing to say to her son, *Because I don't want to, that's why.* Sometimes keeping one's mouth shut was the wiser move.

"Aren't you going to work?"

"Day off." She leaned against the wall, one foot on the stair higher than the other.

"Last time you had a day off, they called and you went to work anyway. All you do is work."

"No, I—" She stopped. He had her there. She'd only had three days off since she started working at the Ranch House. She'd spent those on the pigs and the coffee planting. She reached out with both hands and cupped his face. "Nicholas, if there is something you'd like to do today, we'll do it." She grinned at him. "Within reason, of course."

Nicholas thought a moment but he didn't move away from her hands. "Could we go to the video arcade?" The hopeful look in his eyes stabbed her in the guilt plexus.

She groaned. "I hate that place." At his immediate withdrawal, she clutched on to him and groaned again. "But for you I will do even that."

"With James and Benny?"

"If they can go."

Nicholas let out a whoop that made her ears ring.

— — —

Three boys at the arcade for two hours made her head ring too. They chose pizza for dinner so they could play more video games. Maddy thought working a double shift would have been preferable. She played with her straw in her mug of root beer and watched the boys teasing one another and laughing at some joke.

Seeing Nicholas laugh like that made this worthwhile. Now, if he would only do that with her. At least he could still laugh. Sometimes she wondered if she could.

Benny said something and James threw back his head and roared. Just like his uncle. She caught herself smiling, and she didn't even know what the joke was. Those Waiano males sure did know how to enjoy themselves. It must be genetic.

If only Nicholas had a father worth imitating. Maddy watched as he tossed his hair. Not a terribly impressive mannerism to emulate. The cloud that still spit rain outside seemed to settle around her shoulders, squashing any sunlight the laughing had brought along.

The waiter stopped beside her. "Here's your pizza. Can I get you anything else?"

She shook her head. Not unless he had a new father to give her son. She pasted a smile on her face and began dishing out pizza slices, glad for the boys and their infectious laughter.

"Good pizza," James said, fingering a string of cheese up to his mouth.

"My mom makes good pizza too." Nicholas did the string of cheese to his waving-tongue routine.

Maddy nearly fell off her chair. Was that *her* son giving *his* mother a compliment? "Thanks," she replied, realizing that eating stringy cheese off the tip of your finger definitely improved the taste. And four people doing it at once made for plenty of giggles.

— — —

So after such a good time, why was she awake before dawn again? She'd sat up late working on the figures for her coffee plants. With payday on Monday, she mushed her budget around until she could buy fifteen one-gallon and three five-gallon plants at the nursery. She'd debated between more five gallon and fewer plants, but more plants won out. This would deplete her tip money, too, but that's what that stash was for. Sometimes she thought of opening a checking account, but that would place her here at her father's farm if Gabe was able to crack bank records. And came looking for her.

It was a headache that awakened her, so she got up, took two pills, then lay back down and tried to find a comfortable place in the bed. Realizing it wasn't subsiding, she instead drove to the vantage point in the lava flow where she could watch a fresh day emerge. She left the truck at the end of the road and, grateful for the lightening sky, climbed the ridge so she could sit at the top and watch the sunrise. Gilt rimmed the bottom of the clouds and outlined Mauna Kea. The flanks of the mountain purpled with blacker shadows in the clefts and valleys. Birds twittered in the bits of scrub that had taken a foothold in the ancient lava. Lavender and red hues heightened, and then finally the sun burst from its hiding place within the mountain and flung itself into the sky. Bird song rose along with it and crescendoed, a paean to the morning.

"Thank you, Father God." She whispered the words, wishing she could join the morning chorus and dance like the butterflies kissing the fragile blossoms. She blinked her eyes against the beauty of it all. No other response seemed possible.

Surprised at her murmurings, she crossed her arms over her bent knees and rested her chin on her forearm. *Do I really believe there is a God?* She waited, trying to figure it out. *Can I doubt that there is? Just look around.*

Right at her bootheel a plant had settled in a tiny pocket of dirt and sent forth green leaves and a miniature yellow blossom. The black honeycomb-like lava framed it and shaded it, but it also absorbed enough heat to burn most living things. Unless they found a pocket of protection. Like this seed had.

Her mother had loved this harsh terrain as much as she adored the tumult of flowers on the rainy side of the island. She always looked for treasures such as this, saying that God knew every petal on every flower.

Maddy knew that if she turned her head fast enough, she would see her mother right behind her, laughing and smiling at the glory of the sunrise and the perfection of the fragile flower. Maddy held her breath. She turned her head slowly, so as not to frighten an angel away. Only more black lava with brilliant bits of green and a sky so blue that the line between ocean and air looked drawn by an artist's fine pencil. But the feeling remained and brought with it a tiny sprig of peace.

Could her mother have been mistaken about the reality of a loving God? A heavenly Father who wanted to love His children and them to love Him? Could it be?

Could it not be?

A bleat broke into her thoughts. She listened. The breeze ruffled the strands of hair around her face that had escaped the clip at the base of her head. It came again, plaintive, weeping with distress.

She got to her feet, careful to not cut herself on the sharp lava, and stood perfectly still. The sound came from the south. Walking carefully across the lava clumps, she stopped every couple of feet to listen. Animals could get caught in the lava so easily. Sometimes a fissure cracked with the weight and something could fall into a subterranean cave or just get cut to ribbons in the falling. She jumped to another rock. Her boot slipped and she grabbed for a hold on the lava to keep from falling to her knees.

Looking up, she saw a wild donkey trapped by its leg in a hole. It flung itself about, leaving bloody patches of gray hair on the rocks, and now the battered form was lifeless.

"Oh, you poor thing." *If only I'd been earlier, I might have been able to save you.*

The cry she heard earlier came again. With a groan, Maddy realized it was a donkey foal, probably near death without his mother's milk.

She knew the baby's only hope of survival rested on her, and with unquestioning determination, Maddy surveyed the situation. He was tiny enough that she could carry him to safety.

Weak as he was, the little one made a valiant effort to evade capture. After nearly falling herself, Maddy trapped him in a small canyon and grabbed when he tried to dart by her. He screamed in fright, flailing his legs and throwing his head around.

She took a jab on the chin but clamped her hold around all four feet and lifted him in her arms. "Sorry, fella, but I'm bigger than you and—" she sucked in a breath and hoisted him a bit higher—"you are coming with me."

The fight went out of him and he drooped in her arms.

"Please don't die on me, okay? I can't take any more death this morning." She kept up a running murmur as much as she could between breaths. While he didn't weigh much, carrying anything over such rough terrain and so high in her arms was hard work.

Sweat ran down her forehead and the small of her back. When it dripped in her eyes, the salt burned and made vision even more difficult. The truck seemed miles away. Had she really gone this far or had she missed the truck?

She stopped to catch her breath and look for the green cab. Sun glinted on an object off to her left. With a sigh of relief, she turned toward it and staggered the last few feet. She leaned against the cab, catching her breath and trying to figure what to do. If she put the foal down, the critter would run no matter how weak he was. And he'd just been carried while she walked. Wouldn't take a rocket scientist to figure out who had the most energy. And he might be able to jump out of the pickup bed.

"You are a real problem, kid." One of his soft ears tickled the bruise he'd given her on the point of her chin. Soft as the fur on a panda bear she'd coveted one time in an expensive toy store. How would she drive with him in the cab with her? And what would she do with him when she got home?

"Nicholas, I have a surprise for you!"

"What?" His voice floated down from his bedroom but he sounded awake.

"Come and see." She let the screen door slam and headed back to the truck. Amos glued himself to her side and tried to put his feet on the car sill to sniff the creature on the seat.

"No, Amos, down." Maddy pushed the dog away and studied the foal wrapped in the burlap bag she'd found behind the seat in her father's treasure trove. One hoof stuck out a hole and another showed most of his rump. He was panting like he'd been running in the hot sun.

"We better get some liquid in you, little one, if you are to have any chance of making it." She'd thought of stopping at the vet's, but if there were injunctions against keeping wild burros, the vet would have had to report it. But if they didn't get some water and food into it, the law would be a moot point.

Nicholas wore his habitual frown as he meandered down the steps and over to the truck. "What?"

"Look here, you think you can help me with him?" Maddy stepped back.

"Oh, like wow." Nicholas reached a tentative hand and touched the donkey's shoulder. "Look at those ears." Keeping one hand on the foal's shoulder, he turned to his mother, the stars in his eyes matching those she'd seen in the heavens not that many hours ago. "You mean I can keep him?"

"We'll have to keep him alive first. He might not have eaten for twenty-four hours or more. He is so weak he can hardly fight, poor little thing." Maddy patted Amos as she spoke. "We can put him in that other stall in the barn for now. I'll go to the feed store and get some milk replacer. They must have something for horses like they do calves. And a bottle with a nipple. In the meantime, let's see if we can get some water into him, he's so dehydrated. And the flies have been at his eyes."

All the while she talked, Nicholas crooned to the baby, stroking the burlap sack and the fluffy hair beneath it. "Oh, Mom, he is so cool. We can call him Ears, okay?"

"That suits all right." She laid a hand on her son's shoulder and leaned in to stroke the little body. "Come on, let's get him in the stall so he can be free."

"Can I carry him?" Nicholas looked up, but at the shake of her head he stepped back and let her pick him up.

"He can fight pretty hard in spite of the sack." She grunted as the burro bit her on the arm. "He's taken several bites of me and seems to like the taste." With her package hoisted to her chest, they walked toward the barn. Nicholas kept up a running commentary, stroking the baby's nose all the while. Amos danced beside them, frantic to find out what it was she was carrying.

"Open the stall door." For someone in as good a shape as she was, Maddy was still huffing by the time they reached the barn. "Should . . . have . . . driven him . . . down here." She set her burden down with a sigh of relief. "Go for it, kid. He's all yours."

Nicholas knelt beside the foal and pulled the sack off. With a scramble and a wheeze, the furry little creature scuttled across the stall and stood in the corner, glaring at them and shivering with fear. When Nicholas tried to go to him, he stamped one front hoof and tossed his head, his ears pinned to his skull.

"I thought you said he was weak."

"He was after I chased him around the lava flow. I had to trap him in a little canyon. The way he looks now, he may have a better chance of making it than I thought."

"What happened to his mother?"

She shared the story with him, watching both foal and boy as they studied each other. "So now the main problem is getting him to drink from a bottle. Sure wish we had an agreeable old mare who would adopt him."

"No, he's mine. Here, Ears, come on." The boy knelt on the dirt floor and extended his hand to the foal. Ears made a valiant effort to disappear into the wood.

By the time she returned from the feed store, Ears stood straddle-legged in the corner, his head hanging down as if it were too heavy for him to hold up any longer.

"I'll go mix this in warm water and be right back." She headed for the house at a trot.

"What's going on?" Jesse sat at the table, reading his newspaper.

He must have come down from the graveyard while I was at the feed store, Maddy thought. *Why couldn't he have stayed up there awhile longer?* She gave her father the short version while she mixed the powder with warm water and poured it in the bottle.

"You're not keeping any wild thing here. No good will come of it."

"I'm not letting it loose to die either. It wasn't the foal's fault the mother was injured. How would you like to starve to death up on the lava flows—or anywhere for that matter?" She squirted some of the liquid on her arm. "Besides, he's scared to death. Who knows if he'll make it."

"All that boy of yours needs is something else to die on him."

"Pop, his name is Nicholas." How many times had she said that? Why was he so stubborn? She poured herself a glass of water and turned to face her father. "I know that, so let's pray the foal doesn't die."

"You won't get it to take a bottle," he called as the screen door slammed behind her.

Maddy trotted back to the barn and entered the stall. She set the bottle on the two-by-four railing and smiled at her son. "Okay, let's catch him." The foal threw his head up, eyes rolling in the dimness. When they were three feet from him he made a dash for freedom right between them. Maddy swooped at the right moment and snagged him, lifting him off his feet. Nicholas grabbed the baby's head and kept him from biting his mother again. Between the two of them, they set Ears on the floor and held him secure while Nicholas offered the donkey the bottle.

No such luck. Ears refused the bottle even when they opened his mouth and thrust the nipple in. The milk drooled out his jaw and matted the hair around his mouth.

An hour later they had more milk on them than in him.

"I've got to feed the pigs, so you keep working with him." Maddy handed Nicholas the rope they'd tied around the burro's neck and looped over it's nose. "Calm him down if you can." As she poured grain into the feeder for the sow and her piglets, she marveled at the patience and persistence her son was showing with the little foal. But then, he'd had that with Hector too. *Please, God, don't let that little burro die.* She shook her head. There she went asking a God she wasn't sure she believed in for something He probably didn't care about anyway.

By midafternoon when she had to get ready for work, the donkey was still refusing the life-saving bottle. Nicholas's eyes wore the deep sadness she'd come to think of as normal. Pop kept shaking his head, muttering about wild things and no good. Going to work at the restaurant sounded heavenly. *Why is it whatever I try to do has to turn out bad for Nicholas? Now Ears will die, Nick will blame me, I'm blaming me . . .*

— — —

Maddy called home once in the middle of her shift. Her father said the foal was still alive, but Nicholas hadn't come to the house for dinner.

"Why on earth did you bring that poor little creature home with you? There are animal rescue places on the island, you know."

"I don't know, Pop. It just seemed the best thing to do at the time. I couldn't leave it there to starve to death." She leaned her forehead against the wall by the phone. The headache of the morning was threatening a rerun.

"So instead you brought it home to die in his arms."

"I'm sorry." She hung up the phone. "I'm so sorry, Nicholas."

— — —

When Maddy finally made it home, she noticed a light on in the barn as she climbed wearily from the pickup. Rubbing the back of her neck, she made it to the barn and leaned on the stall door. Nicholas lay sleeping on some old burlap sacks, Ears snugged right up against him. Pop sat propped in the corner, head on his chest, a feeding tube across his spraddled legs. The bottle was empty.

Maddy rubbed her eyes, certain she was hallucinating. Her father asleep with her son and the burro. Ears raised his head at Amos's whine, then flopped back down with the ease of all babies. After a full belly, sleep was the most important thing.

She left them and headed for bed herself.

Her mother used to say Jesse was all bark and no bite, but she'd begun to wonder if the statement still rang true. Now she knew. She could ignore barking. He'd been good to his grandson, and in her mind that was all that mattered.

— — —

"Mom, Mom, you know Ears?" Nicholas stood beside her bed, shaking her shoulder with one hand.

Maddy groaned. Was there a law somewhere that said she should live with sleep deprivation? "What?"

"Grandpa fed Ears through a tube last night and now this morning Ears is running around all happy. Maybe he'll drink from the bottle now. You got to come see him." He shook her again since her eyes had drifted closed.

"Good. Come get me in a year."

"M-o-m."

"I'm coming, I'm coming." She opened her eyes carefully, shielding them from the piercing pain of bright lights. Breathing a sigh of relief, she opened them wide and stretched her hands above her head. No pain.

Her feet hit the floor and she swatted Nicholas on the rear. "Get outa here while I get some clothes on. What time is it?"

"Seven." He evaded a second swat. "Grandpa has breakfast ready."

"Will wonders never cease?" She watched her son whirl out the door and pound down the stairs. Who was this strange child?

Three minutes later she whistled her way into the kitchen. "Omelettes? What is this world coming to?"

"You want salsa on yours or not?" Jesse's gruff rejoinder couldn't dim the light she saw in his eyes. She nodded as he set the plate in front of her. Nicholas brought her a steaming cup of coffee. "Thanks, you guys." Her voice almost broke on the words, but she swallowed the sound and smiled at them both.

— — —

Within days Ears became a permanent part of Nicholas's anatomy, as if there were an umbilical cord between boy and burro. If he strayed at all, Amos brought the furry little beast back to Nick's side.

One evening when business was slow at the restaurant, Maddy came home early and found Ears folded up next to Nick on the floor in front of the television. Her father sat in his chair reading a magazine.

"Nicholas Adam Morton, if that critter makes a mess on this rug, you will be the one to clean it up—after I throw you and it out the door."

Nicholas looked over his shoulder with one of those oh-Mother-how-can-you-say-such-a-thing looks. "He won't. And his name is Ears." He turned back to his program. The burro opened one eye, yawned, and flopped his head back in Nicholas's lap for an ear rubbing.

She could have sworn she caught a wink from her father. He didn't even rustle the pages of the magazine.

"He's not sleeping in the house."

Nicholas shrugged.

Jesse shrugged.

Maddy went to bed.

— — —

By the next coffee-growers meeting, Maddy had forty coffee trees planted. She breathed a sigh of disappointment when she discovered Kam wasn't in the room. While they'd seen each other when dropping the boys off at one house or another, they hadn't said more than "aloha" and "I'll pick them up later." Each time she saw him her heart started its crazy syncopation, but she managed to ignore it. At least, that's what she told herself.

"Are you Maddy Morton?" A raisin-faced man slid into the chair next to her, extending a hand permanently gnarled by hard work. His almond-shaped eyes held the wisdom of the ages.

She nodded and shook his hand.

"I'm Nashi Nakamura. I've been growing coffee down by Captain Cook's all my life. Kam Waiano said you need seedlings?"

She nodded again. "I'm just starting out. My father grew coffee years ago."

"I remember. Hard times for him, eh?"

"You could say that."

"You want some plants, then?"

"Well . . . why, sure, if you don't mind. I could come and dig them later this week."

He shook his head, hair more salt than pepper, swaying with the movement. "No, I bring them to you. My son, he help."

"It'll take me a couple of days to get the ground ready."

His smile warmed her, clear down to the toes of her boots. "Good, good. We bring. Say aloha to your father for me."

She watched him shuffle off, greeting people on all sides as he took his place in the front row. The enormity of his offer sucked her breath out. He didn't know her, so why would he make such an offer?

She refused to admit that she kept watching for Kam to arrive. When he didn't, she also refused to acknowledge that the strange feeling in her stomach had anything to do with his absence. After all, she attended the meeting to learn more about growing coffee, right? She didn't go to see him . . . did she?

A few days later the tractor idled as Maddy stopped to watch the boy, the burro, and the bouncing dog play tag in the shadow of the trees up the hill from where she was terracing. The music of her son's laughter floated back on the breeze and tugged the corners of her mouth into a smile.

A car horn drew her attention down the hill to the house where two pickup trucks had pulled into the yard. One had a bed full of green plants and a metal barrel the size of the bed filled the other. Benny and James had bailed out of one cab and were running up the hill, shrieking for Nicholas.

Mr. Nakamura had said a *few* seedlings. She didn't have half enough terraces cut.

Kam waved at her. Next to the little man from the meeting, he looked like a giant. How come he was here?

"I thought you knew Nashi was my uncle." Kam turned from setting pots of coffee plants on the red dirt. "If you want to cut that next level, we can plant. The boys will help."

"Your plants look very healthy." The old man bowed his head when he greeted her. "I hope we didn't bring too much."

"No, this is wonderful, I mean, thank you." She dipped her head also. "I . . . I can't thank you enough."

"Most happy to bring them."

Maddy looked up to catch a smile on Kam's face that made her heart do a backward somersault—and then a forward flip. She blinked at the bright fire rim that the sun used to outline his head and shoulders. "Thank you," she whispered and climbed back aboard her tractor as if the manehune, the mythical, hard-working little people of Hawaii, were after her.

At noon she went down to the house and called the restaurant to ask if she could have the evening off.

"That should be fine," John replied. "I know you are due for some extra days off with all the overtime you have worked. Besides, we have two new girls that just started on the day shift. One of them is ready for the dinner shift."

Maddy thanked him profusely and stuck her head in the refrigerator. What could she possibly serve these people for lunch?

Another car honking drew her to the front door. Marlea and Edi, Marianna's sister, waved from a minivan.

"Where do you want us to set the picnic up?"

"Oh." Tears clogged her throat. She coughed, blinked, rolled her eyes upward, blinked again, then cleared her throat. "Here on the lanai will be perfect."

"Good." The two women stepped from the van, two younger children piling out after them. They took boxes and coolers from the rear of the van and carried them to the gate Maddy held open.

"I didn't know, I mean I . . ."

"Just show us where to put things." Edi set her load down on the lanai, and taking Maddy's hand in hers, she laid her other over them both. "It is time someone does some good things for you, my child. We are glad to be able to help."

"I'll get the folding table." Maddy spun away and almost ran through the door. She would *not* let them see her cry. A beating she could handle, but this kindness . . .

She stared out the kitchen window, wiping her eyes with a paper towel. Up on the hill, her father was driving the tractor, cutting more terraces. Laughter from the others floated down as the men and boys dug the holes, set the seedlings, and watered them in, using the tank they had brought and a long hose.

She sighed, sniffed, wiped her eyes one more time, and dug in the storage room for the ancient aluminum folding table. The red-and-white oil cloth lay folded right above it. At least she had gotten the house cleaned up before they had all this company, even to washing down the table. Her cheeks burned at the thought of what it looked like before.

As soon as they had the food laid out, she rang the triangle at the back door. Within minutes they'd shut down the machinery and loaded the one pickup to drive down, filling the house and yard with sweaty, laughing men and running, shouting children. Pure chaos. Until Kam clapped his hands.

Silence fell.

"Shall we say grace?" His voice rose above the birdsong. "We thank you, Father, for our friends here, the work of our hands, and the work of your hands. Thank you for the food we are about to eat and may we glorify you in all that we do. And all the people said, amen." Everyone joined him on the final word.

He talked with God like her mother had, as if they were best friends standing right next to each other. Even years ago when she had believed, she'd never felt the familiarity that these two people had with their heavenly Father. Was that something she wanted? She shook her head, reminding herself that she no longer believed in those old tales. *Liar*, she said to herself. *So if I do believe, then what?*

Maddy watched from under her eyelashes as Kam picked up one of the little ones and let the other ride on the top of his shoe. Both of them chattered at him and he answered as if what they had to say was the most important thing in the world.

Just the way he listened to everyone.

He then helped dish up the children's plates and set them in the middle of a blanket that had been spread for the kids. Then he filled his own plate.

Their gazes collided over the pasta salad. Everything else distanced, like a fade-out in a movie. Breathing, thought . . . everything stopped. His eyes searched her soul and seemed to touch the secret places of her heart. How could dark eyes be so full of life? So deep with caring?

Maddy, I watch you and my heart begins to thunder like the drums of my ancestors. Do you not know, can you not feel?

He'd never drowned in sea gray eyes before and now he could not reach the surface.

"Uncle Kam, I want a piece of watermelon, please." A small brown hand pulled at the hem of his khaki shorts.

The moment shattered. He cleared his throat. "Ah . . . okay, Timmy, here you go." Why was he having trouble breathing?

He'd stolen her breath. And the strength from her knees. She took her half-filled plate and plunked down on the middle stair. Falling down would have been terribly embarrasing. Even the thought of it made her cheeks flame. When he sat down beside her, she scooted over, trying to escape the charge that emanated from his body and danced with those from her own.

What is going on here? She raised her iced tea and took a long swallow. Sips wouldn't do at this point. She had to stop the burning.

She ate, answering questions when asked and getting up to serve cake to the children, but later she didn't remember a thing.

Except for refilling glasses of iced tea. When she came to Kam, the urge to lay her hand on his shoulder made her muscles quiver. The pitcher shook, making pouring impossible. At her look of consternation, he placed his hand over hers.

"Thank you." He raised the glass to his lips and swallowed, his eyes watching her over the rim.

"You're welcome." She swallowed in time with him. What on earth was happening?

I f this was falling in love, she didn't want to.

She flipped her pillow over, seeking the cool side. She couldn't ever remember feeling this way about Gabe, not even back in the days of raging teenage hormones.

Whatever happened to your vows of no men in your life?

Good question. She threw back the covers, all but the sheet. A breeze billowed the sheer curtains at her bedroom window and wafted over her face and exposed shoulders. She lifted her chin for it to cool her neck also.

Besides, this wasn't men—this was a man, Kam Waiano. Far more dangerous with his goodness than bad-boy Gabe had ever been. Her walls had taken a long time to get tough enough to withstand the brutality of words and fists, but she was finding that kindness and gentleness could seep in and crumble them.

Could she live without her walls to protect her?

"Tough question, Morton." She rolled to her left side. "You know that since he's a man, he's going to hurt you. That's the nature of the beast." She propped herself up against the wicker headboard, clasping one pillow over her belly. "They all leave."

The brother she adored had left, gone off to war and never returned. Her father left even though his body still lived in this house. Gabe left but brutalized her before going.

And now there was Kam Waiano.

You thought God left you too, a little voice whispered. *But you left Him.*

"That's fine with me," she whispered into the darkness, pounding her fist into the pillow on her lap. "From now on, I'm the one who's doing the leaving." She stared out at the stars upholding the dome of heaven. "But I have nowhere to go."

"I will never leave you nor forsake you."

Where did that come from? But when she thought about it, she knew. "How can a Bible verse that I learned when I was five years old come back to me now?" *If I did the leaving, can I go back?* She closed her eyes and let her mind wander.

"Come to Me, all you who labor and are heavy laden, and I will give you rest. . . . For My yoke is easy and My burden is light." Another verse. Amazing. *"For I have loved you with an everlasting love. I have called you by your name; you are Mine."*

Maddy threw back the covers and made her way down the stairs to the living room, where she took her mother's Bible from the shelf. Back up in her room, she flipped to the concordance and looked up the word *love.* The list of references made her blink. When she turned off the light half an hour later, she tucked the Bible under her pillow and the words away in her heart to add to those stored there so long ago.

— — —

"Mom?"

"What?" She turned from pouring the cake batter into the pan.

"Can I go to Sunday school tomorrow with Benny and James? They said they'd pick me up."

Maddy blinked. "Well, I guess so. If you want."

Nicholas nodded. "I want to go. They have fun there." He left the room, whistling for Amos and Ears.

While the cake baked, Maddy wandered up the hill to look at her coffee plants. She'd have a hundred now if they all survived. So far so good. Hearing a pig squeal, she looked down to where the sow and her month-old piglets were enjoying the mud bath in the shade of the barn. The other gilt was due any day. When they reached about four months, the first litter would be ready to sell. Then maybe she could use that money to buy another gilt or two. And a boar. Surely she could run eleven, twelve head of breeding stock in the space they had. She was already composting the manure and bedding to use as mulch around the coffee plants.

She leaned over and pulled a couple of weeds. She needed a few hours out here with the hoe. On the rainy side of the island, tropical growth could obliterate a planting in a matter of weeks. Glancing up at a squeal she heard higher on the hill, she reminded herself she needed to buy hog wire and fence posts. If the wild pigs ever got in the coffee field, they could have it dug up in no time. After resolving to use her paycheck for fencing, she headed back to the house to take the cake out of the oven. So far, a lot of money going out and none coming in. Wasn't that what her father had warned her about farming?

— — —

That night at work she met Melissa, another of the new girls. Where did John find such human mouses? Was it a requirement for applying at the Ranch House for a job? Was this some kind of sisterhood, for she swore she recognized that haunted look in a woman's eyes every time. That and the fact that Melissa kept looking over her shoulder.

"We got another one," Ruby said, filling breadbaskets for three tables.

Maddy tried to ignore her. Staying out of other people's business was a much safer way to live.

When a group of men came in laughing, Melissa was harder to ignore. She dropped a tray of three dinners.

"That's okay, honey, we've all been there, done that." Ruby knelt down to help clean up the mess. Maddy went for a broom and mop, returning just in time to see Melissa look up at their boss and cringe away from the scowl on his face.

"Sorry, Melissa, I should have been watching closer where I was going," Maddy said with a smile, making sure she was between their boss and the embarrassed woman. When would she learn?

"Other orders are up," snapped John. "I'll get Juan to clean this up. All of you, please be more careful. We have customers waiting."

"Th-thanks." Melissa muttered into the plate pieces she'd set back on the tray.

"No problem." Ruby got to her feet, making sure she caught Maddy's gaze on the way up. She patted the young woman's shoulder and headed for the kitchen.

Leaving the busboy to finish cleaning up, Maddy handed a now wiped-down tray to Melissa and took her own. "Come on, let's get the food out. You need to make sure the cooks know what to re-prepare and then go to the table to apologize to the people waiting. Policy here is to offer them a free dessert if something makes them wait too long."

"Thank you again." Melissa blinked back tears. "You didn't have to do that, you know."

"Forget it. Like Ruby said, we've all lost a tray one way or another over the years." Maddy set her orders on her tray and lifted it to her shoulder. As she turned, she locked gazes with the man waiting for a table . . . a table in her service area. His smile sent the heat roaring upward so that all she wanted was a fan and a quick exit. Figuring she was smarter than a moth near a flame, she took Kam's order as if he were any other customer, even though her hands were shaking. If she didn't watch out, she'd end up with a tray on the floor like Melissa, and two in one night would make John see more than red.

"How are your seedlings coming?"

"Great."

"I hear Nicholas is going to Sunday school tomorrow with Benny and James."

"Uh-huh. Iced tea to drink?"

"Why don't you come too?"

"That isn't on the menu."

"Before your mother died, both she and your father were there every Sunday."

I know that. What's it got to do with me? "Just water, then. Anything else?"

"I'll pick you up at eight-thirty."

"I don't think so. The mahimahi just came off the boat this afternoon."

"Some other time, then?"

"We'll see." She looked up in time to catch the glint in his eyes and the widening of that expressive mouth. *The mouth that was kissing you in your dream.* She stuck the pad in her apron pocket and walked as fast as she could to the kitchen. If only she dared ducking her head under the faucet to cool her face. What a coward he must think her to be.

"You okay?" the head chef asked.

"Yeah, I'm fine."

"Someone bothering you?" He glanced toward the swinging doors.

If you only knew. She forced her lips to smile. "Just got a bit h—warm there for a minute. I'm okay now." Heading back out the door, she could feel her nose growing.

Kam was still nursing an endless glass of iced tea when Leilani put up the Closed sign.

"We're closing." Maddy stopped across the table from him.

"I know, I just thought you might like to go out for a cup of coffee. It's not as good as here but we—we could visit for a bit. Like we did before with Ruby and Ken."

"No tha—" He looked like a puppy that had just been kicked. "Oh, all right." Gracious her answer wasn't, but surprising? Big time. To him no more so than to her.

He quickly covered up the shock and gave her a smile that cut off her breathing. "Good. I'll be waiting right out by my truck. It's parked next to yours." She caught the inflection, as in *if you think I'm going to allow you to run off, you are sadly mistaken.*

She walked back to the coffee bar in time to see Leilani and Ruby swapping high fives. She didn't bother to ask what that was about; she could tell by the looks they gave her and the glee on their faces.

Once she got over her disgruntlement, coffee with Kam was like visiting with an old friend one hasn't seen for years but once together, it's as if no time had passed. As long as she kept the memory of her dreams at bay. The times they snuck up on her she could feel her face flame in an instant, so she hid behind her coffee cup. An hour melted away before she knew it. She glanced at her watch when she had to swallow a yawn.

"I need to get home."

"I know." He reached for her hand. "Thank you."

"For what?"

"For coming with me. We could do this more often."

"We'll see."

"Nicholas says that when you say 'we'll see,' there's a good chance it will happen."

She rolled her eyes. "Oh great. What other family secrets has he been blabbing?"

"Grandpop helped him with Ears." Kam rubbed the palm of her hand with his thumb.

"Grandpop?"

"That's what he said."

"Ah." If she could get her mind off her hand and on the conversation, she might come up with something more ... more ... She snatched her hand back and grabbed her purse. "I have to go." She was halfway to the door before he caught up with her.

"Easy, you can't go until the driver with the keys starts the car." He dangled his keys in front of her.

"Great, next time I'll drive my own truck."

His grin told her he caught the 'next time.' It had slipped out so fast, she'd caught the tip of her tongue trying to stop it.

"Thanks for a good time," she said, sliding out of the pickup as soon as he stopped it next to her truck. "See you later."

"In just a few hours, matter of fact. I'm driving the boys to Sunday school. The invitation still stands."

She stopped her rushing and looked him full in the face. "I'm not ready for that . . . yet. Good night."

At least she didn't say no, Kam thought on the way home. *Thank you, Father, for that and for our time together.*

At least he didn't push me, Maddy thought as her truck took the curves, seemingly without her volition.

She drove into the yard and killed the engine, then sat there, listening to the quiet. When she got out she took the flashlight from the glove box and, with Amos at her side, ambled down to the barn to check on the pigs.

The new gilt lay on her side, a full line of piglets nursing away. Maddy swallowed her shout of joy and counted. Nine healthy babies. She opened the door and stepped inside the stall. The afterbirth lay in a puddle so she knew the farrowing was done. Had Nicholas and Pop seen them? Surely they would have called the restaurant if they knew.

She waited until all the piglets were sleeping and then walked each one under the board to the lamp and safety. The sow grunted and rose on her front quarters to shake her head.

"You want some warm water and grain now, girl?" Maddy scratched the hog's shoulders. "You sure did a fine job, and this your first litter too." She poured some grain in the shallow, flat pan and headed for the house for warm water.

With the pig taken care of, she checked on Ears, who came over to nibble at the grain she offered him. When that was gone, he went back to his pile of grass and flopped down again with a sigh.

"You're right on that, little fluffy one." With her heart still singing, she made her way upstairs and finally sank down on her bed. Pulling her boots off left her only enough energy to throw back the covers and collapse.

M om! Mom! Wake up! The coffee plants . . . "

Maddy hit the floor running.

"Grandpop took his rifle." Nicholas pounded down the stairs behind her.

"How did you know something was wrong?" She thrust her feet into the rubber boots by the back door.

"Amos was barking and barking. He came and got Grandpop. I heard 'em."

While dawn had tinted the clouds, the sun had yet to rise above the line between ocean and sky. Three shots echoed from the hill above them. Amos barked in a frenzy. She could hear Pop yelling too.

Tomorrow I was going to buy fencing. Always late, that's me. The thoughts made her run harder.

The lower rows, the most recently planted, looked fine. She passed them and kept going. More shots. More barking.

But it was too late. The top three terraces looked like a bulldozer driven by a drunk had gone through. Plants uprooted and drainage torn up. Wild pigs on the loose. Maddy clutched her side with one hand, the ache making it hard to breathe.

She knelt and lifted one bruised and wilted plant from the mire. Digging with her hands, she set it back in a hole and tried to prop it up with the stalk of another. The twig tilted and lay flat.

Nicholas tried to do the same, scrabbling in the red mud up to his elbows. "I'll help you, Mom. We'll get more plants." His tears ran through the red dirt and onto his cheeks, where he'd brushed his hair back.

Maddy rested back on her heels. She closed her eyes against the raging pain. Her coffee plants, the ones she'd so carefully scavenged from the older plants up the hill. Why? There was plenty to eat up on the hills. Pure mean, that's what those feral hogs were.

"Shoot 'em all, Pop!" she screamed. "Shoot every last living one of 'em."

"See, h-here's one that's alive. They missed it." The boy took his mother's hand and pointed to a small tree still standing. "Please, Mom, we can get m-more."

Maddy heard him, as if from a long distance. She blinked and looked from her son to where he pointed. His hand shook, his chest heaved.

Maddy gathered him into her arms and, kneeling in the red mud of the ravaged hill, the two hugged each other close.

"I'm sorry, Maddy. I should have come out when Amos first barked." Jesse fought to get his breath. "I only scared them away with the gun—I could hear 'em going through the brush but never got a shot at any."

"If I'd got the fencing up first . . ." She shook her head. "Like you said, Pop, farming's a gamble no matter what way you look at it." Wishing she could look anywhere but at the rooted-up mess, she gave Nicholas another hug and stood next to her father. "You were right again. Guess I'll never learn." She shook her head and continued shaking it while she muttered. "Been a waitress for more than ten years now, and I guess that's all I'll ever be."

"Mom, we can plant again." Nicholas tugged at her arm. "I got some money in my bank—we can use that to buy some coffee plants."

"You're not giving up, are you?" Jesse's eyebrows straight-lined across his forehead.

Maddy stared at the two males in her life who'd been grumbling about the work and griping at the expense of it all.

"I'm not?"

"No!" The two spoke as one. "*We're* not."

"Oh." *They agree on something. Nicholas and Pop agree.* "We?"

"We!"

"Well, I guess *we* better go on down to the barn and look in on all the new babies. They were born just before I got home."

"She hadn't started when I checked at ten." Jesse pulled a navy-and-white handkerchief from his back pocket and blew his nose. "How many?"

"Nine, no runts." Maddy laid a hand on Nicholas's shoulder. "I put them under the light."

Nicholas grinned up at her. "Race you down there."

She brushed red dirt off his nose. "Nope, you'll win. But I bet Ears is hungry too. He glared at me for bothering his sleep."

The sun hung like a gigantic flaming orange above the horizon as the three of them walked down the slope, Amos trotting beside them.

While Jesse and Nicholas admired the new litter, Maddy fed the others. "Time to get an automatic feeder in here for all you hungry little pigs so you'll leave your mother alone." She scratched the sow's back with a stick she kept by the gate for just that purpose.

Ears hee-hawed from his stall. While Nicholas wanted to keep the burro in his room, the little colt had yet to be housebroken. No matter how much the boy begged, on this Maddy stayed firm.

"I'm coming, I'm coming." Nicholas left the farrowing stall and opened the gate for his shadow. "You don't ever eat this early, Ears, so cool it."

— — —

"Mom, you got a Bible I can take with me?" Nicholas called a few hours later as he stood in the doorway, his hair slicked back and the red streaks drained down the shower.

"Should be one up on my bookshelf from when I was a kid." She straightened from putting dishes in the dishwasher.

"*You* went to church?"

She nodded. "Every Sunday."

"Then why don't you come now?"

Her son's question startled her. *What can I say? Because I'm not sure what I believe anymore? But if I don't believe, why am I allowing you to go to church? And why am I suddenly compelled to read the Bible?* She looked at Nicholas. "I'll think about it, okay?"

"Okay." Nicholas left the room in search of a Bible.

"I can't find it," he called down the stairs a few minutes later.

"There's one in the living room," Jesse answered from behind the paper.

"But that's Mother's."

"He can use it."

"I found it." Footsteps thundered back down the stairs. Nicholas held up a black leather volume. "This one?"

"Yes." Her Bible didn't look anywhere near as worn as her mother's. But it had been on the shelf for the last few years. Kind of like her faith had been. She nodded. Definitely needed some thinking here.

Amos barked and a horn honked.

"See ya." Nicholas ran for the car, the screen door slamming behind him.

Maddy poured herself another cup of coffee and ambled into the living room. As usual, it needed dusting. Her father's nest had been refeathered with newspapers and magazines, pipe scrapings filled the ash tray, and a cup wore a dried coffee ring in the bottom. A paper plate that had held pizza lay under the glass-topped coffee table. He and Nicholas lived in this room when she wasn't here. Neither one did well on the pick-up-and-put-away drill.

You should go up and see what you can salvage on the hill. The thought made her sink down on the faded chintz sofa and lean her head back on the cushions. All those weeks of work for nothing. *And it all hinges on money!* She slammed her fist into the sofa cushion, raising a cloud of dust. *You knew better—and now what do you have? How can you be so stupid and never learn?*

Flames flared in her belly, hot and angry, licking at the words she kept muttering in her mind. *Stupid, no good, worthless, dumb, you always act before you think, what's the matter with you, can't you do anything right?* The voice segued from her own to Gabe's.

"If I'd only taken my tip money to buy the fencing." She rolled her head from side to side on the sofa back. "If only." Tears burned at the back of her throat. She knew if she kept this up she'd be bawling and once she started she was afraid she'd never stop. The urge to go upstairs, crawl back in bed, and pull the covers over her head got her to her feet.

Pure disgust made her pass on the stairs and instead get the cleaning supplies out of the cupboard. While the feral pigs made a mockery of her coffee farming, the house needn't be called a pig sty. She clicked the vacuum on, grateful for the roar that helped drown out the crushing words still marching in her mind. With the dusting brush on the end of the wand, she vanquished the spider webs in the corners and the dust on the bookshelves.

"Maddy?"

Lost in her own world, she whirled at the sound of another's voice. The vacuum end knocked several books off the shelf and aimed itself for the lamp on the end table. She grabbed for the lamp as the books hit the floor, one of them scattering papers as it fell.

"Sorry." Jesse stood in the door.

"What?" Maddy clicked off the vacuum so she could hear better.

"I . . . I just thought—" He paused. "Well, maybe if you wanted to go with me into town, I'm going for the fencing, we could go by and get some replacement plants, you know. When Nicholas said he'd use his money to buy you new plants, I . . . I thought . . . well, I've been mighty selfish and—and I know your mother would be takin' me by the ear by now. She was the most generous woman that walked this earth and I . . . I haven't been doing as she would have liked."

Maddy snapped her mouth closed. "Ah . . . oh, Pop." She blinked her eyes and sniffed, then did both again. "Thank you." The words barely croaked by the lump in her throat. "Let me pick up this mess and get cleaned up a bit and I'd be happy to go with you." She stopped to look him full in the face. "Pop, are you sure you can afford this?"

"I'm sure. We've got to be back before Nicholas comes home."

That did it. She knelt to gather the papers together, wiping her eyes on the tail of her shirt. The papers had all come from her mother's Bible. She picked up the worn book and began tucking the small bits of paper back in among the thin pages. Letters, bits of poetry, a funeral announcement. Notes in the margin caught her eye, along with many underlined passages. A thin pad of lined paper was tucked in the back of the book. *Prayer list*, she read, and her gaze traveled down the first page.

Please, Father, take care of Maddy. She is making such a terrible mistake. Bring her home to us.

Another. *A letter from Maddy, a phone call, Father, please.*

There were others with a date at the end, showing when the answer had come. Maddy saw her name on many of the pages, but there were no dates after those.

All those years her mother had been praying for her. All those years she had refused the nudges to call home, afraid of Gabe yelling at her for wasting money on long-distance calls, afraid her parents no longer wanted to hear from her, angry at her father's denouncement.

Her hands shook as she laid the tablet back in place. *Oh, Mother, I failed you so terribly. I should have known. I should have let you know where we were. If only I hadn't been so headstrong, so stubborn.* She set the Bible on the coffee table and returned the other books to the shelf. *And now it's too late. I can't ask for forgiveness and you can't give it. What a waste . . . what a terrible, terrible waste.*

Her nose continued to need wiping all the way to the co-op. When they left the building, they had three one-hundred-foot rolls of hog wire and the steel posts to go with it, along with three five-gallon coffee plants.

"Pop, you can't afford all this."

"How do you know what I can afford and what I can't? I told you I could, remember?"

She swallowed her answer and climbed in the cab. Seemed strange to be on the rider's side. It was like when she was little and so excited because her father asked if she wanted to ride to the store with him. Sometimes they'd stop for an ice cream cone. But all that ended with Mark's death.

She'd spent the rest of her growing years trying to take his place.

Kam arrived shortly after they'd driven the supplies up to the ravaged coffee rows. He'd changed out of his church clothes, as had the boys, and when he got out of the pickup, he reached behind the cab to lift out more coffee plants.

"What are you doing?" Maddy stared at him as if he'd grown donkey ears.

"Nicholas said you had a problem so we came to help." He handed the gallon containers to the boys. "Sorry we couldn't bring bigger ones but they didn't have any more. Said they'd have a new shipment in next week."

He surveyed the damage, shaking his head. "Mean suckers, aren't they?"

No comments on the lack of fencing, no superior looks for her failure, not even a raised eyebrow. Only eyes filled with compassion and a smile that reminded her of a sunrise.

"How about I help Jesse with the fence and the rest of you work on the plants? Edi and Marlea will be by later with lunch." With that, the day's work was organized and with the boys laughing and teasing, it turned into a party instead of a funeral.

"I . . . I hate to be such a burden," Maddy whispered when she ended up next to Kam at the picnic table set up under the blue gum trees in the yard.

"Maddy." He looked over his shoulder, holding a bun filled with barbequed pork. "You don't get it, do you? This isn't about a burden, this is about friends helping each other out. We do that around here."

"But I'm always the helpee, not the helper."

"Your turn will come. That's the way God works."

Maddy looked down the table to where her father sat between Edi and her sister, Marianna. They had him laughing about something—he who hadn't really laughed for who knew how long?

Kam followed her gaze and grinned at her. "He doesn't stand a chance of keeping up the curmudgeon act with those two. They could charm yellow jackets into not stinging." He brushed one away from his plate.

"Yeah, well, why not sic them on those stupid pigs up on the mountain? That's who could use some charm right about now."

"I said they were charmers, not miracle workers. Only good thing for those critters is the business end of a rifle. We should do away with them all, but the cost is prohibitive. They're meaner than sin and multiply like rabbits. Ruined more natural habitats than the dozers. At least we have some control over those."

A burst of laughter came from the other end of the table. How could she have forgotten about the friendliness and caring among the people of her home island? Perhaps because Gabe had put down life on the big island so often she'd begun to believe him.

By the time Maddy had to leave for work, two sides were fenced and the plants that could be salvaged were replanted, along with the new ones. Kam volunteered to take everyone swimming if they could get done before dark, so the boys were taking turns pounding in the fence posts. The heavy post maul slamming down on the steel posts rang through the air like joyful bells.

She hated to leave.

When she arrived at the Ranch House, patrons were lined up clear out the door, sitting on the benches provided for just this kind of situation.

"I called for you to come in early but there was no answer." John glared at her like she'd done something unspeakable.

"Sorry, but I was busy outside. Didn't think to check the answering machine." She crossed the apron strings behind her and tied them in the front. The burgundy fabric felt crisp but she knew that would last only so long. By the time she'd put things in the pockets of the bibless apron a few times, she'd be wishing for a clean one.

Their manager checked his watch. "Well, at least you're on time. Melissa is late."

Maddy glanced at the clock. "Doesn't she start at five too?" The hands said 4:55.

"Yes, but you know waitresses are to arrive fifteen minutes early, like you did." He shook his head and walked off muttering about irresponsible people.

Maddy shrugged. Nothing much she could do about it. The girl wouldn't last long if she consistently showed up late.

She felt the rush of the girl's entrance even before she heard the breathy "Sorry I'm late." Maddy turned to smile at her, but the pancaked makeup crusted over a cut on the girl's lower lip made her grit her teeth.

Melissa saw her response and put a finger up to her mouth. "I . . . I banged myself with the car door. That's why I'm late."

Maddy nodded. "You've got the front section tonight. You better hustle." *Car door my eye. You don't wear a whipped look because you banged yourself with a car door.*

Now, what was she going to do about it?

26

"What happened to Melissa?"

"She says she banged her face on the corner of the car door."

"And you believe that?" Ruby raised an eyebrow.

"I didn't say I believed it, I'm just telling you what she told me."

"Hmm." Ruby took both coffee carafes and began making the rounds.

Maddy finished her shift and headed for home, still trying to decide what, if anything, she should do about Melissa. She knew the car door thing was a cover-up, and it didn't work any better than the pancake makeup.

But if she wanted help, wouldn't she ask?

Would you? Did you?

She squirmed on the truck seat. No, she had never asked for help. Gabe had warned her about that, threatening to hurt the other person more than her.

Fear. Melissa was living in fear just like she had.

That thought brought on another. She hadn't been afraid since the lawyer told her Gabe's mail would be curtailed. At least not afraid of Gabe. That fear was totally different from the ones she had about failing as a mother, a daughter, financially, and, if she were really trying on the honesty thing, as a friend. She thought of turning around and going back. She'd gotten off early and Melissa was on the closing detail.

At the beginning of the driveway she paused. Kam had just shown up when he knew she needed help. He didn't wait to be invited. Was this any different?

Yes. Interfering in a marriage was more private than coffee plants. And no. Melissa needed help from someone who'd been there.

The terror on Melissa's face every time the door opened made Maddy pound on the steering wheel. She threw the truck into reverse and backed out onto the highway. Cranking the wheel, she spun around and roared back to the Ranch House.

The Closed sign was up on the front window as she drove around to the back. What if her husband was here to pick her up? She drove slowly past all the vehicles—empty. She breathed a sigh of relief. Having no clue as to what she was going to do, she entered by the back door and walked on into the dining room.

"Maddy, I thought you left." Ruby gave her a puzzled look.

"I did. Think you can take over so I can talk with Melissa?" Maddy kept her voice low.

"I sure can." Ruby gave her a smile so full of approval that it nearly splashed on the floor. "You, my dear friend, just became an answer to my prayers."

"Wish me luck."

"I'll do far better than that. I'll pray for you some more."

Maddy grunted a noncommittal response and ambled over to where Melissa was cleaning the salad station. "You got a minute?"

"Ah, not really. I have to be out of here on time. I . . ." Her gaze darted around, looking anywhere but at Maddy's face.

"Come on. It'll only take a couple of minutes, and I'll help you finish up afterward."

Melissa looked toward the office.

"He's gone home. I saw him leaving when I pulled in." She took Melissa's hand. "Come on." Pausing at the soft drink machine, she poured herself a Diet Coke and, after a glance at Melissa, made hers Coke. Then, carrying both glasses, she led the way to the back room. Hooking one chair with her foot, she pushed it toward Melissa, then turned the other around and sat with her hands on the back.

"Now let's talk." *Great, you get a gold star for tact.* "First, let me tell you a bit about my history. My husband, Gabe, began with just talking mean, but after we got married, if I didn't do exactly what he wanted — and how I was supposed to know that is beyond me — he took to slapping me around. Then, when he'd had a bit too much to drink, he used his fists. Pretty soon I didn't have any friends, and he took to *borrowing* money from my purse when he felt like it. He started dealing drugs and I ended up in the emergency room more times than I care to count from 'being clumsy.' I became the queen of makeup art and wore most of my shirts buttoned at the collar and the wrists, no matter how hot it was." She paused and waited until Melissa looked up. "Does any of this sound familiar?"

The younger woman nodded, tears filling her eyes. "But . . . but you are so s-strong."

"Having my sweet husband sent to the pen for selling drugs and my filing first for a restraining order and then a divorce were the two things that changed my life. He swore he'd get me, but he won't be out for ten years and he won't find me when he does — if I have to run to the ends of the earth."

"But my baby is only eighteen months old and I —"

"Are the beatings getting worse?"

She shrugged. "Only when he's been drinking. He says he loves me and I . . . and I l-love him."

"Really?"

"He promised it wouldn't happen again."

"And you believe him?"

Melissa waited a long moment and then nodded, her gaze glued to the soda glass clenched in her hands. "I . . . I have to." Her whisper barely traveled the short space between chairs.

"Look. You have to decide. All I can say is if you ever need a place to hide out, you have it with me. No one will know where you are. From there we'll figure out what to do. Okay?" She took a piece of paper out of her pocket and wrote her phone number on it. "Use this, day or night. I'll come get you wherever you are."

Melissa took the paper and studied it. Her lips moved as she memorized the numbers.

That bad. She doesn't even dare have a friend's phone number in her purse.

"Has he ever hurt your baby?"

"Oh no, Buddy would never do that."

Buddy, eh. She'd never yet known anyone named Buddy she dared trust. But then, the crowd she'd run with hadn't been too trustworthy anyway, and Gabe's friends, if they could be called that, didn't earn much in the way of trust either.

"You call if you need me, all right?" Maddy kept her level gaze locked on Melissa's.

Melissa nodded again.

Was that a tiny flicker of hope in her washed blue eyes?

"Come on, let's get your chores done and get out of here." Within a matter of minutes Maddy was back on the road and heading home. Somehow she felt a whole lot better about the situation. Ruby's look of commendation helped her spirits.

Had she been like that? Was she still like that?

The thought brought a shudder of horror.

She had a hard time picturing herself as the beaten mouse Melissa exemplified. But fighting back had been useless too. She just got hurt worse. What a separate world women who were being hit by their mates lived in. Hidden, covered up . . . and lethal.

Back home, Maddy parked the truck in front of the barn and went inside to check on all the babies. Ears yawned when she flashed the light on him, the new babies were all under their light, and the others slept in a pig pile, like pieces of cord wood thrown in a heap. The sow blinked at her and snuffed, not even bothering to raise her head.

Amos then walked with her back to the house, not even glancing up the hill, reassuring her that her plants were as safe as the animals in the barn.

— — —

"Come on, Nicholas, we've got to get you registered for school." Maddy checked her watch. "You said ten o'clock and it's five till."

"I'm coming."

"So is Christmas."

He appeared in clean shorts and a tank top and ambled down the stairs.

"You need a haircut too."

"Today?"

"Might as well get it over with."

"Other kids have their hair long like this." He tossed his head to get the hair out of his eyes.

"Good for them." She checked in her pack for his immunization records, birth certificate, and last year's report card. "Let's get a move on." She studied his hair. "Guess we could buy some barrettes and clip it back."

"M-o-t-h-e-r!"

She heard a snort from behind the paper propped with her father's arms on the kitchen table.

A while later, with Nicholas duly registered for the fourth grade at the Waimea Elementary School, they stopped at the Ice Creamery for shakes.

"Benny said he hopes we both get Mrs. Alioto. Mr. Benson is mean." Nicholas took a deep pull on his straw.

"Oh great. Is there a third choice?"

Nicholas shook his head. "Just two. And James is in third."

"You'll make lots of new friends here. That's the same school I went to, you know."

"Back in the dark ages?" The sparkle in his eyes negated the innocent look he tried for.

— — —

A few days later, when Nicholas came home with a puffy eye and a lip that had obviously been bleeding, Maddy thought back to her earlier statement with regret. "What happened to you?"

"Nothing."

"Nicholas Adam Morton, 'nothing' won't cut it. What happened?"

"Looks like he got in a bit of a fight." Jesse leaned against the doorjamb.

"True?"

Nicholas nodded and hung his head.

"You know what I think of fighting." Maddy clenched her fists at her sides. Another nod.

"Sometimes it can't be helped," Jesse put in.

Maddy glared at her father and returned to her son, lifting his chin so she could inspect the damages. "How come I wasn't called?"

"The principal said one more time and he would call you."

"There won't be another time, will there." This wasn't a question but a command.

"What happened?" Jesse ignored Maddy's warning look and addressed Nicholas.

"Nothing."

"Sure, you and some other kid just decided for no good reason to begin hitting each other."

"Well, no."

"I'm going down there in the morning to sort this out, you can believe me," Maddy stated.

"M-o-m, n-o-o-o." Nicholas's chin squared off and his shoulders followed suit. "You can't do that."

"No, you can't, girl. Nicholas would never live it down." Jesse smiled down at his grandson. "So how did the other guy look?"

"P-o-p!" She turned back to Nicholas. "Do I have your promise this won't happen again?"

He nodded without looking at her, scuffing one sandal on top of the other.

— — —

That night at the restaurant, Kam waited until *his* table was free, then took his seat. "So I hear Nicholas mixed it up with the Kerny boy at school today."

"Whatever happened to 'Hi, how are you?' " Maddy took her order pad out of her pocket.

"Is he okay?"

"Nicholas is just fine. He and his grandfather are in full agreement that some things have to be settled with fists rather than brains." *Just like his father.* But she didn't say that.

"Do you know what it was about?"

She shook her head. "He wouldn't tell me."

"The Kerny boy teased Nicholas about having a jailbird for a father."

Maddy grabbed the back of the chair to keep her knees from buckling. "Oh my . . . I'll kill that kid."

"I just thought you oughta know." Kam's dark eyes beamed with compassion. "You needn't worry about Nicholas. He's a good kid and he's got your strength."

Right now she felt like all her strength had run out her toes. *Poor Nicholas. I gave him such a hard time.* "Thank you." Pulling her gaze from his took more will power than she believed possible.

"You're welcome. Any time." His words felt like a caress.

Her fingers itched to reach out and stroke his dark hair back.

"What'll you have?" Her voice squeaked so she swallowed to clear it.

"What's the special?"

If her gaze weren't drowning in his, she might have tried to be flippant.

— — —

The next evening she found her two men in the barn, with Jesse teaching Nicholas how to feint, keep his elbows in, and watch for the other's weak spot. She left them to it without letting them know she was there.

The call came at three A.M.

"Maddy, phone."

She was already halfway down the stairs. "Who is it?"

"Woman crying." Her father handed her the phone and wandered back into his bedroom.

"Hello?"

"M-Maddy, I . . . I'm so s-scared."

Maddy could barely hear her. "Melissa?"

"Oh, he's coming back." The receiver crashed onto the cradle.

Maddy wished they'd gotten Caller ID but that still wouldn't give her Melissa's address. Glancing up at the kitchen clock, she shook her head. The bar would be closed by now, too, and everyone long gone. She doubted John kept employee addresses at home.

Might Ruby have gotten it? She ran for her purse and fumbled through the bits of paper until she found one that said Ruby and a phone number. Melissa's cry of "he's coming back" played in time with her tapping foot. "Come on, Ruby, pick up."

"Hello?" a man's groggy voice answered.

"Hi, this is Maddy Morton. Is Ruby there?" Of course she was.

"What's wrong?" Ruby's voice carried no hint of being awakened in the dark hours of the morning.

"Melissa called just now, but she hung up before she could give me her address or phone. Do you have it?"

"No. Oh please, God, I wish I did."

"Any idea where she lives?"

"No."

Maddy sank down on the kitchen chair. "Then there's nothing we can do." She rubbed her forehead with the tips of her fingers.

"We can pray."

"Well, you can." *Why didn't I ask for that address? What was the matter with my head?*

"God listens to *all* prayers, girl. He's not like us. Heavenly Father, please care for that poor girl and her little one. Hold back the hand of her angry husband. Send them help since we are unable, for you have promised to protect the weak and right the wrongs. Please be with Maddy so she doesn't worry and feel guilty about this situation. Help her to know this isn't her fault. Give us wisdom in knowing how to help, and we will give you all the praise and glory. In Jesus' precious name and for His sake, amen."

Maddy sucked in a shuddering breath. Her mother might have prayed the same prayer for her even when she wasn't sure what was going on. "Th-thank you. See you at work." A deep sense that Melissa was all right flooded through her, in spite of her knowledge of what the young woman might be going through.

Amos whined at the door and she poured herself a glass of iced tea from the refrigerator before taking it out to the glider on the lanai. Amos sat beside her, one paw up on her knee. She stroked his head and ears as she sipped and marveled at what had just gone on. She should be pacing the floor, madly searching her brain for some hint of where they lived so she could go rushing over there. Instead, all she wanted to do was go back to bed.

She drained the glass, climbed the stairs, and fell back into oblivion.

In the morning she almost thought it had all been a dream. Except for her iced tea glass sitting in the sink.

With Nicholas in school each day, Ears now took to following Maddy around. As soon as she opened the door, he Velcroed himself to her side, as did Amos. They all checked on the pigs, pulled weeds around the house, and watered the coffee plants. When Amos barked at the squealing weaner pigs, Ears sort of brayed.

"He thinks he's a dog." Maddy laughed as she shook her head.

Pop looked up from tinkering with the tractor and grinned at her. A smudge of grease gave him a devilish air. "Might as well be. If they could, those two would climb right on the bus with Nicholas."

Ears nipped Amos on the rump, and Amos, rear in the air and chest to the ground, barked and bounced forward, then back. Ears circled around, his ears flopping. They chased each other, then reversed and came straight at Maddy, skidding into her knees.

"Ya gotta watch 'em. Ears gets any bigger and he'll be knocking you over." Jesse wiped his hands on a rag tucked in one of the overall pockets and climbed up on the tractor seat. This time when he started it, the engine rumbled like it had just come from the factory.

His satisfied nod made Maddy smile. Was this the same man of two months ago?

Her shadows behind her, she headed up to the coffee plants, hoe in hand. While many of the plants they'd doctored made it through and were sending out green sprouts, others had withered and needed to be replaced. She hoed out weeds and built up the circles of dirt around each plant, which kept the water she poured on them from running off.

"One of these days we're going to have a drip system," she told Ears. Amos lay in the shade of a larger plant, pink tongue lolling and blue eyes winking. Ears nudged her knee. When he looked up at her, a huge yawn showed all his teeth and long tongue, and she laughed and bent

LAURAINE SNELLING

down to rub his ears. Nicholas had shown her the little nub not far from the tip of the ear that when rubbed made Ears close his eyes in bliss. "You know what? You look like a stuffed pet with that silly expression on your face."

Ears leaned against her knee.

"You go lay in the shade with Amos; he's a smart one."

But Ears followed behind her and every once in a while practiced his bray. He sounded like a rusty door hinge.

Maddy climbed to the next terrace and started back. Looking over her shoulder, she caught the burro in the act.

"Leave those coffee plants alone, you wind-up toy." She shooshed him away from the plants and checked on a few earlier ones. Ears had been pruning the tender new shoots. He darted away from her flapping hands and angry voice but as soon as she turned back to her work, there he was. This time she caught him with a shoot hanging out of his mouth.

"Danged donkey!" She grabbed her hoe and headed down the hill. "Going to have to keep you penned up, I guess."

She glanced up to see her father trying to keep a straight face. "And don't you say 'I told you so' either." She shook her fist at him. "Or I'll pen you up too." With that, he burst out laughing.

Amos leaped and yipped, Ears brayed, and Maddy couldn't help but laugh along.

— — —

At work that evening she made sure she got Melissa's address and phone number. But since it was the younger woman's day off, she and Ruby could do nothing but guess as to the state of things.

"You think we should call her?" Ruby asked as they both put order slips up on the spinner.

Maddy shook her head. "It could just make things worse."

Thinking about Melissa's state brought back painful memories. Running orders out and serving the guests kept her too busy to think, but on the drive home, with the midnight blackness surrounding her,

244

the images came back again. Gabe drunk, his fists flying. Gabe furious because she didn't have his dinner ready. Gabe threatening her with a knife.

Her stomach roiled, her hands shook. *That's all over. Don't think about it. Don't remember how stupid and weak you were.*

Her father sat on the glider, smoking his pipe. If it hadn't been for the sweet scent of cherry pipe tobacco, she'd have walked right on by.

"How come you're up so late?" She paused with her hand on the door handle.

"Got something I think you better look at." He got to his feet, the glider creaking, one floorboard groaning at his weight. "Come on." He motioned her into the house.

"Nicholas?" Thoughts raced through her mind like millet being chased by a shark.

"No, nothing like that." He handed her a folded-up newspaper and pointed to a story in the second column, halfway down. "Local man indicted as king of drug ring, accessory for murder."

She read swiftly. Another prisoner had confessed and implicated Gabe. While the article used the terms "suspect" and "alleged," it sounded like an open-and-shut case. Accessory to murder, Gabe had probably ordered it. With this new evidence and testimony, he should be sent up for life or a hundred years, whichever came first.

"Good." She dropped the paper on the table. "Hope they nail his sorry hide to the wall."

— — —

Some nights later, when she should have been long asleep, Maddy thumped her pillow again. "You'd think with such good news I would sleep like a baby." She flipped over for the umpteenth time. "I do . . . like a colicky baby," she muttered into the darkness. The coffee plants were growing well, as long as she kept Ears out of the field. Nicholas was doing well in school—in fact, Mrs. Alioto had raved about what a good student he was, how polite, and what a droll sense of humor he had. She wondered about that; he seemed more slapstick to her after watching him with Benny and James and the animals here on the farm. Her father was acting like a real human being and things were going well at work. Melissa even wore a smile these days. She had apologized for calling Maddy that night, saying she'd overreacted.

So why couldn't she sleep?

An image of the tall, broad-shouldered Hawaiian refused to be chased from her mind. He'd been at the restaurant again, teasing her and giving the other waitresses a hard time until everyone was laughing and it was like a big party around closing time. Her middle felt warm just thinking about it. *Face it. Kam Waiano spreads joy wherever he goes. And he openly gives God the glory for everything, but he sure is no weakling. Everybody likes him. Teresa would walk on hot lava coals for him. He even made Melissa giggle like a little kid.*

And he likes you.

She tried to ignore that voice.

And you like him.

She rolled over and sat up on the edge of the bed. These weren't the kind of thoughts she needed right now—or at any time. What she needed was sleep, more hours than she'd been getting. Her body felt like someone had let all the air out and then run over her. She ached from her head to the ends of her toes. Getting up, she padded downstairs to the medicine cabinet and took two pain-killers. Anyone who thought waitressing was a cushy job ought to try it awhile.

Her alarm woke her in time to get Nicholas up so he could feed Ears before he got ready for school. Her father used to say he felt drug through a knothole backwards. If this was what he was referring to, she couldn't agree more.

"Thank you, thank you," she murmured, accepting the cup of coffee her father thrust into her hands when she entered the kitchen. "Can you serve it intravenously?"

"You ever sleep?"

"You heard me up?" At his nod, she shrugged. "Sorry, I tried to be quiet."

"Your mother used to say that when she couldn't sleep, her Bible was the best friend she had. I always could sleep through a hurricane, leastwise that's what she said."

"Nicholas, come on." She raised her voice only enough to float up the stairs and into the room with the door open. She'd called him the first time on her way down.

"I'm coming."

"So what's eatin' on you?" Jesse asked.

"Nothing. Everything. I don't know." She refilled her cup and set boxes of dry cereal on the table while she sipped. "I need to go to the grocery store this morning. If you want anything special, put it on the list."

"Mom, we're having a party for Mrs. Alioto's birthday next week. Can you make cupcakes?"

"Sure." She went over to the calendar. "What day?" She wrote it in and turned back to her son. "Thanks for asking me early."

Nicholas ducked his chin. "I was supposed to ask you last week. Can I have a dollar to put in for her present?"

Jesse pulled out his wallet and laid a dollar bill on the table. "There you go."

Nicholas looked from the dollar to his mother, to his grandfather and back to the dollar. "Thanks." But his look had said far more. This was the first time Pop had given the boy money.

"Thanks, Pop," Maddy said, clearing her throat.

She could still feel the pleasure of the morning when she went in to work later that afternoon. She caught herself humming as she tied her apron strings and sharpened her pencil.

"You sound happy." Ruby came through the door.

Maddy nodded. "I guess I am."

"Praise the good Lord for that. You deserve some happiness, and I'm the first one to say so." Ruby put her purse in her locker and spun the dial. "I saw Nicholas in church Sunday. He sure is a handsome young man."

"Thanks."

"Maybe one of these days I'll see you there too." Her sly smile made Maddy grin.

"Maybe." Maddy smiled more broadly. "Most likely." One eyebrow twitched.

"Well, praise the Lord and pass the ammunition." Ruby walked off chuckling.

Maddy's smile faded when a late Melissa came in the door. Maddy knew there'd been trouble. Gone was the smiling face, the graceful posture, the curled blond hair. Heavy makeup caked under her left eye.

Maddy felt like swearing. No, more than that, the urge to go after Buddy made her hands shake. "You go sit down for a moment and get yourself together. Ruby and I can handle it right now."

"I . . . I can't go back there." Melissa looked over her shoulder as if Buddy were right there and could hear her.

"No problem. Where's the baby?"

"At the sitter's."

"Good. We'll pick him up after work, and the two of you will come to my house, easy as that. No one here will tell that—" She cut off her words, knowing that once she started, she might not stop. "Your secret will be safe with us."

By the time they were halfway through the shift, Maddy wished she could take the girl and her baby out of there now. Melissa jumped every time she heard a male laugh and looked at the door every time it opened.

"She's in trouble, isn't she?" Kam came in toward closing time and took his usual table.

"Who do you mean?" Maddy poised her pencil over the pad.

"You know—Melissa. He's been at her again."

Relief felt warm and sweet flowing through her veins. Maddy nodded.

"I'd like to take that horse's rear and kick him off a cliff."

Maddy blinked at both the tone of voice and the language. "It'll be taken care of."

"You taking her home with you?" His whisper went no further than her ears.

"She'll be taken care of." She raised her order pad. "And what can I get you tonight?"

"Just iced tea and a piece of that macadamia nut pie you created. They ought to give you a bonus for coming up with that recipe."

"Coming right up." She scribbled the order on her pad and tucked her pencil into the hair above her right ear. Giving in to the urge, she laid a hand on his shoulder as she went by. The tingle went right up her shoulder and straight into her heart.

Kam was still there when they put out the Closed sign.

"But what about my car?" Melissa asked, keeping an eye on the door.

"Leave it there for now. Otherwise he'll come looking for it and I don't have a place to hide an automobile at the moment." Maddy dropped her apron in the laundry bin.

"You sure this is all right?" Melissa about wore her fingers out, twining them together.

"I'm sure. Come on." Maddy checked the back lot to see if anyone was lurking out there. All clear. "Does Buddy know where the sitter is?"

"Uh-huh. But he won't start looking for me until I'm late." Melissa put her bag in the truck and headed for her car.

"Where are you going?"

"I have to get the car seat."

Maddy groaned. Time was flying. She got in the truck and started it up, easing over to where Melissa was wrestling the baby's seat out of the back door.

Maddy followed the younger woman's directions and waited in the truck while Melissa went in to pick up her child. She hoped no one looked out of the window to see that anything was different. All had to seem normal in case Buddy came around asking questions.

Each second seemed endless as she kept watching the rearview mirror. Every time a car passed, Maddy kept herself from ducking down. "Come on, come on," she quietly urged.

She only breathed easier when they drove into the yard at her home and shut off the lights. Safe.

Behind them a pair of headlights turned in the drive.

28

Should she head for the old road or stay? It couldn't be Buddy.

The baby whimpered. Melissa shushed him.

The vehicle kept on coming.

"Get down." Maddy stepped out of the truck and slammed the door shut as if it were a normal night.

A pickup swung in beside her, and when the door opened, Maddy breathed a sigh of relief.

Kam.

She put a hand to her heart and took in a much needed breath of air.

"Sorry to scare you, but I got to thinkin', and there's only one way into this place far as most people know, so . . ." He leaned his crossed arms on the top of the cab. "My brother and I figured we'd kind of play gatekeeper out there under the eucalyptus. That all right with you?"

Maddy could hear Melissa crying softly. "Kam, that's so far beyond all right that it isn't even in the same galaxy. I was trying to figure—"

"You don't have to worry tonight."

"Thank you." And she knew she wouldn't. "Come on, Melissa, let's get that boy of yours bedded down and you too."

The guests were asleep within minutes—mother on the sofa, the baby on a pallet on the floor.

For Maddy it took a little longer, but considering the circumstances, not much. She'd stood at the window, seeing the darker shadow the truck made under the already dark trees. How could they sleep sitting up like that in a cramped pickup cab? Both were tall men too.

This is how being cared for and protected feels, she thought as she drifted off. The smile stayed on her face.

— — —

"Mom. Mom, there's a baby on our floor," Nicholas hissed in her ear.

Maddy woke, feeling the smile still in place. "Oh, really?" She snagged her son and gave him a hug, earning her one of *those* looks. "How about not telling anyone we have company, okay?"

"Not even Benny and James?"

"Not even."

"Are they running from the law?" His eyes grew round; she could see the wheels turning in his mind.

"No—and that's all I'll say. Other than I'm not sure how long they'll be here." She swung her feet to the floor and, getting up, walked to the window. The pickup was gone. Knowing better, she still felt a letdown. They'd been there for the night and now they both had jobs to go to. Made perfect sense.

On the way down the stairs, tying her robe around her, she realized why she felt sad. She'd wanted to cook breakfast for them. As a way of thanking them, of course.

"They can have my room if they want to stay. I can sleep in the living room easier."

"Nicholas Adam Morton, you are one fine and generous young man, and I'm so proud of you I could bust right here."

"It's like when we went to stay with Juan, huh, Mom?"

"Yeah, it is."

— — —

"But I can't stay here. He might . . . I mean, I don't want you to get hurt," Melissa said a short time later, twisting her fingers together in that way she had.

Jesse looked at Maddy over the edge of his paper. "No reason why she can't, is there?"

Maddy could have run across the kitchen and hugged him.

"Been a long time since we had a little one around here." Jesse turned the page of his newspaper.

"But I don't even have diapers for him," Melissa said.

"Grocery store does. And I have a feeling some other things might just show up here before long." Jesse winked at Maddy.

He saw the truck out there last night. Maddy grinned around the edge of her coffee cup. "Anyone want a refill?"

True as could be, a minivan arrived an hour later, driven by two women who looked so much alike no one ever doubted they were sisters. Like a traveling child's store, they came complete with a soft-sided playpen to use for a bed, a high chair, and a full wardrobe of toddler clothes—for a boy.

"I wasn't sure of his size, so I brought a variety." Marianna Waiano held up a red tank top, after the introductions. "I threw in the wading pool, too, and some toys because I didn't think you'd have those either." She held out a fluffy teddy bear. "What's your baby's name?"

Melissa sat as if she'd been bumped on the head. "Ah, Michael, after his father. Since everyone calls him, my husband that is, Buddy, this is Michael. Mrs. Waiano, you didn't . . . I mean, I can't pay you."

"Pay us? For what? A bunch of leftover toys and outgrown clothes? We keep things at our house for emergencies and I'd say this is one. Oh, and there's a case of toddler diapers out in the back. Jesse, maybe you could bring those in?" Marianna smiled up at him as he entered the room.

Michael clapped his hands and pushed himself to his feet, heading for Jesse.

"He likes men," Melissa said, "especially men with silver hair."

When a silence fell, Marianna asked the question Maddy had been wanting to ask. "Do you plan to file charges against your husband?"

Melissa looked like she'd been slapped across the face. "I . . . ah . . . oh, I don't want to." She looked to Maddy for support. "Do I have to?"

"That's the only way we can get an injunction to keep him away from you and Michael. Have the police been called in before?" Maddy felt like she was beating a soulful-eyed puppy with a club.

Melissa nodded. "But I couldn't—I just couldn't file charges."

"Because you were afraid he would hurt you worse?"

Melissa shook her head. "Maddy, I love Buddy. And he loves me."

"We always think that and maybe they do, but maybe they hate us, too, and we're too dumb to figure it out. An injunction might force Buddy . . ." Maddy could hardly force herself to say his name, ". . . into treatment both for alcohol and abuse. He's not going to change unless someone or something forces him to, and even then it will be a hard row to hoe."

"You . . . you think I should?"

Maddy looked her straight in the eye. "Yes, I do. And the sooner the better."

"Did you?" The quiver in Melissa's voice went straight to Maddy's solar plexus.

"Not soon enough. Not nearly soon enough."

"I'll stay with Michael if you want to go right now." Edi waggled a fluffy green smiling dinosaur in front of Michael's face. "We'll be just fine here, if Jesse doesn't mind." She glanced up at the man leaning against the doorjamb.

"Not at all."

Was that a blush she saw on her father's face?

By the time Maddy headed up the hill to work for the dinner shift, Melissa had filed for an injunction, it had been granted, and it was now illegal for Buddy to harass her or even come near her for that matter.

But as Melissa said, "Injunctions won't stop Buddy when he goes on a tear."

Maddy believed her with every bone in her body.

The restaurant was full of diners when the door slammed open and Buddy roared in. "Which one of you . . ." A string of filth followed that would have made Gabe proud.

People hunkered down, uncertain if he had a gun or not.

The bartender rushed in through the arch and John came out of his office.

Buddy kept screaming as he accosted each of the employees. "Why ain't she here? She's supposed to be working." The names he called his wife made Maddy see every shade of red, but the desire to protect Melissa kept her still.

"Who took my wife?" he shrieked as the men dragged him out the door. Sirens screamed as the police cars hit the parking lot.

"Sorry, folks," John said, moving around the room. "Please enjoy a dessert on the house. We're sorry to upset your meal like this."

"Boy, he was mad," one little kid said, his eyes as big as his face.

That brought a chuckle from other diners, and Maddy could feel the tension relax. She sucked in a deep breath and let it out slowly, her shoulders dropping and her jaw unclenching. Now maybe the police would throw Buddy in the slammer. If only they could keep him there — forever.

When she told Melissa about it the next morning, she began to cry. "He's going to hurt someone and it's all my fault. I should go home, I can calm him down again, I . . ."

"You are going to stay right here where you are safe." Maddy sat down on the glider and tickled Michael's toes. The chubby little guy giggled and stretched his foot out again. "Buddy's safe in jail."

That afternoon Kam called. "Don't tell Melissa, but Buddy is out.

They didn't have anything to hold him on other than disturbing the peace. Please be careful."

Maddy put a smile on her face and a lilt in her voice. "I will and thank you so much for calling. See you later." After Melissa took Michael upstairs for a nap, she explained to her father what Kam had said.

"Is there a way he can find her?"

"Only way I know of is to follow me home. John won't give out any information, that's for sure." She leaned against the counter at the sink. "He'd have to follow each of us since he has no idea who is helping her."

"Unless he got lucky on the first try."

"True." Little fingers of fear raced up and down her spine. This was her former life all over again. And she had sworn to never let a man make her afraid again.

When she came out of work that night, three police cars sat in the parking lot, ready to escort the workers home.

Kam was parked right beside Maddy's truck. He looked up at her when she stopped beside him. "The benefits of small-town politics. And a police department that cares about preventing incidents."

"Thanks." Maddy knew this escort was a gift from him. He knew everyone and swapped favors whenever he could. This was payback time. "Thanks is such a little word. It's not enough." She struggled with trying to express her feelings. "I . . . y-you make me feel protected and I . . . " She swallowed, took in a breath, and sighed it out. "Just thank you, I guess."

Kam closed his hand over hers on the window frame. "That's enough."

"I . . . please be careful." She turned her hand over and clasped his. "See you."

She flashed her lights at the officer behind her when she drove into her yard. Amos yawned as he greeted her.

Melissa waited on the glider. "He's out, isn't he?"

Maddy nodded. "Yes."

"I called my mother and he's been threatening her. I didn't tell her where I am, though."

"Good thing." Maddy felt like she was trapped in a rerun—only now she wasn't the principle player but a spectator that needed to help save the heroine. The lines were always the same. *If only . . . I should have . . . if I had . . .*

"Tomorrow we can look for a shelter for you if that would make you feel better. Kam said there are several safe houses. They'll help you get on your feet again."

"How does he know all this?"

Maddy shook her head. "Guess their church is active in helping support women's shelters." She'd been surprised to hear that. "They even help train women like us for new jobs, set up interviews, and teach you how to apply and interview. Edi was telling me about it."

"I've got a job, if I can ever go back."

"Yeah, John is holding it for you." Maddy didn't say that she and Ruby begged for him to hold it, promising to work extra shifts because they knew that Melissa would be a good worker when she got rid of Buddy.

Maddy paused and listened to the police sirens scream up the highway. *Must be an accident somewhere.* She turned back to listen to what Melissa was saying. For being such a quiet person, the dam had now burst and she obviously needed to talk. *Been there, done that,* Maddy thought again. *I talked Rita's ear off that first week. I wish I dared send her a letter. Or could call.*

She'd bid Melissa good-night and stopped in the kitchen for a drink of water when she saw the folded paper on the table and an article circled. Gabe had been before the judge. Sure enough, life imprisonment with no parole. That was better than she'd even dreamed. No parole. He could never get out. Never!

She was free.

She felt like dancing around the room, shooting off fireworks, yelling at the top of her lungs, "I am free!"

Two hours later she lay in bed and wondered, *If I'm so free, why can't I go to sleep?* She got up and made her way back downstairs, being careful not to wake Nicholas, who still slept on the sofa. She took her mother's Bible from the shelf where'd they put it to keep it away from Michael's busy little hands and wandered back upstairs. Turning on the light by her bed, she let the pages flop as they would and read first her mother's notes in the margin.

The dear handwriting brought a lump to Maddy's throat. Her mother had such beautiful penmanship, something her daughter had never perfected, among other things.

She read the underlined verses. *"Consider the lilies of the field . . . they neither toil nor spin; yet . . . Solomon in all his glory was not arrayed like one of these. . . . Do not worry about tomorrow, for tomorrow will worry about its own things. Sufficient for the day is its own trouble."*

Her mother had written, *Fear not! I trust in Jesus, for He is my life.*

"Oh, Mother, I need this so badly. I've been so afraid. . . ." She read it again. *"Sufficient for the day is its own trouble."* She lay her hands across the Bible, crossed at the wrists. How could God say fear not? Did He really expect that? How could Jesus be her life? What did that mean? Maddy looked out the window and quietly asked, "God, does my invitation to have Jesus come into my heart back in Bible School still count? In spite of the mess I've made of my life since then?"

She waited, letting the silence seep around her like the finest silk sheet. Memories of her mother flooded her mind. Amelia sitting on the lanai in the early morning with her Bible on her lap. Her mother tending to her flowers and picking fruit in the garden. Her mother dressed for church on Sundays, the smile on her face so peaceful, like she was lit from within.

"I sure hope you are enjoying heaven because I miss you so much here and I know Pop does too."

"Lo, I am with you always." Soft as the breeze the words filled her mind.

She laid the Bible on her nightstand, turned out the light, and snuggled back down, her heart no longer racing. "Jesus, if you are really here with me, inside my heart, what difference will it make?"

Off in the distance she heard the sirens again.

The phone ringing jerked her awake.

The alarm went off at the same time. She stumbled to her feet in time to hear Pop say hello and then call her name.

"I'm coming." She pushed her arms into the sleeves of her robe and tied it as she came down the stairs. "Who is it?"

"Your boss."

Maddy tucked her hair behind her ear and took the receiver. She had to clear her throat to speak. "H-hello?" Already her stomach was tying itself in knots. Unless, of course, he needed more help.

"Maddy, sorry to bother you so early, but I have a suspicion that Melissa is at your house?"

"Why do you ask?" She'd almost blurted out yes. What if Buddy were there forcing John to call? It wouldn't surprise her a bit.

"There's been a terrible accident and the police are trying to find Melissa."

"Accident?" She thought back to the sirens of the night before.

"Her husband was driving, under the influence, I think, and the passenger was killed. He's badly injured. I think if she wants to see him again, she better get to the hospital."

"Kona or Hilo?"

"They airlifted him to Hilo."

"We're on our way." She hung up the phone and took the stairs two at a time.

In fifteen minutes they were driving through pouring rain, leaving baby Michael with Jesse until Edi could get there to help care for him.

Melissa huddled against the truck door, her arms wrapped around her shoulders as if for warmth. "It's all my fault. I should have been home. He was probably out looking for me. What am I going to do?"

Maddy let her run on until she finally couldn't stand it any longer. "Melissa, that might have been you in the passenger seat and Michael in the back. You could both be dead right now."

Melissa started to cry. "I never wanted it to come to this. Why couldn't he stop drinking?"

Now you're asking the right questions, Maddy silently thought. *Buddy made those choices, not you.*

Maddy let Melissa off at the front door of the hospital and went to park. How would she react in a situation like this? What if it were Gabe?

Kam met her at the door and held it open. "Edi called me before she left. She's on her way to your house. You know any more?"

Maddy shook her head. Seeing him there made the sun come out in spite of the dark clouds. He would help her deal with Melissa and Buddy. Could she trust him to always be there for her? Or was that asking too much?

"How bad is he?" Kam asked the nurse coming out of the door of the ICU.

"Hi there, Kam. Is the man a relative of yours too?"

"No, thank God." He turned to Maddy. "This fine nurse is my second cousin on my mother's side. Jan Kioto, Maddy Morton. We're friends of Melissa's."

"That poor girl needs a few friends. If I were her, I'd no more go see that creep than . . ." Jan caught herself and smiled sheepishly. "Sorry, not very professional of me."

"That's okay, we agree."

"She's been here in the ER more times than I like to count, and it is always her being 'clumsy.' Does she think we're stupid or something?"

Maddy flinched. She'd said the same thing. Every injury had always been her fault.

"How bad is he?" Kam repeated as he took Maddy's elbow and drew her out of the way of an incoming gurney. He kept his hand on her arm.

"He could go either way at this point. And if he lives, who knows? There's major trauma to the head and spine. Not as bad as the other guy, of course. He's down in the morgue. They both had blood levels above 2.0."

"Is he conscious?"

"Heavens no."

"Can we go be with Melissa, then?" Maddy could see her standing by the bed, her shoulders shaking.

"Well . . . since you're her immediate family and all." Jan winked at them and held the door open wide.

Maddy stood next to the bed with both her arms around Melissa, holding her while she cried. She didn't bother to even look at the broken body lying in the bed. Far as she was concerned, Buddy no longer existed. Unless he hurt Melissa again.

When the nurses came in to monitor the patient, they all went out into the hallway.

"Could you please take me home so I can get my car and a change of clothes? I'll pick up Michael and take him to my mother's house."

Melissa stood taller somehow and an air of confidence had entered her voice.

"Of course. But you don't need to be alone now."

"I've been alone a long time, Maddy, as you well know. Right now I'm safe too."

The house seemed empty when Maddy got home. Edi and Jesse had offered to take Michael to his grandmother's when Melissa called earlier. Nicholas was in school. All the confusion was gone. Maddy poured herself a glass of iced tea and took it out to the glider. What a few days this had been. And what an ending. The *"fear not, for I am with you"* verse kept running through her head. So often lately she'd felt protected, like someone was taking care of her—besides Kam and her father, that is. *"Perfect love casts out fear."* She couldn't remember when she'd memorized that one.

"Oh, Mother, what a gift you had given me, and I haven't used it all these years. How different they might have been." But she turned from the bad memories and thought again of the verses.

Sometime later, a car drove in. It was Edi returning her father.

"That child is a real charmer," Edi said as she came up the walk. "Isn't he, Jess?"

Jess? Maddy looked at her father, but he wasn't taking his eyes off Edi. Maddy nearly choked on her tea.

Edi sat next to Maddy, and Jesse leaned against the railing. "I've been meaning to call you and then all this came up. Kam's thirty-fifth birthday is next week, and we want you and Jess"—she sent him a warm smile—"and Nicholas to come. Please don't say no."

"We won't . . . I mean, we'll come." Maddy glanced at her father to catch his nod.

"Good. Then one other thing. I'd like to buy one of your hogs for the luau. Kam said they were about ready. Are they?"

Maddy nodded. "Only one problem. You can't buy one. I will provide the luau pig as our gift." She again caught her father's nod.

"But that's not fair that a guest should bring all that." Edi's hands

fluttered and she stuttered a bit. She was not used to being contra-
dicted.

"Please." Maddy softened her voice. "It means a lot to me to be able
to do this."

"All right, then." Edi gave in graciously. "And thank you. I want
this to be the best luau ever. My oldest nephew—and my favorite, but
don't tell anyone—will only turn thirty-five once. A milestone, wouldn't
you say? Oh, and did I tell you it is to be a surprise? We'll meet Sunday
afternoon at one at Marlea's house, since she is on the beach."

— — —

The next few days were a kaleidoscope of busyness. Visits to the
hospital for Melissa's sake. Selling the first batch of hogs. Sending the
luau pig to be slaughtered. Working at the Ranch House and watering
her coffee plants. With the proceeds from the hog sale, she bought two
more gilts and a boar, just like she'd hoped.

On Sunday she and Jesse took Nicholas to Sunday school and then
all of them went to church. Maddy couldn't believe her father hadn't
given her a hard time about attending the service, but when Edi came
over and sat with them, she knew why. Kam sang in the choir and had
a solo for the choral piece. His voice captured Maddy's heart and lifted
it to soar with both voice and organ.

Pastor Andrew Kamaki stepped into the pulpit as the notes drifted
off.

"Grace and peace to you from God our Father and our Lord Jesus
Christ." His rich voice rolled over the congregation, full of the peace of
which he spoke.

If Maddy heard nothing else, those words settled in her heart and
soul. Grace and peace. She'd needed them so badly. And been given
them so richly. She returned to the present to hear him read from the
Bible in front of him. " 'I have come that they might have life, and that
they may have it more abundantly.' " He bowed his head. "Shall we
pray?" The rustles subsided. Someone coughed. And then silence.

"Heavenly Father, we come to you this day a broken people in need of your love and forgiveness. We praise you, for you are God and without you we flounder. You are the shepherd and we are the sheep of your pastures. Thank you for never deserting us, no matter how far we stray, no matter how long. You came for us." More silence.

Maddy fought to keep breath coming into her lungs and then leaving. *You came for us.* Had God been seeking her? Had He, the God of the universe, come for her?

"In Jesus' precious name and for His sake, He who died for us, Amen."

Died for us. Died for me. Me, Amanda Marie Hernandez Morton.

Nicholas tucked his hand under her arm and smiled up at her.

She fought the tears, finding it hard at times to see the minister. *He came for me. He didn't wait.* She sniffed again. When she looked up, Kam smiled directly into her soul.

She couldn't smile back, for if she did she knew her composure would crumble and she would have to leave.

The benediction was nearly her undoing.

"The Lord bless you and keep you. The Lord look upon you with favor and give you His peace. Amen."

The age-old words sifted until they found the minute cracks in the walls she'd so carefully constructed, and like the walls of an ancient city, hers came tumbling down. She had to hang on to the pew in front of her to keep from crumbling. The hymn book shook so badly that Nicholas took over holding it.

"You okay, Mom?" Concern and fear darkened his eyes, taking away the sparkle that had come back to live there.

She nodded. "Tears are for joy, too, okay?"

He returned to singing with a vengeance.

Every time she tried to sing a word, her throat clogged and the tears ran faster. Finally she quit trying and studied the cross. The sun streaming through the stained-glass windows burnished the gold metal, setting it afire. It glinted, seeming to pulse with a life all its own. The cross.

That's what it was all about. And here she'd been running away for so long. Right then, for the life of her, she could no longer understand why.

Here was where she belonged, at the foot of the cross. It was so simple.

She followed the congregation out the door, shook hands with Pastor Andrew, and greeted others, though she didn't remember any of it later. She nodded when her father said he'd ride with Edi and when Nicholas asked to go with Benny and James.

The drive home passed in a blur of tears. She felt like someone had uncapped a spring and the water continued to flow whether she wanted it to or not. Knowing that she needed to get things ready for the luau, she changed her clothes and climbed the hill to her mother's grave.

"I'm home, Mom. I'm really home." She sat in the shade of the mimosa tree and poured forth the events of the last years. "And so, you see your prayers were answered. I'm just so sorry you aren't here to rejoice with me. But if what the Bible says is true, you've got a pretty good crowd around you to party with."

She dried her eyes on her shirt tail and walked back down to the house. Upstairs she took the Bible from the stand by her bed and withdrew her mother's prayer list. After one of the many *please bring Maddy home both to me and to you*, she wrote the day's date.

Maddy stood in front of the closet. She had nothing to wear. Jeans and shirts. That was it.

Would anything of her mother's fit? She hurried downstairs and into her father's room, the one place in the house that hadn't succumbed to her cleaning supplies. Sure enough, all her mother's clothes still hung in the closet as if she'd only gone on a trip and would be home soon. Maddy sorted through them until she came to a navy cotton skirt and a white short-sleeved blouse with navy trim. She took them outside and shook the dust out, then tossed them in the dryer with a damp cloth and a sheet of fabric softener. If only she had gotten to cleaning that room, too, but then she might have packed her mother's things away or even given them away.

Shoes! She suddenly realized she couldn't wear her boots with this, and the grunge look of her tennis shoes wouldn't do either.

Would her mother's sandals fit? She looked in the pocket of the shoe bag hanging near the clothes. A pair of white sandals looked a bit mildewed, but she wiped them clean and slid her feet into them. A bit tight, but she unbuckled the straps and reset them in the last hole. They'd do. In front of the bathroom mirror, she unbraided her hair and brushed it out so it hung in waves down her back. Taking the top and sides, she held them back with two tortoiseshell combs she found in a drawer, again gifts from her mother.

As she left, she looked in the mirror and nodded. New woman—inside and out. At the gate she turned and snipped a blossom off the Plumeria bush, tucking it into the hair above her right ear.

— — —

"Surprise! Happy Birthday! Surprise!"

Kam blinked and began shaking his head. The children rushed him, shouting and laughing. "How'd you do this?" He looked at his mother and sister, then around the gathered group.

It seemed half the island was there and each person wanted to greet him and shake his hand, hug him, or thump his back. His gaze flicked over a tall, slender woman with a creamy blossom in her hair and he took a step backward.

"Maddy?" The crowd parted as he headed toward her. If he was the ship, she was the lighthouse.

She could feel her cheeks flaming as everyone looked at her but she straightened her spine and held her ground.

"You . . . you're gorgeous. I . . ." He took her hand, lacing his fingers through hers. "I . . ." Hearing snickers from those around, he turned to the crowd. "Would you please excuse us for a few minutes, I need to get something straight here." He imprisoned her hand in his and dragged her along with him. "We'll be back soon. Go on with the party."

"Kam, you can't leave your guests like this." Maddy sputtered as he pulled her along, but it did little good.

"Sure I can, it's *my* birthday, and I just got the greatest gift of all."

"You have? What's that?"

"You!"

Some ways up the beach, he slowed and drew her closer. "Okay, Ms. Morton, what happened to you in church this morning? I don't think I heard a word Pastor Andrew said, 'cause all I could do was watch your face and wish I could leap out of that choir loft and hold you."

"I came home."

He turned to face her, now holding both of her hands in his. "Good."

Giggles erupted behind them.

"Okay, guys, go look for floats or something." He waved his hand at the three boys. "Now get."

Benny, James, and Nicholas ran off up the beach toward the rocks where black crabs lived along with a myriad of other creatures. They could be busy for hours.

"Now, as you were saying."

"I realized Christ died for me and has been calling me back. That's all."

"That's all?" His mouth dropped open and then creased again in a heart-stopping smile.

She smiled up at him, her eyes misting again. "Pretty cool, huh?"

Kam nodded. "Pretty cool. Way cool, in fact. I've been praying for you."

"So had my mother."

He nodded. "Among others." Hand in hand, he led her to the shallows where wavelets washed the sand. They both took off their shoes and let the warm water kiss their feet. "I have so many things I want us to talk about, but right now all I want to do is kiss you."

"So what's stopping you?" Maddy couldn't believe she said that.

He turned toward her, searching her eyes, looking deep within.

She felt the tingle begin with another wave caressing her feet and work its way up to blossom as heat upon her cheeks.

He lowered his head.

She raised her chin. The world fell silent but for the swish of the waves. She struggled to keep her eyelids from drifting closed.

"Uncle Kam, look what we found."

The shriek shattered the moment and jerked them apart.

Benny reached them first. "Look." He held up a blue glass ball, a float from long-ago Japanese fishing nets. "We found it like you said. For your birthday."

Kam took the softball-sized float and held it to the light. The world exploded in flashing sunbeams, all rimmed with ocean blue. The perfect sphere, a circle never ending.

"For you," the boys said in unison.

"For us." Kam handed it to Maddy.

The sphere felt warm in her hands, alive like the moment.

"We better get back."

"I know." With one hand in his, she cupped the glass ball in her other.

"They were getting all mushy," Benny announced when they got back to the crowd.

"Gooey," added James.

Nicholas's shining eyes spoke for him as he stood beside his mother and gazed up at the man who still held her hand.

The rest of the party passed in a haze for Maddy. Everywhere she turned, she felt Kam's gaze resting on her. The food was phenomenal. When they uncovered the pig, roasting in its bed of coals under the heap of sand, everyone cheered at the sight of the full hog.

"We have a real luau hog, thanks to Maddy Morton and her family!" Edi announced, clapping her hands. "She raises them, you know, so if you ever want a whole hog, you go talk with Maddy."

While the men cut the meat, the women set out the food. The table seemed to stretch for a mile, piled high with authentic Hawaiian dishes.

But by the time they finished, bones and empty bowls were all that were left.

When the guitars, mandolins, ukuleles, and drums came out, the singing and dancing began. As dusk fell, the fire blazed higher and the tide changed, bringing the song of the waves closer to underlay the melody. The instruments softened, a chant whispered and grew. Kam took up the melody, his voice rich and full. Edi stepped into the firelight, raised her hands toward the heavens, and with swaying hips and lyrical hands, danced the ancient love story he sang.

Maddy didn't understand the words, but that wasn't necessary. The hands told the story, the music captured her heart, and firelight bronzed the cheeks of the man singing from his soul—for her.

Hours later, when Kam finally captured her lips at the gate to her father's house, she sighed into his embrace, knowing again she was home.

"We have a lot of talking to do," Kam whispered sometime later, his hand stroking her hair and down her back.

"I know." She smiled up at him. "Later. Good night." Their hands lingered as they drew apart, loath to let go. "Happy Birthday."

The wind kicked up in the trees, as if blown from a mighty mouth. Maddy's skirt was plastered to her legs as she made her way up the walk. But in light of the wonder she was feeling, she barely noticed how the wind had started so abruptly.

Y ou got what?"

"An offer on my place here." Jesse held the paper out for her to see. "Came right out of the blue."

Maddy, sweaty from cleaning trenches above the coffee plants in case the predicted storm really did hit, wiped her hands on her pants before reaching for the letter. She whistled at the amount on the bottom line.

"Why now?"

"They say they want a place to build condos and the view here is good."

"That's true." *Why now after all the work she'd put into the place? And how could her father turn down an offer like this?* "Have you talked with them?" *And not told me?*

The glare he gave her shouted offense. "Big a surprise to me as to you." He took the paper out of her shaking hands. "I'll have to think on it."

"You do that." Maddy couldn't have stopped the screen door from slamming if she'd tried. The wind kicked up dried eucalyptus leaves, swirling them around in a death dance. How could this be? Right now, when she was trying to get ready for a freak storm? The reports talked of near hurricane-force winds. It was so out of season—typhoons usually came in the spring.

School let out early. Nicholas leaped off the bus and ran up the drive, whistling for Ears and Amos as he came. The burro answered from his pen in the barn as Amos danced around him, barking and yipping his delight.

Maddy watched the familiar scene from up on the hill where she'd gone back to trenching. For some reason, the tractor refused to start just when she needed it. Pop was screwing closed the shutters on the house to protect the windows. He'd drop the bars in place last.

The wind buffeted her, trying to tear her from her tasks. The worst was predicted for later in the night. The coffee plants bowed before the onslaught, giving obeisance to the power behind the storm.

Maddy muttered a prayer as she worked. The wind kept snatching her breath away. *He can't sell this land.* Storms within and storms without. Right now she wasn't sure which was worse.

Nicholas stopped working and pointed to the barn. "But, Mom, I have to bring Ears to the house. What if the barn blows down?"

Maddy couldn't help thinking, *If the barn goes, my hogs go and who cares if he sells this place?* "All right, but he has to stay in the kitchen so you can clean up after him easier."

"Thanks, Mom." Nicholas ran to the barn to bring in his friend.

The rain began its torrent.

"Maddy, get down to the house." Jesse appeared like an apparition out of the streaming curtain. "They're announcing that the storm is veering off to the south. It should let up here soon."

Maddy kneaded her fists into her aching back. She'd deepened the highest trench a good foot. That should hold it. "Okay."

"I made dinner."

"Thanks." She took her shovel and pick and followed her father down the hill. Water ran in her eyes so fast she could barely see.

The rain had indeed let up when she saw car lights coming up the drive. Kam knocked at the door moments later. "Hi, came to see how you are. Your phone is out."

"Probably that eucalyptus limb took it out. I saw it go." Jesse ushered him into the kitchen, where Amos and Ears nosed him in search of treats.

"You eaten yet?" Maddy controlled the urge to run into his arms and plaster herself to his chest.

Kam shook his head. "Been out warning folks that might not of heard the sirens."

"Did they go off?" Maddy brushed a strand of hair behind her ear. At least she'd dried off and changed clothes before dishing up the spaghetti.

"Most of them."

"Hi, Kam." Nicholas came down the stairs. He, too, wore clean dry clothes.

"Hi, yourself. Your friend here has not only gotten lots bigger but lots nosier."

"I know. I hide treats in my pockets and he tries to find them." Nicholas pulled the burro away from Kam. "Come on, Ears. Mind your manners." Ears shook his head, his namesakes flopping against Nicholas's chin.

"Do you have everything you need? Batteries, candles, water jugs, canned food?"

"Yep, we've done this before, you know." Jesse crossed the room to refill his cup of coffee. "You want some?"

"Sure." Kam took the place at the table Jesse pointed him to. "Thanks."

His smile took Maddy's breath away when she set a plate of spaghetti before him. "The bread's in the basket." Somehow her hand found its way to his shoulder and would have remained there had she not dragged it away so she could dish up the rest of the plates. On the way back, she paused, listening to the quiet. The storm had passed.

They sat around the table visiting after the plates were emptied — of seconds for both Kam and Nicholas.

"You got a minute?" Jesse asked. "I want to show you something."

Nicholas slipped to the floor to play with Ears and Amos, who both tried to climb in his lap.

"Sure." Kam waved away the half-empty plate of cookies, then shrugged and took another anyway. "These are mighty good. Dried papaya chunks sure do taste good no matter how they're used."

Jesse handed him the paper from the development company. "Know anything about these folks?"

Kam read the letter and whistled when he finished. He studied the name on the letterhead. "YK Development. That's the Yoshida group. They've been buying up whatever land they can get their hands on. Have a good reputation so far, meeting all the codes and such. You want to sell?"

"I don't know. Guess I have to think about it with an offer like that. What do you think?"

"I think it stinks." Nicholas flung himself to his feet, scattering his buddies. "You can't sell our home! Not now! I like it here!" He glared at his grandfather. "Moving stinks." He threw himself up the stairs, his feet thundering on the steps. Ears started to follow him, but Maddy grabbed him around the neck. Amos whined.

Jesse cleared his throat. "Well, we certainly got his opinion. I didn't say we were selling, just that I have to think about it. We could buy someplace really nice with that kind of money."

Maddy couldn't help but agree with her son. The whole idea stunk.

"I better be going." Kam got to his feet.

"Warning! Warning!" The words from the radio caught their attention. "Radar shows the storm turning. If it continues on the new northerly course, it will hit the southern tip of the island in about thirty minutes. Stay off the roads and batten down. We've got a monster coming."

The last comment was uttered with awe.

Maddy grabbed her slicker and rain hat from the pegs by the back porch and splashed her way out the back gate. The rain had started again, but with her flashlight she could see the way.

"Where are you going?" Kam caught up with her.

"I've got to deepen that trench at the top of the planting or all the coffee plants will be washed away."

"We don't have much time." He kept pace with her.

"I know." She flashed the light in the trench to see it already half full of water from the earlier rain. "You want to start over there?" She pointed to the place where this trench ran into the downhill one.

He took the shovel she offered and walked off, visible only by the circle of light that proceeded him.

The winds kicked up and the rain intensified as Maddy flung shovel after shovelful on top of the low side of the trench. If they had sand bags, it would have been more effective, but she didn't have time to search for any. Besides, if Pop had some, he'd have brought them out.

They continued, shovel by shovel, moving as much water as dirt. Stab, hit the shovel edge with the sole of her boot, and lift. The water in the trench was halfway up her calves in spite of the trenching she knew Kam was doing at the other end, but water poured from rivers coming down the hill. If only they had the tractor and blade, they could deflect some of the runoff higher up.

But *if onlys* never paid off. Push and lift. Her shoulders screamed in agony.

"Get down to the house!" Jesse tried to grab her shovel.

"You go!" She dug some more.

"Maddy, you can't do any more. One of those trees could take you out with it." Kam said this.

"No!" Her shriek couldn't be heard above the wind. She felt herself hoisted in strong arms and thrown over Kam's shoulder.

"We are going down. Now!"

Rain pounded his head while Maddy pounded his back as they

slipped and slid their way down the hill. He didn't set her down until they stood on the lanai. The wind tried to grab the door from him but he held firm. "Get in the house."

She obeyed and collapsed on the bench in the laundry room. When he finally had the door closed again, he stood with head bowed, trying to get his breath.

It was over. Her plants would be washed down the hill, chewed up by the muck. If the barn made it through, it would be a miracle. She closed her eyes and leaned back against the wall.

"Maddy! Maddy!"

The voice came from some far-off place that she never wanted to return to.

"Maddy!"

She opened her eyes to find Kam shaking her and calling her name. "Go away."

"Let's get you out of these wet clothes and then you can sleep all you want." He tipped up her chin and looked in her eyes. "Do you need help?"

She shook her head. When her fingers began to fumble with the buttons on her shirt, he left the room, only to come back later with towels and her robe, handing them to her through the door.

What difference does it make? All is lost. Pop was right, coffee is jinxed on this place. He might as well sell it.

Maddy finally pulled herself upstairs to get some dry clothes and brought Nicholas down with her. The hallway was the safest place in the house, so they all gathered there. But no matter how hard she fought, she could no longer stay awake.

— — —

What is that noise? She burrowed closer into the warmth at her side and pillowing her head. She sniffed. Kam, she was leaning against Kam in the hallway during the wayward typhoon.

But when she tried to straighten up, his arm kept her close.

"You are fine, Maddy, just go on back to sleep if you like."

The idea was incredibly appealing, but now that she had permission to sleep, her stubborn eyes stayed wide awake. In the glimmer of the lantern, she could see Amos, Ears, and Nicholas in a tangled heap on a mattress someone had pulled in for them. She looked around.

"Where's Pop?"

"Sound asleep in his bedroom. Said he was as safe there with the window shuttered and the bed was far more comfortable than the floor and wall."

"And you've been . . ."

"Oh, sleeping and listening, praying and watching."

"Watching what?" The listening and sleeping part she understood.

"You sleep." His breath tickled her ear and when she tilted her head, her lips were right in line with his mouth. Kam kissed her. "Umm, you taste as good as you look."

"Mister, you have got bad eyesight." She touched her hair and it felt like clay-filled rope gone hard in the sun. "Is there mud on my face?" She scrinched her nose and could feel the mud crack, like she'd just had a facial. "Don't answer. I can tell." She looked up at him. "You know what, Waiano?" He shrugged. "I don't like being manhandled."

"I don't like playing caveman, either, but I do what has to be done. If you think I was going to leave you up there to get blown away, think again."

"Oh, you got a point there."

The screech of nails being pulled from wood made her shudder. Would the house hold or—she didn't dare contemplate the *or*. *God, I tried to trust you and look what happened.*

Maddy gazed at Kam. "Talk to me."

A crash from outside made her burrow into his broad shoulder.

"Please." She knew if she held her hand out, it would shake as badly as leaves in a storm. That is, if there were any leaves left. Or trees, for that matter.

"What do you want to know?"

"About when you were a kid."

"You would pick that." The silence inside stretched while the storm outside raged. "Well, my father left for Vietnam when I was seven. Marlea was six, Benjamin four, Ann Marie was two, and Josie was just a baby."

"Go on," she said after waiting patiently. She looked up to make sure he wasn't asleep. No, his eyes were open, seeing into the distant past.

"My father told me I was to take care of my mother and my brother and sisters, that I was the man of the house until he returned. He never came back."

"Benjamin? I didn't know you had a brother."

"He died." The words lay stark before them.

"Oh, Kam, I'm so sorry." She looked up to watch his face. Right now it appeared carved of granite. "You don't have to talk about it if you don't want to." She raised her hand and stroked his cheek.

She could feel his ribs when he sucked in a lungful of air and let it all out again. "No, it may be better if I tell someone."

The wind roared and screeched. Trees crashed and yet they sat still, waiting.

"If I had done what my father said and watched Benjamin more carefully, he would be alive today."

"Ah." *Now I understand so much. You live with "if onlys" too.*

"Mother told us to stay in the yard. But I wanted to go pick the fruit. The guava tree was ripe and we loved guava juice. But Benny followed me, and when I wasn't watching he climbed a tree; and when he fell out, he hit his head and that was it."

"Oh, Kam, and you try so hard to make up for this. It wasn't your fault—it was an accident."

"I should have been watching better. He was so little."

Maddy shook her head and, raising on her knees, took his face between the palms of her hands. "Look at me, Kam Waiano. You cannot undo the past, and if I understand what we believe, Jesus Christ forgives our sins. He did it once and for all so we don't have to carry the terrible burdens of past sins and stupid mistakes." She stared deep into his eyes, searching his soul like he seemed to do hers. She saw the moisture well and glisten on his long eyelashes before dripping down his face.

He wrapped his arms around her, buried his head in her arms, and sobbed like a small child.

"There, there, now." She smoothed his hair and let him cry. Great sobs shook them both in their intensity.

When he finally dried his eyes with his fingertips, she smoothed more of the tears away from his cheeks. "Mahalo."

"Yes, my friend, mahalo." Maddy glanced over to see Amos perk his ears and whine.

Sure enough, the storm had passed. The silence sent chills up and down Maddy's back.

"The eye." Kam removed his arm from around her and got to his feet.

It seemed like only minutes until the force struck again. The house shuddered like it was being lifted off the foundation. The roar of an unleashed freight train built in intensity until Maddy wanted to cover her ears and howl along with it.

Would it never end? Would there be anything left when it did?

31

Birdsong awakened her.

Amos barked outside.

Maddy pushed herself to her feet, using the wall behind her as support. Sunlight poured in the window. Her watch said ten A.M. *Where is everybody?*

Ears brayed and Amos barked again. The two must be playing in the yard. If there was any yard left.

She thought of crawling up the stairs and into bed, but cleaning off first was more than she could handle at the moment. She staggered into the living room. She could tell two windows were blown out because the shutters were already open.

How did I sleep through all this activity?

Stepping out the back door, she shuddered. All the shrubs along what used to be the fence were gone. The garden looked like a monstrous, hungry bug had ravaged it. One of the Blue Gums by the house took a corner off the porch roof as it fell.

The barn—minus some parts—was still standing.

"The barn is standing." She let out a whoop and tore down the lane. In the barn she could see daylight in many places where the shingles were missing, but the pigs were fine. She counted swiftly. All nine babies still there.

"Thank you, God, we have something to start over with."

She heard Nicholas whistle for Amos. It sounded like from up on the hill. Wandering back outside, she finally forced herself to look upward. She started from the top of the hill. Trees lay like fallen giants. Only one mimosa still shaded her mother's grave. The hill ran red with blood—at least, that's what the gash looked like.

All my hard work—gone. No more coffee plants. Pop can sell out and we can start somewhere else with the hogs.

She wandered up the hill, watching Kam, Jesse, and Nicholas with stupefied eyes as they worked on the mangled plants. "Why bother?" she asked when she drew even with them. "There's nothing left to save. Besides, you're just going to sell anyway."

"Who's going to sell?" Jesse pounded another stake home while Nicholas tied up the badly bent coffee plant.

"You are."

"Says who."

"Grandpop said he wasn't letting any old developer take away our home." Nicholas brushed his hair back with a red-coated hand. Now his forehead matched.

"Really?"

"Yep." He sounded just like her father.

"Pop, this is a waste of time. Like you said and Kam too. Coffee doesn't do well on this side of the island."

"You know your mother would say we've got enough to start over— maybe even half."

Maddy clapped her mouth shut. She caught Kam's gaze. He was shaking his head and trying to keep from . . . laughing? What was there to laugh about?

"You know, for someone who practically gave her life to save the plants at the beginning of the storm, you sure lost your grit."

"Along with most of the plants."

"But you've got some left. Plus the hogs. That's far more than many people have. You should listen to the radio—it will break your heart."

Maddy stared at him. He was right. They had so much to be thankful for. She turned and looked out across the island to the sea. Most of the trees were down. A house far below them was gone, its garage stood with no roof. Other buildings were in various stages of destruction.

"Two people died, so far. There are a lot of injuries."

"I . . . I'm sorry. I didn't think."

Kam walked over to her and put his arm around her shoulders. "Lots of people are in shock right now. Soon as we get that tree cleared out of the driveway, I'll be leaving. Thank God for cell phones—I was able to check with my family. Other than damaged cars and pieces of roof missing, they are all okay."

"Thank God for that."

"I do. And for you. The thought of losing you to a typhoon over a bunch of coffee plants . . ." He shook his head. "Sheer insanity."

"Sorry."

"You should be. I got bruises on my back from where you pounded on me."

Nicholas looked up at Maddy while stroking Ears. "You said we shouldn't hit other people, that we should settle our differences with brain power, not muscles."

"I know what I said. Thank you, Nicholas."

"You said—"

"All right. Enough . . ." She felt her stomach rumbling and gurgling. "Anyone else hungry besides me?"

At their collective nods, she leaned her head against Kam's shoulder for a moment. "Then I better get us something to eat."

"I'll go work on that old generator, see if I can get it going." Pop strolled beside them down the hill. "Should have done that long ago.

Barn really needs a new roof now, and I can't put off painting the house any longer. Sure did let things go, didn't I?"

Maddy recognized a rhetorical question when she heard one.

"I'll help you." Nicholas looked up at his grandfather. "I bet there's no school for months."

"Thanks, son." Jesse clamped a hand on his grandson's shoulder. "I bet there isn't either . . . for weeks, anyway."

By evening they'd cleared the upper branches of the eucalyptus tree with the chain saw, enough so that Kam could get his pickup out. If the tree had fallen north instead of east, the cars or the house would have taken the damage.

Maddy kept counting up the things to be thankful for.

"When I get back we have some talking to do." Kam covered her hand with his.

"Promises, promises."

Kam reached inside the truck at the ringing of his cell phone. "I'll be right there." He hung up and turned back to Maddy. "You mind taking some of the homeless if need be?"

"Not at all."

"See you then." He dropped a kiss on the end of her nose and drove off.

"Mushy," Nicholas said, shaking his head.

— — —

Maddy was just heading up to work with the remaining coffee plants the next morning when she heard a car crackling over the smaller drying branches of the fallen eucalyptus tree. While the sky was pinking, the sun had yet to show itself.

"Who can that be?" she asked Amos. Amos obliged by rounding the corner of the house and making a couple of halfhearted yips. Obviously he knew who it was or he'd have set up a ruckus.

The prickles up the back of her neck went into full alert as soon as she heard the voice—the same voice she was fairly certain had whispered "I love you" sometime during the storm. But she couldn't ask. What if she'd been hallucinating?

"Hi."

"Hi yourself."

"I brought you something." Kam handed her the Honolulu newspaper, folded open to the second section. "There, third column."

Maddy scanned the article, her breath catching in her throat. Four prisoners at the penitentiary had taken advantage of the brief power outage during the typhoon to try to escape. Two were caught and two were killed. Gabino Hernandez was listed as one of the casualties.

"Oh, dear Lord." Maddy closed her eyes and shook her head. *Leave it to him, always looking for the out.* She opened her eyes to find Kam staring at her, his eyes so full of love and concern, she felt bathed in it. "S-so, I . . . I'm free." *Strange, that's the first thing to come to my mind.* "There's no way he can come for us."

She checked inside again. Shouldn't she be sad? Grieving? No such feelings existed.

"I wouldn't have let him anyway." Kam's quiet voice carried all the strength she had come to realize lay within him.

"I know." And she did know.

"How will Nicholas take this?"

"I have an idea he will feel much the same way I do and maybe now he can let go of the anger and fear too." She leaned her head against Kam's chest and treasured the feel of his arms circling her. *Safe, I'm safe. Thank you, God, I'm safe.*

"There's something else for you to see." His breath stirred the hair around her ear.

"What more could there be?"

Kam beckoned with one crooked finger. Puzzled, she followed back out to his truck. In the back were five coffee plants in five-gallon containers. "That's all I could find. I know they look a little worse for wear but . . ."

Maddy stroked one of the shiny green leaves. A couple of branches were bare, but that would soon be remedied. "They're wonderful." She looked up at him, stars shining in her eyes. "And so are you." The words came out gravelly, like she hadn't said those kind of words for a long time. If ever.

"I . . . I have a question for you." Then he turned and looked over his shoulder. "Come on." He grabbed her hand and pulled her after him. Up the hill as fast as they could navigate through all the mud and debris. Up above the wounded coffee field.

They were both panting when he stopped, put his hands on her shoulders, and turned her to face the east. "See that?"

"Other than the destruction across the island, I see the sun about to pop up."

"That's right. Another sunrise. The other night I wasn't sure I—we—would ever see another."

The rim glowed gold at the edge of the horizon.

"Maddy, as faithfully as the sun rises every day, I promise to love you."

The rim became a dancing fire. Maddy's eyes burned.

"Will you marry me?"

The shimmering disk grew.

Her breath caught on the boulder in her throat. *Can I trust this man?* she wondered. But she knew she already had . . . with her life.

"Yes, on one condition."

"Condition?" His arms tightened around her middle.

"That we greet sunrises like this on a regular basis."

"Like this?"

She turned her face up to his. "And this." Their lips met in a kiss that caused the sun to burst free from its night bonds and smile benevolently on Hawaii and the two who were locked in each other's arms.